under *the* spotlight

A Jamieson Brothers Novel

Angie Stanton

under *the* spotlight

A Jamieson Brothers Novel

HARPER TEEN
An Imprint of HarperCollins*Publishers*

Library of Congress Control Number: 2014955503
ISBN 978-0-06-227260-7 (pbk.)

Typography by Andrea Vandergrift
15 16 17 18 19   CG/RRDH   10 9 8 7 6 5 4 3 2 1
❖
First Edition

For Kristi

I love how bright your light shines

1

Garrett's head pounded, and not from the hangover that would greet him with the sunrise, but from being slammed against the wall. Or maybe it was from the few punches that came later when he crashed to the floor of Ye Ole Boston Brew Pub and knocked his head on the beer-stained tile.

He rubbed his unshaven face, and dried blood flaked into his hand. *Great.* He needed a shower and an aspirin, but the Boston city jail offered neither. Where the hell was Peter? It had been over an hour.

The sharp edge of the narrow bench he lay on cut into his back, making his already battered body even more sore. He only hoped the other guy felt worse. The jerk had the audacity to call him washed up. For Christ's sake, he was only twenty-two. He'd accomplished more in the last five years than that asshole would in a lifetime.

Reaching for his phone, he remembered the cops had taken it, along with his wallet and keys. Damn it.

"Garrett Jamieson," a bored cop with thinning hair announced, unlocking the cell. "You're free to go."

"About damn time," Garrett huffed, rising slowly. He tugged his shirt into place, smoothed back his hair, and followed the officer down a long corridor past several cells with other perps. He couldn't wait to get away from this hellhole. The officer opened a solid metal security door, and Garrett walked through, relieved to be free.

In the far corner of the waiting room, studying the Most Wanted posters, his brother waited, wearing faded jeans and a gray T-shirt.

"Hey Peter," he called. "See anyone you know?"

Peter turned with a smirk on his face and his hair still ruffled from bed. "Just checking to make sure your ugly mug isn't up here."

Garrett sneered. "It wasn't my fault."

"Never is." Peter sighed. "You realize this is becoming an annoying habit. You're lucky your Jag is still in the shop from your crash last week, otherwise you might have added drunk driving to your record."

"Stop acting like an old woman."

"You have more to worry about than me. Dad isn't going to be happy about this."

"No reason Dad needs to hear about it."

"You're kidding yourself if you think you can keep this

under wraps. A couple of photographers are outside. You're busted. Again."

Garrett stepped to the counter and signed his discharge papers.

"At least I know how to live a little. You're tied down to a ball and chain."

His brother grinned with a smile that melted millions of young girls' hearts. "Well, I happen to have the hottest ball and chain on the planet."

Garrett rolled his eyes as he collected his personal effects. Peter was so in love it made Garrett ill. It's not like he wasn't glad for his brother, but Peter and Libby were so damned happy all the time, he wanted to puke.

"Yeah, and you're missing out on the best years of your life," Garrett snapped.

"How's that? I've been watching you drink yourself into oblivion, rack up speeding tickets, and pick a fight every chance you get. You don't look too happy to me."

"You ever think that maybe you're to blame?"

"How do you figure that?" Peter asked, opening the door to exit the police station and ducking his head as cameras flashed.

"Seriously?" Garrett stopped suddenly. "You're the one who broke up the band."

2

"*Nuggett,* hold still," Riley scolded the wiggling little dog. She held him at arm's length with one hand and aimed the sink sprayer at the disgusting little canine. Riley tried to flip her long red hair over her shoulder and out of the spray zone, but it kept falling back in front of her.

"Riley, what are you doing?" asked Logan, a fellow runner with her at Sound Sync Studio. He was only a year older than she. He wore his shoulder-length hair in thick dreads along with a neatly trimmed beard.

"Living the dream," she said, wrestling with the pint-size troublemaker, determined he wouldn't get the best of her.

"Now dog baths are part of our duties?" Logan leaned back against the break room counter and watched.

"Only when the dog has the runs and rolls in it." She wrinkled her nose as she found another soiled area on Nuggett's white fur.

"You're shitting me," he said with a smirk.

"That's not funny." She used her shoulder to push her wet hair from her face.

"Well, at least now I know my life could be worse," he said in a defeated tone.

"What happened?"

"Oh, just another meltdown from Candace Capri. The woman can't carry a tune nearly as well as she thinks she can." He turned and purposely banged his head against the cupboard door. "Remind me why we keep coming back here?"

Logan had been the first person Riley met when she started at the recording studio three months ago. He'd saved her from making huge mistakes a number of times. Poor guy. He seemed to get assigned to all the difficult artists lately. Unless of course, you counted Nuggett, the lapdog of a classical singer who fed him Manhattans and jellybeans.

"Well, it might be the big bucks we make working from noon until two a.m. every day," she teased, watching him out of the corner of her eye.

Logan glared, and Riley bit back a smile.

"Or rubbing shoulders with the greatest musicians of our day."

"You mean those arrogant, entitled prima donnas," Logan said.

She laughed. When she took this job at one of the most prestigious recording studios in Chicago, she knew she'd be dealing with some big egos. Riley had dabbled in this world a long time ago and witnessed it firsthand.

"Fine. How about it's your desperate yearning to help create the perfect album while working insane hours."

"And barely making enough money to feed my cat," Logan added.

"That's it! I knew there was a reason." She waved the hose in the air.

Logan ducked away from the spray and pointed under Nuggett's neck. "You missed a spot."

"Thanks." As she sprayed the little mutt's neck, he tried to bite the water. "So what happened?" She took the dish soap and squirted a blob on Nuggett's back. The dog now resembled a drowned rat.

"Ms. Capri spent half the night arguing with the bass player over the intro. Four hours into the session he stormed off, swearing that she was tone deaf and couldn't find high C even if she was sitting at a piano. At this rate they won't be done with the album for another three months."

"That sucks. I'm sorry. But on the bright side, I heard that Fever Pitch is coming in. That ought to be epic." She lathered up Nuggett.

"Seriously? I gotta get in on that session," Logan said.

"Too late. I already asked." She grinned.

"You're killing me. You keep flaunting your girly ways and you'll be producing soon."

"Yeah, 'cause this is the look guys go for." She looked down at her drenched T-shirt and faded jeans with the frayed bottoms. She wore her hair down, and other than mascara and eyeliner, rarely wore makeup. There were enough glamorous singers strutting around in designer clothes with camera-ready faces.

Riley paled in comparison, which was fine with her. Lurking in the background, setting up equipment, and running errands was a more comfortable gig.

Ron, one of the lead engineers, stuck his balding head in. "There you are, Riley. You're a difficult girl to find."

"I've been right here, having spa time with Nuggett while his owner lays down vocals. What's up?"

"Good news. Not only has Barry agreed to let you in on the Fever Pitch sessions, he wants you to take a shot as assistant producer."

"Oh my God! Are you serious? I've been begging Barry for a month to give me a chance at the sound board." Nuggett tried to jump out of the sink. Riley quickly grabbed his slippery little body and held him tight, the ends of her long hair falling onto his sudsy back.

"It worked. And not a bad gig either." Ron smiled, knowing how much Riley wanted a career in the recording industry. This was an awesome first step.

Logan crossed his arms and shook his head. "See, there's those girly ways again. I'm doomed. I might as well give up."

"Yup, that's me. Oh so alluring." She swiped a glob of lather from Nuggett onto Logan's shoulder.

3

Garrett drummed his fingers in rapid succession on the steering wheel, willing the Boston traffic to move faster. Rush hour should be long over by now, so what was the big holdup? Was it all the tourists who bombarded the city each summer?

Then he realized there was a concert at the Pavilion. He smacked his hand against the steering wheel and swore. It should be Jamieson causing traffic jams, not some piece-of-shit group that some oily promoter threw together. The greed to cash in on tween lust for bubblegum pop was out of hand.

It had been three months since his brothers, Peter and Adam, had blindsided him with quitting the band. His blood boiled whenever he thought of it, which was most of the time.

No matter how hard he tried, his brothers wouldn't

back down. At the height of their career, the two walked away, without a care in the world. And tonight Garrett had to spend a whole evening with his family, minus Adam, who had hopped a plane to Tanzania to shadow a *National Geographic* photographer.

Garrett finally reached the restaurant, squealed into the driveway, and stopped in front of the doors.

"Good evening, sir," the parking attendant said. The pimple-faced valet couldn't be much older than eighteen.

"Hi. Park it in a double spot, would ya? I just got it back from the shop." Garrett scooped up a massive bouquet of flowers and a small, professionally wrapped package from the passenger's seat.

"Absolutely. Enjoy your dinner."

Garrett jogged up the steps and entered the restaurant.

"Good evening, Mr. Jamieson. The rest of your party is already seated. If you would please follow me," the maître d' said.

Forcing a smile, he followed the man through the crowded restaurant to a smaller dining room toward the back. A few heads turned, but not nearly as many as if he'd appeared with Peter and Adam. It was impossible not to notice their star quality as a group, but alone, he'd become invisible. Garrett tamped down his irritation as he arrived at the table.

"There you are," his mother said, rising. Her bright eyes sparkled with joy at having the family together.

"Happy birthday, Mom." He greeted her with a warm hug and a kiss on the cheek, and then gave her the flowers.

"Oh my gosh, they're beautiful. Calla lilies. You always remember." She smiled, happy over the littlest things.

"I could never forget your favorite flowers. We have Dad for that." He grinned at his father. "Hey, Peter. Libby." He nodded to his brother and his longtime girlfriend.

"Hi, Garrett," Libby said with a smile.

Peter nodded as he sipped his water.

Garrett took a seat between his father and Peter. He was the fifth wheel at this little soiree. Seemed like he was always the odd man out these days.

"Running a bit late, aren't you?" His father raised an eyebrow.

"Sorry about that. I got a late start and traffic was insane." He bit back the urge to mention the concert was the cause of the backup. He couldn't say it without starting an argument.

"It's no problem. We ordered a couple of appetizers while we were waiting. Ah, here they are," his mother said.

The waiter set down the plates.

"Could I get a beer, please?" Garrett ordered.

His father frowned.

"What? I'm twenty-two, Dad."

"Maybe you should cut back," his dad said.

"Why? It's not hurting anyone." Garrett's jaw tightened.

"Isn't it?" his dad said with a pointed look.

"Jett, try the shrimp. It's delicious," his mother smoothly interrupted, placing a hand on her husband's arm.

His father turned his attention back to Garrett's mother and they enjoyed a mostly amiable dinner of small talk about Libby's summer art class, Peter's new hobby of rock-climbing, and his mother telling of a walking group she wanted their dad to join.

"If I wanted to take a walk, I don't need a coordinated group to do it. I'll open the door and go," his dad said.

"Yes, I know, but I'd like to see you be more active," his mother replied, concerned, but then changed the subject. "I really wish Adam could have been here. There's such a void without him."

"I'm sure he's having the time of his life photographing exotic safari animals," Libby said.

"He would have been here if the band stayed together," Garrett muttered, "but everyone seemed to want to trash all those years of work, and for what? So Adam could play amateur photographer and Peter can write indie rock music?"

Peter kicked him under the table.

"What? You know this is bullshit. We should be onstage or in the recording studio. No one in their right mind quits at the height of their career!"

"Garrett, please," Peter said in a steady tone. "Tonight is about Mom's birthday, not business. If you want to have it out again, you'll have to wait."

"Hell, I do. I'll never stop arguing the point." He downed the rest of his beer.

His mother sighed and looked away.

"Garrett, perhaps it's time to focus your attention on your own life. You have a few things to get in order, don't you think?" his father said.

"You're going to make this about me? That's perfect. I'm the only one who ever took the band seriously." He leaned back in his chair and crossed his arms.

"That's a load of crap and you know it," Peter said.

"Is it? I was the one driving to keep us at the top."

"And you burned us out! If it were up to you, we'd never have a day off. What's the point of being at the top if you can't enjoy life?"

"You love being onstage. You can't deny it."

"You're right. I do. But at what price?"

"Don't do me any favors, I don't expect you to get it when you're in such a hurry to play house."

"Boys, keep your voices down. Please," his mother said.

"Excuse me?" Peter said through clenched teeth. "It seems that all I've done the past month is do *you* favors. Three times I've picked you up drunk or bailed you out of jail."

"Is that true, Garrett?" His mom looked horrified.

Garrett frowned. He hadn't planned on her finding out, let alone his dad.

"Garrett, let's take a walk." His father stood.

He was about to resist, but the stern expression on his father's face changed his mind. "Fine." He tossed his linen napkin on the table and rose.

"Honey, go ahead and enjoy dessert without us." His dad kissed his mother's cheek and then led the way out onto the street.

Garrett glanced back at the restaurant. Great, now he felt like a total dick. "Dad. We don't need to ruin Mom's birthday by leaving."

"I think you've already taken care of that." He walked down the sidewalk, leaving Garrett no choice but to follow.

They walked in silence for two blocks before his father lit up a cigarette.

"Does Mom know you're smoking again?"

Dad eyed him. "What do you think?"

Ever since his dad's heart attack a couple of years ago, he'd been forbidden to touch a cigarette.

"We're all going to die someday. I'd prefer to live life my way." He took a long drag and blew it out. "Son. I know this has been tough for you. I see you floundering, with no direction."

Garrett bristled. His dad made him sound weak. "I've got it under control."

"That's good, because I'd hate to see what out of control looks like."

They walked along the quiet streets. The concert at the

Pavilion would have started by now.

His father interrupted his thoughts. "Have you given any consideration to what you'd like to do?"

"Yeah, I'd like to be on tour with Jamieson."

"Garrett, your life is just getting started, and you have a lot of years ahead of you. You've had remarkable success, but life is filled with unexpected twists and turns."

"And this one is bullshit."

"Bands break up all the time. You boys started this at such a young age. It's no surprise that things changed."

"Dad, I get that. It doesn't mean I have to like it."

"No, but how a man deals with adversity defines him. Do you want to be a washed-up young rocker who becomes more famous for his screwups than his achievements?"

"Of course not."

"Then it's time to pull yourself together and get on with life." His dad settled his commanding gaze on Garrett.

"And do what?" Garrett sighed as they walked on.

"Whatever you want. You've certainly got the resources for it. You could go to college. That was always your mother's and my dream for you and your brothers. But then that got put on the back burner."

"Garrett Jamieson sitting in a freshman English lit class? I don't think so." He bristled at the idea.

"Have you considered going solo?"

"A little, but I don't know if I'm solo artist material."

As a group, Jamieson was in perfect sync. As a solo

act, he didn't think he was strong enough. He was no idiot. He didn't have the voice and charisma of Peter, who could make girls scream with one look or shake of his hair. And Adam was bursting with charm and showmanship. Everyone loved him. Garrett was basically the intense, mysterious member of the group.

"What do you think? Could I make it going solo?"

"You want my honest opinion? I think it would be a career ender. You'd be chasing after the success of Jamieson and you'd never catch it."

Garrett's heart dropped. "Gee, Dad. Thanks for crushing my dreams."

"It's time for new dreams, son."

He stepped in front of his dad and walked backward so he could face him. "But this has always been my dream. I have no other dreams or skills. I can't do anything other than perform."

"That's not true. You're damn good at making decisions that helped Jamieson become successful. Everything from selecting songs for the albums, production, and promotion. You have a talent for the business side of the industry."

Garrett fell back in step beside him. "I had to. That first business manager we hired was a total idiot."

His dad laughed. "No, Garrett. You have a talent for finding the gems among the dust. Peter may have written the songs, but you always knew which ones would hit it big."

He'd never thought of it that way. He figured they'd gotten lucky.

"Have you ever thought about producing records? You like having control of things, and as a producer, you'd be calling the shots. You could select what artists to work with."

Garrett perked up. "I've never considered that before. Dad, you're brilliant!"

"We have enough contacts. I'm sure we can call in a couple favors, maybe find someone to show you the ropes a little, give you a chance to do some hands-on learning."

Finally, something he could get his head around. He could take some fresh new band, teach them the ropes, and produce their album. Hell, he could make his name all over again as a music producer. Not to mention showing up his brothers. They could wither away in the shadows while he struck it big without them.

4

Two days later, Riley patched the last cords into the sound board. She checked every last setup detail, finding everything in order. She may have been working as an entry-level runner for the past three months, but she'd soaked up every bit of knowledge she could from the engineers and their assistants.

"How's it look?" Ron asked, entering the control room. She still couldn't believe that he was giving her this opportunity.

"I think we're about set. I'm entering the track names now, so all we need is the band." Working with Fever Pitch was the best thing that had happened in a long time. It sure made up for the Nuggett fiasco.

"Great. Let me take a look." Ron settled into the middle seat in front of the board and pushed up his glasses. He'd be adjusting all the input levels, making sure they captured exactly the right sound. As assistant engineer, Riley would cue the tracks, set the recording, save and mark each take, patch in different mics as needed, and occasionally adjust equipment.

"I'm going to grab some coffee while it's still fresh. Can I bring you some?"

"Thanks. That'd be great," Ron said.

Fetching coffee was a runner's job, but Riley didn't mind. Plus, she didn't feel like waiting around for Logan. He was still a little sore that she got this session.

As she finished pouring the two coffees in the break room, Tara rushed up, her long dangly earrings swinging like wind chimes in a storm. "Did you see who just arrived?" she asked, her tongue piercing flashing into view.

"No, who?"

"Garrett Jamieson! Can you believe it?" Tara's face flushed with excitement.

The band, Jamieson, was huge. They'd recorded their last two albums here, and Barry Goldman, the owner of Sound Sync Studio, had won a Grammy for producing their *Triple Threat* album, as did the band. The award hung prominently in the lobby along with awards from other big artists like Graphite Angels and Fever Pitch. "Seriously? I thought Jamieson broke up. Is he here to do solo work?"

"I don't know, but he's meeting with Barry right now. Riley, you should see him. He is even better looking in person." Tara fanned herself. "Wanna come peek through the meeting room door with me and check him out?"

"I'd love to, but I'm in Studio B. I get to assist Ron and Barry with Fever Pitch." If it were any other day, she'd have been next to Tara sneaking a fangirl look at the superstar. She had several of their hits on her favorites playlist.

"That's right, I forgot. Good luck. I better get back before they're out of their meeting. Would it be weird if I asked for his autograph? Here?" Tara stuck out her chest and smiled with a naughty twinkle in her eye.

"Go for it." Riley laughed and carried the hot coffees back to the control room, shaking her head.

"Here you go." She handed a coffee to Ron, and set the other on a table next to her spot at the control board. As she was about to sit, the door opened.

Barry, the producer on the album, entered. He stood tall, always wore jeans and a T-shirt, and so far had been an awesome boss. "Ron, Riley. I'd like to introduce you to a special guest."

In walked Garrett Jamieson, with dark hair pushed off his face, a confident set to his jaw, and a commanding intensity in his eyes.

"Garrett, meet Ron Slater and Riley Parks. They'll be working with us today on Fever Pitch's new album."

Garrett stepped forward. The way he moved in his tailored shirt, dark designer jeans, and Sperrys gave him an air of casual confidence.

Ron stood and shook his hand. "Nice to meet you. Congratulations on the Grammy for your *Triple Threat* album."

"Thanks. We couldn't have done it without Barry. He's a genius." Garrett's eyes traveled to Riley, and he smiled. "Nice to meet you." His voice softened.

She shook his hand, noting his solid grip and the way his gray eyes sparkled. "Great to meet you!"

Riley tried to control her breath. It wasn't every day she bumped into a superstar barely a few years older than her. Jamieson's music had soothed her through many difficult days. She first discovered them on YouTube when they were getting their start. The three band members were as popular as their music was chart topping.

Garrett scanned Riley from head to toe, then abruptly turned his back on her. Riley's smile fell. Had she failed some secret test?

"Barry, I can't thank you enough for giving me this opportunity," Garrett said.

"It's nothing. We're glad to have you here for as long as you want," Barry answered.

What opportunity was he talking about? Was Garrett going to sing on Fever Pitch's album? She couldn't quite see that happening.

A musician with curly hair hanging in his eyes and a dense beard entered the recording studio and picked up a saxophone.

"The rest of the band is running late," Barry said. "But we met with Tony, and he's ready to lay his tracks, so let's get started."

Barry took the producer's chair on the right side of the sound board. The man was a genius. Riley always learned a ton when he was at the helm.

As she was about to take her seat, Garrett slipped into her chair.

She stared, dumbfounded, as he examined the board, taking in all the connections and settings she'd made. He picked up her coffee from the adjacent table and took a sip.

Her jaw dropped. "Excuse me," she said, a little more snappish than she meant to in front of her boss.

All three men at the sound board turned to look at her. She stared at Garrett pointedly.

"What?" he said.

She glanced at Ron, who shrugged. Barry looked annoyed at the interruption.

"Uh. That's my coffee."

"Oh. Sorry about that," Garrett said. "I prefer mine black, anyway." He handed her the cup.

Riley held her coffee as she waited for him to realize he'd taken her place at the board, and get up. But he didn't.

"Do you mind?" Garrett asked.

She stared at him in confusion. "What?"

"Coffee. Black."

Was he really that stupid?

"Riley, please fetch Garrett a cup of black coffee," Ron said, interrupting her frozen shock at Garrett's audacity.

"But . . ."

"Riley." Ron leveled a knowing gaze at her. "The coffee, please."

She spun on her heel and left.

"This is bull!" Riley dumped her coffee down the drain. Five minutes ago she'd have loved to share coffee with the famous Garrett Jamieson, but now, it was tainted.

Logan jumped out of the splash zone. "Whoa. They throw you out already? That's got to be a record."

"No! Garrett Jamieson just hijacked my job. He walked in, tossed around his gold records, and stole my chair. And my coffee." She pulled a fresh mug from the cupboard and slammed it on the counter.

"That sucks." Logan frowned.

She pulled out the coffeepot to find it empty and shoved it back on the burner. "Great. Doesn't anyone know how to make a damn pot of coffee around here?"

She grabbed the empty coffeepot again and filled it with water. "Why can't anything ever go my way?"

"Don't be so down. I'm sure Garrett's only here for a couple of hours and then he'll disappear with some groupie."

"I hope he catches something itchy." Riley poured water in the pot, tossed a few scoops of coffee grounds into the filter, and pressed BREW.

Tara walked in. "Are you guys talking about Garrett? Oh my God, Riley, I heard he's in Studio B with you? You are so lucky." Her eyes glittered—she was starstruck like a true fangirl.

"Yup. Real lucky." Riley leaned against the counter, her arms crossed.

"Why aren't you in there? I wouldn't leave his side," Tara said.

"He wants coffee," she muttered.

"I wonder if he's looking to put together a new band. Or maybe he's going solo," Tara speculated.

"I don't think so. He's not good enough," Logan said.

"How can you say that? I'd buy his music." Tara sat on the break table and reached for a hard candy from a basket.

"Trust me. He could never make it solo. He might have a pretty face, but his voice isn't good enough to go it alone," Logan said.

"Such a pity." Tara sighed as if she somehow had a vested interest in the superstar.

Riley pulled out the coffeepot, filled up her mug, and then filled the other mug halfway. She splashed some creamer in hers, then filled Garrett's the rest of the way, turning his black coffee a light shade of beige.

"Isn't that a lot of cream?" Tara asked, popping a candy in her mouth.

"Just the way he likes it," she said, smirking.

Riley carried the mugs back to the control room and handed the one that was more cream than coffee to Garrett.

"Here you go," she whispered in his ear, irritated when

she noticed how good his cologne smelled.

"Thanks." His cocky smile would have brought Tara melting to the floor, but Riley found it patronizing. He took a sip and startled. He looked in the mug. "I said black."

"You did? I'm sorry, I guess I didn't catch that." She smiled.

Garrett narrowed his eyes as she took a seat on the couch at the back of the room and sipped her steaming coffee.

The next hours dragged and Riley's patience waned as Garrett ineptly set up the tracks. Riley rearranged mics, brought in take-out food, and fetched guitar strings from Fever Pitch's van. Garrett was so busy trying not to fail, he didn't notice the daggers she stared at his back.

The night grew late as Barry messed with the snare drum, trying to get the perfect sound. Not too tinny, and yet not hollow either. Riley was fighting to keep her eyes open when her phone rang at one a.m. She checked the number. It was her little sister, Britta. Not a good sign this time of night. Riley slipped out of the control room.

"Hey, Britta, what's up?"

"Can you come home? I'm scared." Her sister's voice wobbled.

"I'm working right now. What's going on? Where's Mom?"

"I don't know. She never came home. She had the early shift and said she'd be home tonight, but she's not."

"I'm sure Mom's fine. She's probably out with friends again," Riley said, mustering a chipper voice, but inside, her irritation steamed that her mother was still pulling her disappearing stunts.

"The police brought Matt home. They caught him trying to break into the school. The officers were mad that Mom wasn't here. I lied and told them she'd be back soon."

Riley leaned her head against the wall and sighed. "Put Matt on the phone."

"Matt! Riley wants to talk to you," Britta called out to her fifteen-year-old brother.

Riley glanced up and discovered Garrett watching her through the control room window and turned her back.

"No," Riley heard her brother yell from the background.

Britta came back on the line. "He won't talk. He's mad because some guy stole his phone. He keeps throwing things. He already broke a lamp and a dish."

"Britta, just go to bed. Mom will be home when you wake up." Couldn't her mom see that her kids needed her? Of course not. That would mean she'd have to think about someone other than herself for a change.

"No, she won't. Twice last week she didn't come home at all. And there are some guys drinking outside behind the bar. They're really loud and it's too hot in here to close the window."

Riley checked on the band and the guys in the control room. They'd have to deal without her. She wasn't doing anything important anyhow. "Listen, curl up on the couch with your pillow and try to sleep. I'll get there as soon as I can."

5

After a thirty-minute trip on the "L," Riley arrived at her mom's small apartment located over a dive bar. She'd been so happy to move out from this place and in with her best friend, Erika, a few months ago. Riley thought she had escaped the chaos, but kept getting called back to deal with each new crisis.

Outside the building she found her younger brother holding a cigarette and drinking a beer with a couple of other teenage derelicts.

"Matt, what the hell are you doing?"

He looked up, not surprised to see her. "Just hanging." He inhaled on his cigarette.

"Well, you're done. Get upstairs. Britta's scared and you getting dragged home by the cops didn't help."

"They're a bunch of assholes. I wasn't doing anything wrong."

Riley grabbed his beer, poured it on the sidewalk, and tossed the bottle into a nearby trash bin. "Of course not. You never are. Come on."

She pushed him toward the door. He threw down his cigarette and took the steps to their second-floor apartment. Riley stepped on the butt, crushing it as she followed him up the creaky wooden steps.

Inside she was greeted by the stink of trash that should have been taken out days ago. Nothing had changed since her last visit home. Why she thought it might, she didn't know. Eternal optimism, she guessed.

Britta sat with her legs curled under her in the corner of the threadbare couch, eyes glazed, watching some reality show with a bunch of women screaming at each other.

"Hey, Britta," Riley said.

Britta turned her tired eyes on her sister. "You're here!" She ran across the room and hugged Riley around the waist. Riley hugged Britta and rubbed her back, brushing her tangled mess of fine red hair out of the way.

"Of course I am. I told you I would, but you should be asleep. You've got summer school tomorrow."

"Mom never makes me go. I want to stay here with you."

"I'm only here until Mom gets home. I have to work."

"Can't you call in sick? Just this once?" Britta yawned.

"Sorry, I need this job. But I'll be here the rest of the night. It's quiet outside now, so you should jump into your own bed. It'll be cooler in there."

"You promise you're staying?" Britta asked, used to being let down.

"I promise," she said, looking into Britta's innocent eyes.

"Okay, but don't leave before I wake up tomorrow."

"I won't." She hugged Britta one more time and pointed her toward her bedroom.

"Good night," Britta said, and disappeared into her room.

Riley turned to find Matt in the kitchen, digging into a bag of Cheetos. "What were you thinking leaving her alone all night? You know she gets scared. And breaking into the school? What's wrong with you?"

"She was fine. And I didn't break into the school. Jimmy did. His older brother left some pot in his locker and paid Jimmy to get it out before summer weight training on Monday."

"You know better than to get mixed up with that. You can't keep pulling this stuff. You've gotta keep your nose clean." She picked up a fast-food bag and threw it in the trash.

"Stop freakin' out. I've got it under control."

She pulled the trash bag tight and lifted it out of the wastebasket. "Oh yeah, so under control you can't bother to take the trash out?"

"Why should I when I've got you here to do it?" He grinned.

She leveled him a murderous glare. "Matt, you have to do better than this. You can't be screwing up all the time. It's going to catch up with you."

"Not everyone has a famous singer to find us jobs," he said, referring to Jason Edgette, the amazing judge from Riley's run on the reality singing show, *Chart Toppers*. He'd helped Riley land the job at Sound Sync Studio.

"No, but you've got to prove to people you know how to work hard and that you can be responsible. No one's going to trust you with a job if all you do is smoke, drink, and get into trouble."

"Whatever, I'm going to bed." He went to his room and shut the door, leaving her alone. Where the heck was her mother? Out with her girlfriends again, or sleeping with some loser?

Riley took the trash bag and placed it in the hallway. She could see Britta's efforts at keeping the apartment clean. The gossip magazines her mom loved were stacked neatly on the scratched coffee table, and the mismatched kitchen table chairs were all pushed in. Dirty dishes were stacked neatly by the sink. Riley hated leaving Britta here on her own, but she tried to help as much as she could.

After washing the dishes, she lay down on the couch. Her mom still wasn't home. Riley should be used to her mother's disappearing acts, but she really thought her mom would do better now that Riley wasn't around to handle things. Except that here she was, dealing with it all again.

All Riley wanted was to get a fresh start. A new life.

One that was a couple steps up from this crappy apartment and her often unemployed mother.

Riley had rented a cracker box of an apartment with her friend and worked at an awesome job at the studio. It was totally entry level, but she didn't care. All she needed was a chance to prove herself. Of course, Garrett had stomped all over that. She sighed, closed her eyes, and let exhaustion take over.

Riley woke a few hours later to the sound of someone fumbling with the door lock. The door opened and she heard the trash bag get knocked over. She opened a weary eye and spied her mom tossing her designer handbag on the counter.

Riley pushed herself upright. "A little late, aren't you?"

"Oh, you startled me!" her mom said, swaying on her feet. "What are you doing here?"

"Britta was scared to death and begged me to come. God, Mom. You didn't even bother to call home."

"Lenny had some friends in town and invited me over after work. I was fine." She kicked her heels into the corner.

"I wasn't worried about you. How about your ten-year-old daughter?"

"Matt was here, there was nothing to worry about." She dropped onto the couch.

"Actually, he wasn't. At least not until the cops brought him home."

Her mom picked up a pack of cigarettes off the coffee table, pulled one out, and lit up. "What'd he do this time?"

"Broke into the school."

Her mom laughed and then coughed. She brushed her red hair out of her face. "That's a first. Usually he's trying to skip out of that place."

Riley got a whiff of her mother's breath. "Are you still drunk?"

"Of course not." She took a long drag off her cigarette.

Riley was used to her lying. "You should probably get in the shower. Don't you have to work at nine?"

"I'm going in a little late today. Bill won't mind."

"Mom, please don't lose this job."

"Why don't you worry about your own business? If you'd have done that five years ago, we'd all be a lot better off right now." She stared at Riley with a look of utter disappointment.

Riley's gut ached at the sudden attack.

Her mother stood. "I'm going to bed." She disappeared into her bedroom and kicked the door closed. Riley hoped she remembered to put out her cigarette before she dropped off to sleep.

So here it was. Again. Anytime Riley called her mother out about acting responsibly, her mom blamed her. Riley had a chance to change all their lives five years ago. If she hadn't screwed up, she could have raised them all out of the gutter and into something more respectable.

She couldn't fight the guilt over disappointing her family. She'd done the best she could. But it wasn't enough.

No matter what Riley said or did, her mom didn't really care about her kids. She never had, not unless there was something in it for her.

6

A taxi dropped Garrett off at a trendy Michigan Avenue hotel at two a.m. He tipped the driver and entered the lobby, which featured a rotunda seating area, art deco coffee tables, and low-hanging chandeliers.

"Welcome to the Acadia. May I help you?" a twenty-something reception clerk asked.

"Hi, I'm checking in. You should have a reservation for Garrett Jamieson."

A smile lit the clerk's face and he clicked away at the keyboard. "I thought I recognized you. We're so happy to have you staying with us. Yes, here's your reservation. We've been holding the penthouse suite for you. It boasts a beautiful city view and has its own terrace."

"That sounds perfect. I've had a long day." He'd taken an early flight out of Boston this morning and gone straight to the studio. He craved a stocked mini bar and putting his feet up.

A young couple burst through the door, clearly intoxicated and giggling. The guy wore a sharp suit, and the glossy blond woman on his arm shimmered in a sexy dress and heels.

Garrett smiled, pulled out his wallet, and tossed his platinum card on the marble counter.

The clerk ran his card and handed him his room key. "Here you go. The elevator is around the corner."

"Thank you," Garrett said, stepping away from the counter.

The young couple came forward. "Hi, reservation for Walker. We've got a suite," the guy said.

Garrett slipped the wallet in his back pocket. He leaned over to untangle the strap on his messenger bag from his guitar case handle.

The clerk's wide forehead wrinkled. "Let me see."

The wife slipped her arm under her husband's jacket, as if she wanted to crawl right in. The guy smiled and kissed her.

"I'm sorry, sir. There are no more suites available."

"That can't be right," the young woman said. "I made this reservation over a month ago. It's our anniversary. We spent our honeymoon here. Please check again."

"Of course, I'll take another look," he said, but grimaced.

Garrett had a sneaking suspicion he'd just taken their room. "Excuse me," he said to the desk clerk. "I think you gave me the wrong key. I requested a room on a lower floor."

He set his key on the counter and pushed it forward. "I'm not a fan of heights." He smiled at the couple.

"Are you certain?" the clerk asked.

"Absolutely," Garrett said.

The clerk issued him a new key, and a few minutes later, Garrett entered his hotel room. He went to the window and discovered a perfect view of the office building next door. If he craned his neck he could see the street.

The small room lacked the energy of his hotel stays with his family. Now that he thought about it, he'd never really traveled without them before. He tossed the keycard on the desk, snatched a beer from the mini bar, and relaxed into a comfortable chair.

He'd made it through the day. Walking into that studio had been one of the hardest things he'd ever done. Much harder than breaking into the business or pitching record companies. It was him alone, with no one to fall back on or to stand by his side.

Garrett had wondered how Barry would feel about his request to learn the ropes of producing after all the music he had produced for Jamieson. But his concerns were unfounded. Barry welcomed Garrett to spend as much time at Sound Sync as he wanted, which made showing up alone, without his band, a little easier to stomach.

He was tempted to call Peter and shoot the shit with him, but it was the middle of the night back in Boston. Plus, he was still pissed at him and didn't want any of Peter's bullshit encouragement about trying a new direction. If it weren't for his brothers, Garrett wouldn't be in this predicament.

He took a swig of his beer and sighed. The recording session had gone pretty well. It took a bit to get the hang of things in the control room. He'd messed around on the control boards during the recording of Jamieson's albums, but he'd never been scrutinized like he was today.

The chick with the red hair and cute little diamond nose stud had been drilling lasers at his back the whole time. He didn't know what her problem was, but if she was like most women, she'd enlighten him eventually.

The next day, despite a poor night's sleep and more family drama than usual, Riley was back in the live room of Studio B, finishing the guitar setup for Fever Pitch.

Logan, Ron, Nick, and a couple other guys were gathered around the monitor in the control room, laughing. Must be nice to sit around, but she refused to take the slacker route. Still, they were having a heck of a good time. She didn't know what was so funny, but then they noticed her watching, broke into huge grins, and gave her a thumbs-up.

Okay, whatever.

As she taped down a cord so no absentminded guitar genius would trip over it, Nick, one of the assistant engineers, spoke through the talk-back speaker.

"Hey, Riley, nice feathers in your hair."

She glanced up. What the heck was he talking about? Feathers? She'd never worn feathers in her . . .

No!

Riley dropped everything and rushed into the control room. She stopped short when she discovered a YouTube video playing.

The blood drained from her face.

They were watching old YouTube videos of *Chart Toppers*.

"Riley, we didn't know you were a star," Ron said, not taking his eyes off the screen.

"Look at you. You're adorable," said Logan.

Riley couldn't believe it. She'd worked so hard to forget that time of her life. The only one here who knew about her dismal run on the reality singing show was Barry, who owned the studio, and he had agreed not to tell. The only reason he knew was because Jason Edgette, the nicest of the judges and mentors on the show, had contacted Barry to get her a job interview.

"Check out those round little cheeks and freckles. How old were you?" Ron asked.

"Thirteen," Riley mumbled, unsure what to do now that her secret was out. She looked around the control room, feeling trapped. This would ruin everything.

She wanted to make a name for herself here as a

dedicated, hard worker with a talented ear. She wanted to be a sound engineer someday, but how would that be possible now? All they would think of when they saw her was the kid who lost on *Chart Toppers*.

She needed to act professional right now, but all she really wanted was to rush out of the studio and hide behind the Dumpster.

And then, to make matters worse, Garrett walked in. "What's going on?" he asked, noticing the crowded room. His eyes dashed over her. Riley had slept on the couch last night, wore the same jeans from yesterday, and had borrowed a top from her mom that fit tighter than she liked. She folded her arms across her chest.

"Our very own little Riley was on *Chart Toppers*! Look at that outfit. It's like she's trying to be a rocker," said Tim, another runner and a total tool. He always wore a navy ski cap and never tied his shoes.

Garrett joined the mob watching the video. Riley's face flamed with embarrassment.

"You've got pipes, girl. Why didn't you tell us?" Nick said.

She needed to get out of there, but she was assigned to this studio today.

Tim brought up another video. She silently groaned. It was her first Fight for Your Life Challenge.

Memories flooded back. She'd been so upset that day. Each week the pressure became more unbearable, and her mom kept demanding she do better.

Her mom had lost her job again, and blamed Riley. She'd left work to come out to Hollywood to be with Riley during the live performances. The bills piled up at home, and if Riley won, it would make a big difference for her family, but the other contestants were so good.

Riley's husky voice sounded from the monitor. To her it sounded like wailing. She remembered trying not to cry. She was in the bottom two and would be sent home unless she could change the judges' minds with this last-ditch effort.

"That's Riley!" Garrett said, looking at the monitor, then at her, and back at the monitor again. "You can see her feisty side, even back then." He laughed.

"Turn it up," Nick said, moving closer to the screen.

The guys ate up her embarrassment. She turned away from the monitor and focused on the studio setup she'd just finished. They continued to joke as the video played on.

Riley couldn't take it any longer. "Turn it off," she said.

"No way, this stuff is pure gold," Tim said.

The door opened and Barry walked in. "What the hell is everyone doing in here? Does no one work anymore? Destiny's Demise is waiting for their engineer in Studio D, the setup in Studio A needs to be finished, and Logan, answer your calls. Your band is waiting to be picked up at their hotel."

"Yes, sir," Logan answered. He gave Riley a quick

thumbs-up before rushing out of the room. She rolled her eyes.

"Sorry, Barry," said Nick. "Did you know that Riley was on *Chart Toppers*?"

Barry looked in her direction and must have sensed her embarrassment. "Party's over, guys. Back to work."

The group dispersed, but Garrett remained. He didn't say a word. With a small curl of a smile, he studied Riley.

"Hanging around so you can gloat? Go ahead and get it over with. It ought to make your day for the big superstar to make fun of me as a kid."

Garrett leaned back in his chair. His eyes seemed to soak in every detail about her. She squirmed.

He stood and smirked. "It makes my day, all right. You have no idea."

"Whatever. Now would you leave? I have work to do."

He walked past, so close she wanted to give him a push. "I'm going, but just so you know, this changes everything."

"How's that?" she asked.

"I'm going to produce your record."

And he had the audacity to walk out the door.

"The hell you are!" She trailed after him.

He turned and laughed, all confident, as if he could do anything he wanted.

"You can't produce something that doesn't exist," she snapped.

"Then we'll have to make it exist."

Riley couldn't ignore his cocky smile. She wanted to smack him. "You're not hearing me. This isn't happening. I don't sing anymore. I don't even hum in the shower. And I'm definitely not recording a record with you, or anyone else!"

Garrett didn't seem fazed. He raised an eyebrow and gave her a half smile, half sneer. "We'll see."

7

Riley slammed the apartment door, rattling the pictures on the wall. Ten hours later and she was still steaming.

"Have a good night at work?" her roommate asked from her spot on the couch where she balanced a bowl of cereal on her knees and aimed the remote at the TV.

"I'm gonna kill him." Riley tossed her bag at the armchair.

"Kill who?"

"Garrett Jamieson."

Erika put down the remote. "Excuse me? As in the hot, intense Garrett from the band Jamieson?"

"I'd say more like the entitled, arrogant jerk, but yes. That's the one."

"You met him? At work?"

"Yes, but I wish I hadn't." Riley dropped onto the couch next to her.

"Why not? My God, have you looked at the guy? If it were me, I think I would have melted into a puddle right in front of him."

Riley rolled her eyes. "He showed up yesterday and took over my first chance to sit at the board with Ron and Barry. He's horrible."

"Yeah, bummer. What else? Did he try to corner you in the supply closet? Steal your lunch?"

"Not funny." Riley beelined for the fridge, but inside nothing looked good or within its expiration date. She swung the door shut. "You know you could be a little more supportive here."

"There's a half bag of chocolate chips hiding behind the macaroni. How's that for supportive?"

"It'll work." She dug into the cupboard and fished out the chocolate, along with a jar of peanut butter.

"So what did he do?"

Riley grabbed a spoon then closed the drawer with her hip and returned to the living room. "He said he's going to produce my record." She filled her spoon with a huge dollop of peanut butter and then dipped it into the chocolate chips.

"What record?"

"Exactly!" She nibbled off a chunk of chocolate and peanut butter and savored the sweet, creamy taste.

"Why would he think you have a record to produce?"

"Because he heard me sing."

Erika dropped her spoonful of cereal back in the bowl. "Back the truck up!"

"Someone at work found me on YouTube and played all those horrible videos from when I was on *Chart Toppers*. Even worse, practically everyone saw them." She bit off more peanut butter.

Erika grimaced. "That sucks."

Riley nodded with her mouth full. "You know how hard I've worked to put that behind me. Now I have to deal with it all over again."

"It was a long time ago. They'll be curious for a while and then forget about it."

Riley had met Erika freshman year when her friend moved from Cleveland to South Chicago. Erika seemed like the only person on the planet who didn't know about her appearance on *Chart Toppers*, and even better, Erika didn't care, which made her the perfect new best friend.

"But what about Garrett? I didn't like the way he was staring at me. Kind of like I was a fresh piece of meat that he was deciding how to devour."

"Um, that sounds kind of fun."

Riley glared at her.

"Sorry. He can't make you do anything you don't want to."

"Thank you!" She waved her spoon in the air.

"He might be the hottest guy around, but why would you want to spend more time with him? He might try to kiss you and take you out, but don't let him!"

"Okay, you can stop being supportive now," Riley said, even though Erika was right. Garrett was good-looking, and there was something interesting about him. But there was no way he would ever get Riley to sing. Ever.

8

Riley entered the studio the next day hoping to go unnoticed and bury herself in work.

"Riley!" Tara called out. "I saw your videos. Why didn't you tell me you were on *Chart Toppers*? That is so cool. I had no idea!"

"Hi, Tara. No time to talk. Busy night." She kept her head down and kept walking.

"Wait! You've got to tell me about Jason Edgette. I was totally in love with him back in high school. Is he as hot in person as he is onscreen?"

Riley stopped. "I wouldn't know, Tara. I was thirteen. He was thirty."

"Oh." Tara frowned. "Garrett's looking for you."

"Great," she mumbled.

As Riley moved through the building, it appeared everyone knew about her turn on the reality show.

"Nice video," said some grinning tech guy who she'd never even talked to before.

She turned into the break room to find one of the runners, Tim, buying chips out of the vending machine.

"Riley, you should come jam with my band sometime."

She forced a smile and went to the equipment storage room to escape the badgering and closed the door. She put her hand against it and took a deep breath. They were just messing with her, but she didn't really want to deal with it.

She turned and found Logan, wearing a Bob Marley T-shirt and surrounded by piles of tangled cords. "That looks fun. They're more messed up than your dreads."

"Can you give me a hand? Ron needs these straightened out and ready to use in a half hour."

"Sure." She dropped down next to him on the floor and grabbed a pile, glad to have something mindless to occupy her.

They worked silently for almost a full minute before Logan ruined it.

"You gonna tell me about those videos, or do I have to drag it out of you?"

Riley sighed. "Not you, too."

"Everyone's curious. We're the people behind the scenes. We work for the people who have made it. You know that every one of us has dreamed of hitting it big. You actually did. That makes you special."

"I didn't make it big. Not even close. I got on a reality

47

show that ate me alive. I embarrassed myself, apparently until the end of time."

Logan looked at her, dumbfounded. "Why do you think that?"

"You've seen the videos. I lost it on national television," she said, examining the tangled mess.

Logan stopped working. "You were a kid. No one cares about that stuff."

Yeah, tell that to my mom and the kids at school. She shook her head. "The whole thing was a huge mistake. I was this kid with a dream and a little bit of talent. I had no business appearing on that show." She pulled the end of the cord through the knots. "Most of those people had voice coaches and had been trying to break through for years. They were in bands and had street smarts."

"But there were a bunch of kids your age, too, weren't there?"

She thought of Kylie, who had been her best friend on the show. Kylie had done voiceovers on two animated movies and sung in talent contests.

"True, but even the kids my age were pretty savvy. They had stage mothers, and performed in commercials or regional theater. They were little divas."

"Really?"

While she and Riley had been the same age, Kylie was already seasoned in the business. She came in second on the show and hit it big with a successful recording contract.

"Oh yeah. I was the token poor kid, way out of my league."

"But you came in sixth."

She raised an eyebrow. "And you know this how?"

"So I looked you up. Sue me. Riley, tens of thousands of people try out for those shows. You made it to the top six! That's incredible. You have an amazing voice. And if you had been a little older, you probably would have done even better."

Jason Edgette had said that, too.

"You should try out for one of those shows again, or get in a band."

"Nah," she said, wrestling with a knotted cord. "I don't sing anymore."

Logan's jaw dropped. "That's the saddest thing I've ever heard."

"Hardly," she said with a laugh.

"And why did you stop singing?"

Riley sighed. She really didn't want to go into this, but she liked Logan. "As I said, my last show on *Chart Toppers* went really bad. My mom didn't take my getting the boot very well, and when we got home and I started back to school, the kids were horrible. To be fair it wasn't all the kids, but there was a definite group of bullies that wouldn't let it go. I couldn't escape it."

Like Greg Hensen, a popular kid who hung out with Jordan Marx, a cute boy she really liked. In gym class,

Greg wailed out the song she'd performed, mimicking her in front of the whole class, acting overdramatic and sobbing. Everyone laughed, including Jordan. Riley'd run to the locker room in tears.

"In choir, I'd hear kids saying that they could have done better and how I never deserved to be on the show."

"That sucks," Logan said with sympathy.

"I quit choir. I didn't try out for the spring musical. I kind of disappeared from everything for a while. I skipped school for a few days until the principal called my mom."

Riley yanked at the cords. That period had been the worst in her entire life.

"You know they were jealous."

"Of what?"

"Of you getting all that attention. Of having a natural talent. Kids are mean that way."

"I suppose, but at the time, I needed to lick my wounds. That show was brutal. It looks all exciting and fun when you're sitting at home, but it's not when you're on it. They tell you what to do every minute, that you're too short, or your hair's too thin, or that they don't like the way you hold the mic. I wouldn't wish it on anyone."

"I'm sorry it was so horrible, but that was a long time ago and I think you should reconsider."

"Thanks, but I'm happy exactly where I am."

The door opened and Barry popped in. "Riley, there you are."

"Hi, Barry. What's up?"

"About the other day. I didn't know Garrett Jamieson was coming in until right before it happened. His manager called me as Garrett was literally stepping out of his cab. I owed him a favor."

"It's fine," she lied. It wasn't fine, but what could she do? She was the youngest person at the studio. Damn if that didn't feel like déjà vu. She was always the youngest and most inexperienced in this business.

"I'll make it up to you," Barry said.

Riley smiled at her boss. "Seriously, it's okay. I'm just so happy to have this job."

"You'll get your chance to shine, I promise. In fact there's something big coming up that I think you're going to love. The schedule isn't nailed down, but it could be in the next day or so. But in the meantime could you help Garrett mic up the drums in Studio D?"

"Are you saying your new assistant engineer can't set up mics?" She couldn't hide the disbelief in her voice.

Barry smiled and nodded. "That's what I'm saying. But give the guy a break. He's used to being behind the mic, not setting up twenty for a drum kit."

Riley bit her lip before she said something she regretted. She glanced at Logan, who was struggling not to laugh, then stood and wiped off her jeans. "I'll take care of it."

"Thanks," Barry said. "And by the way, nice pipes. You ever think maybe you're on the wrong side of the mic, too?"

She sighed audibly, and, rather than answer, escaped to help Garrett Jamieson.

But Garrett wasn't in the live room or the control room. She looked in the records room and even checked the reception area, but Tara wasn't there to ask. Garrett wasn't reading *Rolling Stone* in one of the comfortable chairs as she half expected, either.

As she was ready to give up and complete the setup herself, she noticed the open door to the mic storage room. He probably didn't know the difference between a condenser mic and a ribbon mic. She rounded the corner, ready to give the confused superstar an equipment lesson, but was startled when she found a pouty-lipped Tara up against the wall looking quite satisfied as Garrett leaned in close, his hand on the wall above her, and his mouth close to hers.

Oh, for Pete's sake, it was high school all over again.

"Hello," she called out. "I hear you need help plugging in a mic." She laced the words with sarcasm.

Garrett turned with the grace of a wildcat, his eyes darting over her.

What a colossal jerk. She didn't need his approval, or anyone else's, for that matter. Still, her face warmed at his all too obvious study of her appearance, and she wished she'd worn something nicer.

"Well, there you are," he drawled. "Tara, thanks for your help. I'll catch up with you later."

"Anytime," Tara purred as she strolled back to her desk.

"Making yourself comfortable, I see," Riley said.

Garrett watched the seductive sway of Tara's retreating curves. "Just getting my lay of the land."

"The studio is the other way." Riley pointed the opposite direction down the hall.

"Are you always this friendly?" he asked.

She wanted to spit out something smart and sassy, but nothing came to mind. "Come on." She headed for the recording studio, not glancing back to see if he followed.

"Is there something in particular I did to piss you off?" He walked next to her with an easy gait.

Riley practically choked. Gee, maybe stealing her chance to be assistant engineer the other day, or his big announcement that he planned to produce her records. "No. Not at all," she said, jaw clenched.

They entered the live room where the drum kit dominated. A mic bin sat on a cart and a couple stands lay on the floor.

"Let's get started." She selected a cardioid mic from the bin, attached it to a stand, and placed it in front of the kick drum. "Grab a couple of small diaphragm mics."

Garrett fished them from the bin and handed one over. At least he knew his mics. "Put the other on that stand, would you?" She attached it to the stand and placed it next to the snare.

"Why are you scrubbing around working an entry-level job like this?" he asked.

Her shoulders tensed. She screwed the stand mount tighter and reached for another.

"What? It's not that tough a question." He held out another mic. She snatched it from his hand.

"I can't believe you're criticizing my job, heck, every job here."

"You know that's not what I'm talking about," he said.

She ignored him. "This job might be below you, but most of us are thankful to be working in an industry we love."

"Bull. You don't love doing all the grunt work. When you were a little kid, you weren't dreaming of running around a recording studio fetching coffee and walking some washed-up singer's dog."

She chewed on the inside of her lip, fighting to hold back her words. He was baiting her. Her dreams had been much grander, but that was then.

"You belong up on a stage."

She glared at him.

"What? Did I hit a nerve?"

She turned her back and placed the stand under the center of the snare.

"You know I'm right. You need to get behind a mic and sing."

She flashed back to the fear she experienced onstage those last few times. Each time the stakes grew higher, the pressure mounted. She was so afraid to let everyone down and yet that's exactly what she did. In grand style, too.

She'd struggled to hold it together with all those cameras rolling, the judges ready to publicly rip her performance apart, and her mother promising their lives would be gold if only she could win.

Her chest tightened, and she forced down her panic.

"So now you're giving me the silent treatment?"

Riley snapped back to the present. "You know nothing about me, Garrett. You have no idea what I've done or not done, so shut it and let's get this job finished."

She reached for another stand, but Garrett stepped in front of her.

"That's not exactly true. I know that singing has been your dream since you were five years old. I know you used to wait outside the stage door of the Chicago Theater when you were young and try to get autographs. I know that you created your own harmonies to all the popular rock songs that your mom played on the radio so you could sing along as if it were a duet."

Oh God, why did he have to dig into her past? Her body raged with frustration and her face became shamefully hot.

"I know you, Riley. Admit it," he said in his cocky tone.

She turned on him. "You don't know jack. Just because you spent all night watching old YouTube videos and reading press from my time on *Chart Toppers* doesn't mean you know me. That was five years ago. Hell, it was before Jamieson hit it big. I'm not the same person. That starstruck little girl grew up."

He laughed. "No. That girl is using a job at a recording

studio to hide. If you don't care about this industry, why aren't you in college getting a degree in accounting or becoming an art teacher?"

She stopped what she was doing and turned on him. "Because my mother blew all the money I made on that show before I could even drive. That's why."

Garrett's eyes widened and his jaw dropped.

She returned to her task. "Didn't expect that, did you? The same woman who exposed all my deepest secrets to the press during the show also wasted what was supposed to be my college money on new clothes for herself, parties, and weekend jaunts to Vegas."

"I didn't know."

"Of course you didn't. Now butt out of my life." She grabbed another piece of equipment and crouched to attach the mic directly to the snare.

He stayed silent for a minute.

"Riley, I really want to work with you. I think we can make some great music together. Let go of your past and move on. Hell, we can show your mother you're the real deal after all."

"What's the matter with you?" she snapped. "Did you eat paint chips as a kid? I'm not singing for you or anyone else. You can't walk in here and tell me what to do. That's not how it works." She twisted the screw on another mic stand.

Garrett kneeled next to her. "That's exactly how it

works. When opportunities arise, you have to snatch them up. This is a golden opportunity."

"Go bother someone else with your deal."

"I don't want anyone else. I've seen the videos. There's no one else out there that sounds like you. You're original. You've got heart and guts."

He placed his hand on her arm, and for that moment he seemed sincere.

"Why are you doing all this? You don't even like me."

He shrugged. "Well, if you wore a little more makeup and dressed like a girl, I would. But we can hire people to take care of that."

Riley stood and stepped away. "You arrogant ass. Let me give you a little tip. This isn't gonna happen."

"We'll see," he said with a smug grin.

She stormed out.

9

Garrett and pop singer Candace Capri entered the artists' lounge the next day to grab lunch from the buffet. Candace was all curves and big hair, and he couldn't wait to get more familiar with her. Her first album had only produced one hit, but if the song hit big enough the label was willing to back a second album.

He wished he'd been the one to produce this album, but he'd been too late. If he could convince Riley to get over her personal baggage, she'd be the perfect project to help launch his producing career.

"Garrett Jamieson! No way, man," a familiar voice called.

Garrett turned to find Brad Stone and Eric Gehrke of the Jade Monkeys. They were an indie rock band who'd hired Jamieson as their opening act back when he and his brothers first started out.

"You've gotta be kidding me!" The guys hugged like long-lost fraternity brothers. "Do you know Candace?" Garrett included her into their circle.

"We met last year at the Grammys," Eric said, his six-foot-three-inch stature towering over her.

"Nice to see you again," she said. Her phone beeped. Candace checked the screen. "Excuse me, I've got to take this."

"So, what the heck are you doing here?" Garrett couldn't wipe the goofy grin off his face.

"We're trying to wrap up our album, but we've had a little personality issue, and our backup vocalist is a no-show. What are you doing here? I heard the band split up. That's gotta suck."

"It's a long story, but basically I'm going to start producing records."

"No way! That's awesome. I can see you as a producer. Where are you staying?" Eric asked.

"I've got a room at the Acadia."

"No, you don't want to stay there. Come to my place," Brad said. "I have a condo in the Marina Towers that sits empty most of the time."

"Seriously?"

"Hell, yes. It's a lot more private than a hotel, plus the House of Blues is right there, so you have a built-in night life," Brad said.

"Sounds perfect, but I might be in town for a while."

"We're only in town off and on for the next week or so, then we're on tour. You should take him up on it," Eric said.

"All right. I will. Thanks." Garrett couldn't believe his luck. He loved how people in the industry stuck together. "You know, as far as you needing a backup singer, I bet Barry can drum someone up."

"You think? That would be awesome, 'cause until we get those tracks laid, we're sitting in purgatory," Brad said.

Garrett noticed Riley at the fridge in the corner, adding bottled water and sodas. An idea struck. He fought back a grin. This was too damn easy.

"In fact, there might be a solution sooner than you think. See that girl over there?" He tilted his head toward Riley. "She was a finalist on *Chart Toppers* a couple of years back. I've heard her sing. She's amazing."

"No kidding. That'd solve the problem and save us a chunk on studio time. Think she'll do it?" Brad asked.

"Sing backup on your next hit album? She'd be a fool not to. Let me talk to her." Garrett grabbed an olive off the table and popped it in his mouth.

He came up behind Riley. "So this is where you've been hiding." She turned and bumped right into him.

"Whoa!" Riley fumbled the armload of bottled water, dropping three. "Geez, dude. You ever hear of personal space?" She kneeled down to pick up the bottles.

Garrett took a step back and nudged a water bottle toward her with his foot. "I've got a proposition for you."

"No," she said without looking up.

"You haven't even heard what I have to offer."

"I don't care what you have to offer. The answer will always be no."

Garrett kneeled down next to her and caught a whiff of her perfume. Something slightly floral, but with a bit of spice.

He spoke softly in her ear. "There's this great advancement opportunity for you here at the studio."

Riley glanced up.

"In Studio C with the Jade Monkeys."

She stood, all the bottles in her arms again. This time her expression showed excited interest instead of derision. "They need a new assistant engineer at the board?"

"Well, no. Not right now, but they might later. What they need is someone who can sing some backup tracks."

She curled her lip in a snarl. "Is that right?"

"You'd be perfect. I told them you'd do it, so you can't say no." He leaned casually against the table and crossed his arms, waiting. She'd be pissed at him, but she couldn't say no with the band a mere ten feet away. She'd thank him later.

"Oh really? And what's in this for you?"

"Nothing. Think of me as the problem solver. They need a kick-ass singer, and you have a kick-ass voice. You need help getting back in the game, and I'm here to provide it."

Riley set the bottles of water into a tub of ice on the table behind her. She glanced at the Jade Monkeys, who dished up their plates, then back at Garrett.

"Why is it that whenever I spend more than two minutes near you, I feel the need to use hand sanitizer?"

"Come on. You know you want to sing with them. Here, I'll introduce you." He took her by the arm before she could say no, and pulled her over to the guys. "Eric, Brad, I'd like you to meet—"

But Riley interrupted. "Hi guys, it's nice to see you again. I heard the final mix for your single 'Monsters Under the Bed.' It sounds like a hit to me."

"Thanks, we love what Barry did with it. It'll be the lead single off the album," Brad said.

Garrett looked from Riley, to the guys, and back again. "Oh, you've met. Good. I talked to Riley and she'd be happy to—"

"Thanks so much for the offer," Riley said. "Seriously, I'm flattered, but I don't sing anymore. Trust me, I'd ruin your album. But did you know that Garrett sings a great falsetto? In fact, I hear he's looking for a new gig. His last band kicked him out."

Garrett pierced her with a glare. Brad and Eric grinned.

"I've gotta run. But be sure to give Garrett a chance. He loves ballads. See ya!"

She punched Garrett lightly on the arm and walked out, letting the door fly shut behind her.

Eric burst out laughing.

"You've definitely got her under control." Brad chuckled. "Got any other ideas?"

Garrett stared at the closed door. Maybe Riley won that one, but he'd get her next time. No way was this little flit of a girl going to best him.

10

The next couple of days were a pain in the butt with Garrett's constant pressure to convince her to sing.

"That's all right. You probably don't have that great of a voice anymore anyway," he'd said yesterday in a poor attempt at reverse psychology.

"You got that right. I peaked at thirteen and it's all gone down the drain since then."

But he couldn't dampen her spirits. The Graphite Angels were in the building. A lot of big bands came through Sound Sync Studio, but to Riley, the Graphite Angels were the biggest. She loved their music, their lyrics, and their unique style. No one else on the planet had done as much for rock as they had.

When she was little, her mom played their music constantly. Riley could sing every word to every song. The Graphite Angels had shaped the way she sang from a tender age as she mimicked the rough, throaty tone of Steven Hunter, the lead singer. She'd even performed their megahit "Eclipse" while on the reality show. It was one of the few memories of the show that she was proud of.

And now, Steven Hunter and the rest of the band were here, and Barry made sure Riley was, too. She wouldn't be at the console, but she would be in the room, a fly on the wall, witnessing the iconic band make their magic.

Riley prepared the live room for vocals. The group had recorded the other tracks in the spring before she started working there, and before the band took a hiatus due to one of the members' sudden rehab stint.

Now they were back and she was setting up mics for Steven Hunter. Her stomach churned with excitement as she set up three different types of mics. She wasn't sure what he preferred and she wanted him to be happy. She set up a Copperhead, a SM7B, and then the big boy Miktek CV4, and attached a pop filter on each one.

She placed a stool nearby in case Steven wanted to sit. When everything was perfect, she took a spot in the back corner of the control room, out of the way. She had to keep her fangirl euphoria under wraps. Artists hated working with tech staff who couldn't stay professional and objective. For that reason, she wasn't sure she should even meet them. Riley didn't trust herself not to squeal with excitement. She just wanted to watch from afar. Maybe breathe some of the same air in the building, and if luck was on her side, sneak a picture of them in action.

Garrett and Ron entered. "Is everything ready?" Ron asked.

"Yes, it's all set," she answered. Garrett looked eager to strike up a conversation, so she studied the paperwork on her clipboard. Why did he have to be here? She'd successfully avoided him the last couple of days.

The door opened and Barry entered, along with Steven Hunter and the guys that made up the Graphite Angels. Another man who she didn't recognize carried a video camera on his shoulder.

One wouldn't know that these aging tattooed rockers, still sporting long hair and a cocky swagger, were such massive talent. Riley felt dwarfed in their presence, while Garrett could stand proudly with them as an equal and didn't need to be embarrassed.

Barry started the introductions. "Steven, Jon, Teddy, Frank, I'd like you to meet your crew for today. You remember Ron from last spring. And we have a special guest who's been working with us for the past couple of weeks, Garrett Jamieson."

Garrett nodded and smiled.

Barry turned to Riley and winked, knowing how starstruck she must be. Her nerves tightened like the snare on a drum.

Oh my God, he was going to introduce her. She pasted on a smile that she hoped looked casual and not like a fangirl.

"And we also have Riley Parks assisting us . . ."

Steven Hunter interrupted. "Did you say Garrett Jamieson? Well, I'll be damned. Your brother is dating my daughter, Marti."

Riley's smile fell as Steven failed to notice her when Garrett was in the same room. She looked away, as if not devastated that Garrett stole her one moment with the superstar.

Steven stepped forward, shook Garrett's hand, and pulled him into a bear hug. "Hell, boy, we're practically family."

Garrett laughed. "Yes, sir. Just about."

Steven wore several chains and pendants, purple brocade pants, a white shirt unbuttoned to his waist, and a mustard-colored jacket with a long scarf. The man didn't disappoint. "How is Adam? I heard he was off taking pictures in some foreign country."

"That's right. He's in Tanzania."

Garrett acted unfazed by the presence of rock royalty as he chatted it up with Steven. But Riley was ticked that he kept stepping into situations where he wasn't welcome. At least not by her.

"Marti called me when he left. She was a big sobbing baby, but she'll get over it. Hey, I heard the band broke up. Something about Peter having throat problems."

Riley could see the light suddenly dim in Garrett's eyes at Steven's words. She'd heard rumors about his brother having vocal problems, but she didn't know if they were true.

"Not exactly the thing you want to happen when you're at the top of your game," Garrett said.

"Damn straight. It's a shame. Any chance you'll be getting back together?"

"It doesn't look that way. Which is why I'm here. I'm hoping to hone my skills in another part of the industry."

"Smart boy. Well, if there's anything you need, let me know." Steven patted him on the shoulder.

"Thank you, sir."

"All riiiiight!" Steven half sang, half screamed in his iconic voice. "Let's get this party started."

Everyone laughed. The other Graphite Angels settled onto the couches, the camera guy set the video camera on a tripod, and Steven removed his bright jacket.

Riley couldn't help the stab of envy from watching Garrett shake hands and talk with Steven while she'd been overlooked entirely. She probably would have said or done something embarrassing anyway. Sitting back in her corner to watch, she shook off the disappointment.

Steven entered the live room, taking in the empty space. He looked above him at the acoustically friendly ceiling tiles and the portable sound walls she had placed around the three microphones to create an open booth. Soloists usually recorded in the small isolation booth, but Steven Hunter was claustrophobic, so he always recorded in the main live room.

He approached the three mics and smiled at the bevy

of choices. "Check, check, check," he said into each one. In the control room, they adjusted the knobs and slide buttons.

He sang an opening refrain from one of his songs, again trying each mic as the guys at the console recorded the samples.

"Hey, what do you think?" Steven asked.

Barry hit the talk-back button. "The SM7B sounds a bit hollow. Why don't you step in and listen to the other two."

Steven reentered the control room. Ron instructed Garrett to play back the other two versions. He pulled them up right away. He no longer fumbled around at the control board. At least the guy was a quick learner and wasn't going to embarrass Barry with shoddy work.

The team discussed the sounds of each mic with the band, narrowing down the last two mics. Ron, as assistant engineer, fine-tuned the balance of the feed. Steven returned to the live room.

"Can I get some water?" Steven asked.

This was Riley's job. Her pulse quickened as she hopped off her stool and fetched a bottle of water from the small fridge between rooms. She entered the live room, trying to act professional and low key.

She set the bottle on a small table next to the mics and snuck a quick peek at Steven.

"Thanks," he said, glancing at her briefly before Barry piped through to give it another try.

Riley's heart soared. Steven Hunter had actually spoken to her! She slipped from the room.

The sound check process took twenty minutes. When Riley first started at the studio, she'd been surprised at how much time it took to make sure each mic produced the desired sound, and the Graphite Angels were very specific in what they wanted.

"We're getting a hollow sound off the Copperhead mic," Jon, the bass player, said.

"Riley, would you adjust the pop filter closer to the mic?" Barry asked.

"Sure." She slipped back into the live room where Steven stood. "Excuse me. I'm going to adjust the filter a little."

Riley kept her eyes trained on her task, not wanting to openly stare at the megastar. He stepped back and took a swig of water. She sensed his eyes on her as her fingers fumbled with the adjustment knobs as if this were her first day on the job.

"I swear they're hiring kids younger and younger. You don't look any older than my daughter, Marti, and she's still in high school."

"I'm eighteen." Riley offered up a smile.

She glanced up and caught Garrett staring at her, then he quickly looked away. Could he possibly be jealous that she was talking with Steven? She fought to keep a smirk off her face.

"You must know someone pretty high up to have gotten a gig here at your age."

"Just lucky," she said.

But she knew it was Jason Edgette who'd helped her, contacting her every so often to see how she was. As soon as she graduated and he learned she couldn't even afford community college, he contacted Barry.

"No one is just lucky, kid. Must be that rockin' red hair of yours," he teased.

Riley dipped her head to hide the blush that crossed her cheeks. She finished adjusting the filter. "There you go. That should sound better."

She hightailed it from the room and fought to act cool as she reentered the control room.

Steven tested the new mic placement.

"Much better. Let's try the first verse," Barry said.

Garrett hit the PLAY button and the loud pulsing notes of her favorite Graphite Angels song pumped through the room. A grin spread across her face as Steven Hunter sang those familiar lyrics. His voice delivered the gritty tones that made him famous. Looking around the room, she noticed everyone on staff smiling, including Garrett.

It wasn't every day they got to hear a legend sing one of the most popular rock songs of all time.

"That was great, Steven," Barry said. "But I want to tighten up the sound a touch. Hang on." He looked at Riley. "Adjust the pop filter a little closer."

"Got it." She returned to the live room and loosened the filter, moving it closer to the mic for a sharper sound. This time her hands moved deftly.

"Something about you seems really familiar," Steven said, studying her. "You wouldn't somehow be friends with my daughter, would you?"

"No." She smiled at the unlikeliness of her knowing his daughter. "I've never met her. There you go. See if that works better." She stepped away.

"I'll think of it. I always do. So what do you want to do with your life? You want to make records?"

She glanced into the control room where everyone listened in on their conversation. "Yes, I'd like to be a sound engineer." She loved talking to Steven, but would have preferred it be private.

"With a face like yours you should be onstage. Do you sing?"

She avoided looking at the all-knowing faces of her coworkers. "No. Not since I was a kid."

"Ha! That's a good one. You're about a split second from puberty."

Her face warmed. "I'll let you get back to work." She ducked out before he could ask her more.

As she entered the control room, Garrett rolled his eyes. She ignored him and picked up her clipboard.

"Check, check," Steven said into the mic. Then he let out another of his signature wails, and the Sound Sync staff laughed, while the band members went unfazed.

Garrett shot her an arrogant smirk and pressed the talk-back button. "Hey, Steven, I just realized where you recognize Riley from."

She almost bolted off her stool to duct tape his mouth.

"Riley was a contestant on *Chart Toppers* a couple of years back."

11

Steven studied Riley through the control room window. She tried to fade into the woodwork.

"Well, hot damn, Garrett, you're right!" Then Steven said to Riley, "You were that adorable little powerhouse that rocked *Chart Toppers*."

Everyone turned to stare at her.

She smiled weakly.

"See, I knew I recognized you. You were damn good, too." Steven looked at Barry. "You should have seen her. I'm hangin' in my living room, mellowing with a smoke in front of the tube, and this little firecracker trots on stage and blows the judges right off the panel."

Riley chewed the edge of her lip.

"She must have been what, ten years old?"

"Thirteen," she said under her breath.

"Hell, the vocals coming out of her were impossible for

her age. I couldn't believe it. I'm telling you. It was mind-blowing."

Despite Riley's embarrassment at being called out, her heart soared from his compliments.

"And then she sang her own rendition of 'Eclipse' that was freakin' brilliant."

Riley remembered. That song launched her into the competition's top ten. It was also the last time she sang anything she chose.

"You should sing it for him," Garrett said.

Riley felt the blood drain from her face.

"Hell yes, the band's gotta hear this!" Steven waited in the live room like a kid with a new toy to show off.

She couldn't move. She could barely breathe. She certainly couldn't sing.

Garrett leaned back in his chair and eyed her in amusement. Ron waited expectantly as if she were supposed to pop right up and break into song. The cameraman aimed his lens at her. She'd forgotten about him.

"What are you waiting for? Get in there and sing," Garrett said.

"I can't." She seethed, clenching her fists, despising Garrett more than ever.

"Come on, Red! Let's make some music!" Steven called out, waving her in.

Garrett stepped over and spoke in her ear. "You're seriously going to tell Steven Hunter that you won't sing with him? Get the hell off your ass and go." He practically shoved her out of the room.

Riley moved like a zombie. She couldn't sing in front of all these people, and definitely not in front of Steven Hunter. She entered the live room trying to figure out how to escape.

"Why didn't you tell me you were on *Chart Toppers*? I can't believe I'm meeting you. The way you sang our song was brilliant. I've heard a lot of renditions, most of them a disaster, but yours was genius. Did someone write that version for you?"

"No. I used to sing along to the radio and make up my own countermelodies."

Steven looked at the guys in the control booth, who'd all taken a new interest in her. "Brilliant, what did I tell ya?"

Despite the awesome compliment, Riley wanted to crawl behind an amplifier and hide.

Steven turned back to her, excitement in his eyes. "You've gotta sing it for me. Don't make a grown man beg."

"I don't know. I haven't sung in front of anyone in a really long time." The last time she sang publicly, she'd cried and blubbered through the song. Riley fought the urge to vomit.

"Seriously? That's a crime right there."

"I'm really nervous. I haven't sung since I was on the show," she whispered, hoping that would make him understand and give up.

"Aw, Red, there's nothing to be nervous about. We're all friends here." He spread his arms and indicated the guys in the control room, too.

She pictured cocky Garrett probably laughing from behind the safety of the console. She wanted to run away and hide, but it wasn't an option.

"Tell you what. We'll sing together. Hey guys, can someone bring in another headset for Red?"

Her stomach dropped.

Before she knew it, she wore a headset and stood in front of a mic, next to Steven Hunter. The rest of the band, her boss, coworkers, and Garrett Jamieson watched. It was a good thing she didn't have to hold a mic or they'd see her hands shaking.

The music cued up and Steven started to sing. She missed the entrance.

"Come on, join me," he said between the lines.

She looked at the control room again and back at Steven. She sang with him, barely making a sound. Steven laughed.

"Oh, Red, you gotta get behind that sound. They gotta hear you in Pittsburgh."

Inside the booth, she saw everyone laugh. She bit her lip.

Steven turned on them. "Hey, assholes. Give the kid a break. In fact, someone kill the lights in the control room."

He covered the mic with his hand and spoke only to her. "Ignore those idiots. They don't know how hard it is to be the one in front of the mic."

The control room went dark and suddenly it was only her and Steven. He removed his scarf and tied it to the mic.

"There, now we've got some style. Let's try it again. We'll take it easy. It's just you and me, kid."

Riley smiled weakly. She suddenly wanted to do this. When would she ever get another chance? She rubbed her sweaty hands on her jeans.

The music began and this time she came in when he did. She smiled as she heard their voices blend, like they did when she sang to his songs on the radio so many years ago.

Steven didn't overpower her voice, instead, he met her at the same volume, giving her the confidence to continue. With each line she sang, she became stronger. Excitement mixed in with the dread, making the experience not quite so terrifying. She put a little umph behind her voice and powered up. Steven grinned.

He jammed with the music, making the whole performance look effortless. Riley giggled as he played air guitar during the musical interlude.

When the song ended, Riley sighed in relief. She did it!

"Nice job," Steven said. "Let's do it again. Only this time I want you to forget everything around you. It's you, me, and the music. I want you to bring it. I want to hear those harmonies. And I want you to belt those big notes. No holding back."

"Okay," she agreed. It surprised her how eager she was to try again. The first time she had been lame. She'd been tentative. Now she wanted to prove she could do better.

"Hit it, boys," Steven called out.

The music pulsed with the low thump of bass and she hit the opening line with guts. Steven fist-pumped the air as they sang the chorus. Her heart raced with adrenaline.

Steven rocked out next to her. She wanted to burst into tears or laughter at the insanity of singing with him. It was unreal. It was beyond a dream come true. It was somewhere in the stratosphere of impossible.

When the final chorus came, Steven whispered, "Let's bring this baby home. We gotta lay it all bare. No holding back. Ya with me?"

She nodded. They came in on the last chorus together, and for that little bit of time she pretended nothing in the world existed except singing with Steven Hunter. She put every ounce of power behind her voice. Her countermelody blended with his melody. As she belted out the final notes, Steven ad-libbed some of his crazy famous riffs.

The song ended, and she couldn't fight back her grin.

Steven high-fived her and let out a rock star whoop. "Hot damn, she's still got it!" He looked into the darkened control room. "What do you think of that, you tone-deaf mutes? Stop picking on little girls."

Barry's voice sounded over the intercom. "I'll be damned. That was amazing."

Riley's heart thudded loudly in her chest. She hadn't sung like that since, well, since the show. Her hands still shook, but she'd just sung with an icon.

Steven looked her in the eyes. "You've got pipes, Red! You need to stop hiding behind the glass and get out and use that God-given talent of yours."

"Thank you. That was amazing."

"The countermelody you sang was genius. Mind if I use it?" he asked.

"Of course not. That would be great." She grinned. "I'll never forget this."

"Damn straight you won't. Okay, have we got everyone awake in there now? Let's get down and dirty and make some music."

Dazed, Riley walked out of the live room. This had to be the greatest moment of her entire life.

She hesitated before the door to the control room. Her chest tightened and she braced for the guys' reaction. Applause greeted her.

"Where'd you get that voice? You sing like an old soul," Ron said.

Riley dipped her head and smiled. She'd never seek out compliments, but they were nice to hear.

"If I didn't just watch those notes come out of her myself, I never would have believed it," Barry said.

On the far side of the room by the control console, Garrett tilted his head in an *I told you so* kind of way.

Riley took a seat on her stool. While she enjoyed the compliments, all this attention over her singing dredged up insecurities from long ago.

Thankfully Barry took charge and got the group back on track. "Steven, we're ready when you are."

12

Garrett watched Riley as she stood toe-to-toe with Steven Hunter and started to sing. Damn, he wished he had the guts to get out there and sing with him, but he hadn't been asked. Scrappy little ginger-haired Riley, the most unlikely person in the building, won the honor.

He still couldn't believe how well the girl full of sass could sing. And not like a thirteen-year-old on a reality show, but like a rocker. He'd watched her YouTube videos, but nothing prepared him for when she opened up and revealed that huge, soulful voice. It defied odds.

"Please tell me you're recording this," Ron said, as blown away as Garrett.

"Oh yeah." Garrett had actually decided to record it as a joke and play it back to Riley the next time she made him feel like a fool. But the joke was on him. No one sang like that after taking a five-year hiatus, but somehow

Riley did. She had a natural gift. That was the only explanation.

He noticed the cameraman recording video as well, and smiled.

"She doesn't even look nervous," Ron said.

She didn't. Her hands were in her front pockets, her foot tapped to the beat, and her whole body pulsed to the music.

"Barry, where did you find this kid?" Teddy, the band's drummer, asked.

A sly smile crossed Barry's face. "Jason Edgette called me up and asked me to give her a job."

"Didn't he used to judge *Chart Toppers*?" Garrett asked.

"He did. He told me Riley was special. I had no idea she could do this." He shook his head in disbelief.

"There's no one in the industry that sounds like her. She has the most original voice I've heard in a long time," said Frank, the chain-smoking band member.

"But can she hit the high note?" Garrett asked.

"No way," Ron said.

They all quieted as the key changed and the momentum of the song built.

"Wait for it, wait for it," Teddy said.

Garrett leaned forward in anticipation. He was rooting for Riley, and he wasn't sure why.

"Here it comes," Frank said.

Riley looked at Steven, he nodded, and together they belted that note to the heavens. Riley nailed it in all her raspy glory.

Inside the darkened control room, everyone cheered.

"No freakin' way, man," another said.

"Look at Steven. Have you ever seen him so impressed?" Frank laughed. "She almost outsang him. We gotta find a way to use this video."

Garrett had never seen Riley look so pleased with herself, certainly not since he'd met her, and why shouldn't she? She was a dynamo.

Barry hit the talk-back button. "I'll be damned. That was amazing."

"Thank you," Riley said.

Barry laughed.

Garrett couldn't believe her subdued response to Barry's compliment. Wasn't she aware of his far-reaching influence in the music industry? Suddenly all the pieces of his life fit together. Riley was an unturned stone waiting to be discovered.

She might have resisted the idea before, but now that he'd witnessed this impromptu jam session, there was no way he'd let her turn him down.

How awesome would it be to launch his career as a record producer by putting out a hit? He certainly had the connections, and he'd just fallen upon a surefire star. He just needed some backing from the boss.

"Barry, would you be okay if I worked with Riley and put together a demo?"

"I'd love to hear her lay down some tracks for real, but it may not be as easy as you think," Barry said.

"Why's that?"

"I think you might find the artist a bit reluctant to cooperate." He smirked, clearly knowing something Garrett didn't.

"Don't worry, I can be very persuasive." Riley didn't stand a chance. Now that he'd seen a real sample of how she could sing, he'd give her the full-court press.

The door opened and Riley slipped into the room. They all applauded.

She dipped her head, wearing a timid smile, and he was drawn to her even more. Her shy modesty was a rarity in this business.

"If I hadn't just heard you myself, I never would have believed it," Teddy said.

Riley glanced Garrett's way. He raised an eyebrow and smiled. He couldn't wait to talk to her alone. She averted her eyes and took her seat.

Barry hit the talk-back button. "Steven, we're ready when you are."

Garrett shifted his attention to the task at hand and queued up the track. They worked the song for an hour, listening for every spot that could be improved. Steven was a pro. As wild as his reputation was, in the studio, he worked with pure professionalism and drive, as well as plenty of laughs.

When Barry called a break, Garrett waited for Riley outside the control room.

"Riley, hold up a sec," he said as she came through the doorway.

"What?" she asked, not stopping.

"You were phenomenal."

"Thanks," she said, and glanced away as if not wanting to talk about it.

"I talked to Barry and you're not gonna believe the great opportunity I've got for you."

Her attention snapped back to him. She stiffened. "What are you talking about?" she asked, her tone cautious.

"He gave me the go-ahead. We're gonna record a demo together."

"Excuse me?"

"Not as in a duo. I'm going to produce, you're going to sing."

"I told you before. This . . . is not going to happen."

"Oh, come on. The way you sing makes people sit up and take notice. You have natural talent. You can't ignore it anymore. I'm going to put you back up onstage under the spotlights and make you famous."

"No." She crossed her arms.

"What do you mean no?"

"I mean. Hell no!" She raised her voice and her face turned red.

"Let me start over. Apparently you don't understand." He stepped closer and put his arm around her shoulder. He could smell the sweetness of her hair. "You have a product that is waiting to be discovered and I have the motive, smarts, and contacts to make it happen. I'm going to make you a lot of money."

She brushed his arm away. "Thanks. But, I'll pass."

"Riley, no one passes. Opportunities like this don't come around more than once in life."

"Well, I do." She stomped off.

13

That weekend, Riley walked with Erika through Lincoln Park to the baseball field to find a guy Erika liked from work.

"How are things at the studio? Is Garrett still bugging you to sing for him?" Erika asked as they walked toward the ball fields.

"All the time. The guy doesn't know how to take no for an answer. I might mess with him and say yes just to bring me a day or two of peace before he figures out I'm yanking his chain."

The sun beat down and the light summer breeze off Lake Michigan cooled their skin. Squirrels darted about as a jogger passed.

"Nice. Oh, there's the field, over there." Erika pointed, and they followed the sidewalk toward the concession stand and bleachers.

"So who is this guy we're here to stalk?" Riley asked.

"I'm not stalking. He told me to come. His name is Chad and he works in the warehouse."

"Hang on, I want to get something to eat." Riley stopped at the concession stand. "Popcorn, please," Riley said to the shaggy-haired sales kid, and handed over her money. She turned to Erika. "So, has Chad asked you out yet?"

Erika leaned back against the counter, searching the ball field for him. "No. We're still doing the mating dance."

"Huh?"

"He comes to the store floor pretending he needs help buying a cell phone case for his sister's birthday. I do reconnaissance on the break room like a double agent so I can just happen to take my break at the same time."

"How very James Bond of you." Riley took her change and the popcorn. She followed Erika to the metal bleachers, where they climbed to the third row.

"This is a delicate situation. If I show too much interest, he'll run scared. If I'm too easy, he'll take the goods and disappear before round two." Erika craned her neck, trying to find Chad.

"That sounds like our receptionist, Tara. She's definitely doing the mating dance wrong. She's more of an instant-gratification kind of girl. She's been drooling over Garrett Jamieson ever since he showed up."

"Well, he is a hottie."

"Yeah, but then I met him and he ruined the whole image by speaking."

"There he is."

Riley turned her head, expecting to see Garrett. "Where?"

Erika pointed and then waved to a tall, solid guy playing second base. He waved back, then returned his attention to the batter.

Riley's heart fell when she realized Erika wasn't referring to Garrett, which was confusing and stupid because she didn't even like him. She focused on the guy out on the field. "Looks cute. At least from a distance with a baseball cap on." Riley took a handful of popcorn.

"Trust me, he is. So, is it true that Garrett's a total man whore?"

"Where'd you hear that?"

"Online, where else?"

"It wouldn't surprise me. You know, you take a perfectly hot guy, make him a superstar, and he becomes an insta-jerk, who thinks the world revolves around him and that anything in heels can't resist him."

"Good thing you wear flats." Erika grinned.

Riley tossed some popcorn at her, and they giggled.

The inning ended and as the rest of the guys on Chad's team ran to the bench, he beelined straight for Erika.

"Hey." He climbed the bleachers and sat next to her. He wore a blue Cubs hat, and had a crooked nose and a friendly smile.

"Hi," Erika said, her voice suddenly high-pitched.

Riley held back a smile.

"Chad, this is my friend Riley."

"Hi," he said.

"Nice to meet you." Riley noticed how he angled his body toward Erika's, but stared at Riley, and more specifically her hair. She glanced at Erika with a raised eyebrow.

"How's the game going?" Erika tried to draw Chad's attention back to her.

"I'm sorry, but you look really familiar," he said to Riley.

"I do?" She was pretty sure she'd never met him before.

"I could swear I've just seen you."

"Unless you hang around the recording studio where she works, it's not likely. That's the only place she ever goes."

"That's it! In a recording studio. On YouTube."

Riley groaned. Not more YouTube videos from *Chart Toppers*. She glanced at Erika and silently begged for help.

"Oh, that was a long time ago. I can't believe you even recognized her. She was in, like, middle school," Erika said.

"No, I swear to God it couldn't have been that long ago. She was singing with Steven Hunter. That hair is kind of hard to miss."

"Are you serious?" Erika asked.

"What!" Only a handful of people knew she'd sung with Steven.

"We were messing around waiting for a shipment and my friend from work was playing a bunch of vintage rock. Then this version of 'Eclipse' with Steven Hunter came on.

The only reason I noticed is that it was a different version of the song. A cooler version."

Erika pulled out her phone and started searching. "I've gotta see this."

Riley's gut tightened into a knot.

"Hey, Chad, you gonna play ball or suck face?" a teammate hollered.

"I gotta go. I'll catch you guys later." He adjusted his cap, smiled at Erika, and ran onto the field.

"Okay," Erika answered, now focused on her phone. "How is there a new video of you on YouTube? I mean, there hasn't been anything new since *Chart Toppers*."

Riley watched Erika's phone as she brought up the site and tapped in the name "Steven Hunter." "I have no idea. No, wait. There was a guy with a video camera. He was with the band. Oh my God, he filmed the whole thing."

She leaned back against the seat behind her, defeated.

"I think this might be it."

Riley scooted up to watch.

"Look at you! With Steven Hunter," Erika squealed.

"I still can't believe it happened."

"Well, now you have proof."

They watched as the video played and she and Steven sang. Riley's pulse raced as if she were experiencing the whole thing for the first time.

"Geez, Riley. Look at you rock it out."

"I was so scared." But on the tiny video screen, she

looked totally into it. She had given herself over to the moment, and now that she watched, she felt sort of proud.

"You don't look nervous. And look, the video has over a hundred thousand views."

"How is that possible? This happened only a couple of days ago."

"It's Steven Hunter. Of course the video has gone viral." The song ended and Erika pounded her feet on the metal bleachers. "You are all over YouTube! This is so cool!"

Riley slumped against the row behind her and shook her head. "This is not good."

"Oh, stop overreacting. You're not in high school anymore. Nothing bad's going to happen."

Still, a shadow of dread hung over her. The whole idea of being noticed, being under the microscope again, made her stomach sick. "I can't believe someone posted that video. Why would they do that?"

"Because it's kick-ass!"

Riley sat up. "Oh my God, I know who did it."

"Who?"

"Garrett. And I'm gonna kill him."

14

Riley stepped onto the Chart Toppers stage. The stylist had dressed her in an obnoxious orange dress with a big flouncy skirt, high-top sneakers, and yards of long necklaces draped around her neck. The woman from hair and makeup had pulled her hair into a ponytail high on the left side of her head.

The lights came up and Riley sensed the eyes of four thousand audience members staring at her. The cameras loomed from every direction. Her mentor and judge, Desiree Diamond, introduced her as the best new artist the show had ever discovered.

The peppy beat of the bubblegum pop song Desiree had selected for her blared through the sound system. Riley tried to bounce to the chippy tune, but felt like a fool. She trotted around the stage singing "Girls Just Want to Have Fun."

She'd never heard the song until five days ago, but

Desiree assured her it was a huge hit in its day. This decades-old song would determine if she stayed on the show or got sent home on the next flight. So she gave it her best effort.

When the song ended, Riley, out of breath, took center stage. This was the worst part of the show. The judges would critique her performance. She braced herself.

Morton King, a distinguished African-American record producer, spoke first. "I hate the outfit, and I hate the song. You looked like an eight-year-old jumping around a bouncy tent at a birthday party."

Despite her desire to agree with the opinionated judge, Riley kept a smile pasted on her face.

"Riley, you didn't connect with the song. If you want to stay in the competition, you're going to have to work harder," Desiree said.

"Thank you, I will," she said, trying to look voteworthy, but wanting to scream in frustration.

"Riley, did you pick that outfit?" asked judge Jason Edgette, a successful recording artist.

"God no," Riley blurted before she could stop herself. She laughed nervously.

Jason turned to Desiree. "Why would you put her in such a hideous outfit? It's no wonder she couldn't relate to the song."

Desiree faked a happy tone. "I think she looks adorable, and the costume goes perfectly with the theme of the song."

"Maybe it did back in the 1980s. You made her look ridiculous," Jason said.

Riley didn't know whether to feel like an idiot or to thank Jason for defending her.

The host of the show joined her onstage. "Okay, audience, what do you think? Did you like the outfit?"

The audience erupted into loud boos. How would she ever stay on the show when she was being humiliated on national television?

Riley woke with a start. She hadn't suffered those bad dreams in a long time. That is, until Garrett arrived and started trying to force her to sing. And now, with the YouTube video reminding people of the girl who failed on *Chart Toppers*, she panicked that the whole thing would happen again. Garrett had to stop. He needed to butt out.

She tried to calm herself down as she showered and dressed for work, but by the time she reached Sound Sync, her temper was like a ticking time bomb.

Not ten feet into the studio, she spotted Garrett drinking coffee and hanging out with Tim. She drilled Garrett with a lethal glare as she stormed past him and into the employee lounge to store her bag. He appeared a moment later.

"Good morning to you, too. Have a nice weekend?" he drawled, all cool and casual in his high-priced jeans and topsiders.

Riley tried to ignore him.

"Nice video. Looks like you're a star again." He laughed.

Riley came at him full force. She shoved him in the chest, knocking him against the wall, spilling his coffee down the front of his shirt.

"Whoa! What's your problem?"

She grabbed the front of his shirt and shook him. "You had no right to post that video. Take it down."

"Look at Riley, all riled up. It's adorable. If I didn't know you better, I'd say you might kick a puppy."

"You *don't* know me! So butt out of my life."

"Why would I do that when it's so fun to mess with you?"

"Oh my God, you are such a bastard! No wonder your brothers quit the band. They couldn't stand being around you."

Garrett flinched, but didn't respond. Was it pain she saw reflected in his eyes?

"Now take the video down or you'll live to regret it."

He set down his coffee cup and adjusted his shirt. "As much as I'm enjoying your fiery little tirade and would like to take credit for it, I didn't post the video."

"You're lying."

"I wish I were. It was a brilliant move and goes to prove my point that you need to record some music and get your ass back onstage. Plus, from the look of things, you could use the money."

Her face burned with embarrassment. He was right

about the money. Her clothes were old and her jeans frayed, but they were clean. "Screw you," she said.

His mouth curled into a smirk. "No thanks, you're not my type."

"Am I your type?" Tara appeared carrying a courier envelope.

Garrett's eyes dashed over Tara in her low-cut top and clinging skirt.

"Hey, Riley, this just arrived for you." She handed over the envelope.

"What is it?" Riley asked.

"Probably a subpoena. Have you broken any laws lately?" Garrett commented.

"No one's talking to you," she snapped, and accepted the envelope. She didn't recognize the company name or return address.

She tore it open and pulled out a few sheets of paper, clipped together. Scrawled across the stationery was a note.

Hey Red,
Great jam session!
Thanks for the footage.
Living the dream, baby!
Steven Hunter

She removed the paper clip. Behind the note was a form with her name printed on it and a little green tab with an arrow that read SIGN HERE.

"What is it?" Tara asked.

"It's a note from Steven Hunter and some sort of a release form."

She looked at the next page and her jaw dropped. "Oh my God!" Her hand shook as she stared at the corporate check made out to Riley Parks for five thousand dollars.

Garrett leaned in to see. "Looks like your money problems are over. Not bad for ten minutes' worth of work."

Riley leaned against the bathroom stall door. She needed a minute to breathe and make sure she wasn't dreaming. She read her name on the check over and over and counted the zeroes to make sure she hadn't misread it.

Five thousand dollars.

She closed her eyes and sighed. This money could do so much. She could finally get ahead. She wouldn't have to live paycheck to paycheck. She could go shopping!

No, that would be stupid. She needed to get as much mileage out of this money as she could. Maybe she could go to school. That had been her plan until she found out her mom spent her college money. Maybe she could get a business degree. Something where she could have a job like Barry's. He was the smartest businessman she knew, not that she knew many. He found a way to combine music and business. That would be perfect. Of course, five thousand would barely get her started, but it was a lot bigger start than she had an hour ago.

She leafed through the documents and stopped at the

release form. There was a lot of legal mumbo jumbo about rights, indemnification, and breach of contract. She had no idea what it all meant or what exactly she was supposed to sign off on, but Barry would know.

She snuck out of the bathroom and beelined for Barry's office.

"Oh. Sorry." She startled when she saw Logan at the small table in the owner's office. "Have you seen Barry?"

"He should be back in a minute. He had to go put out a fire in Studio C. Literally. Candace Capri lit candles all over the studio to set the mood. Barry was afraid the smoke alarm would go off and trigger the sprinkler system. What a lousy way to ruin thousands of dollars in equipment."

Riley's heart thumped loud in her chest. She couldn't bear to keep her news from Logan. "Want to see something incredible?"

"Sure." He put down his papers.

With her hand shaking, she set the letter and check in front of him.

"Holy moly!"

"I know. Right? This is totally insane."

"Why is Steven Hunter giving you all this money?"

She scooped up the papers. "I think it's for the video we shot."

"I saw the video, but I wasn't going to say anything. I figured you'd be totally pissed."

"I was. I thought Garrett posted it, but I think the

Graphite Angels did. And now, well, I don't know what to think."

"Hard to get mad when you're looking at all those zeroes."

"Exactly." Her phone buzzed, and she looked at it to find a text from her mom. Before she could read it, Barry walked in shaking his head.

"I swear this day couldn't get any nuttier."

"Actually, I think it might." Riley put away her phone and held out the documents.

"What's this?" He pulled glasses from his shirt pocket and slid them on. He read the check, glanced at Riley over his rims, and whistled.

"Here's the letter and a release document I'm supposed to sign. I'm not sure exactly what I'd be signing off on and thought you might be able to explain it."

"Let's take a look," he said, accepting the papers and rounding his desk to sit.

Logan scooped up his log sheets. "I'll get out of here and let you guys talk." He closed the door behind him.

Riley sat across from Barry.

"I think the papers are asking me to allow the Graphite Angels to use that YouTube video, but I don't really understand a lot of those clauses."

Barry scanned the document for a minute before answering. "That's pretty much it, but it's also giving them permission to use your version of the song in any future recordings and performances, as well as using the video for any promotional or entertainment purposes they wish."

"How could they use it for promotional purposes? It's only a video of a studio session. It's not even that good."

"They may not plan on using it that way, but they want the rights to do so, should it come up." He paused and removed his glasses.

"Honestly, that studio jam session you did with Steven Hunter was PR gold. You may not see it that way, but here's an older band that wants to stay relevant to a new generation. If I were them, I'd blast that video everywhere. Not only is it their signature song, but it's done with a new melodic twist, thanks to you, and it features a dynamic young voice that most people don't know."

"Oh." She didn't like the idea of the video being blasted anywhere, but the odds of that were low. Plus, people didn't know who she was, so other than putting up with her coworkers' jibes, it shouldn't affect her that much.

"All in all, I'd say it's a fair deal. Unless, of course, you plan on launching your own career and want control over what is put out about you. Have your feelings on the subject changed?"

"God, no!"

"If that's the case, I don't think this will mean too much, other than some cash in your pocket."

"So you think it's okay to sign?"

Barry smiled. "Yes. I think it's fine to sign. You can

always call a lawyer to take a look at it."

"Oh no. I trust you. If you think it's okay, I'm good with that."

"Congratulations. What are you going to do with all this money? I hope this doesn't mean you're going to quit."

Riley smiled. "Oh gosh, no. I love working here. I'm putting this in the bank where it's safe."

"Good idea."

As she left Barry's office, the stress from the last few days disappeared.

15

"*Logan,* hold up," Garrett called as he saw Logan leave Barry's office.

"Hey, Garrett."

He walked with Logan. "You've worked here a while, haven't you?"

"Yeah, almost a year now. Why? You need some help with something?"

"I do, but it's not what you think." Garrett kept running into brick walls trying to get Riley to record with him. Time to find another way to convince her.

"Now you have me interested."

"I realize I've gotten off on the wrong foot with Riley." Logan fought back a smile.

"Okay, so it's public knowledge she can't stand me."

"I never said that," he laughed.

"You didn't need to. Riley's not very subtle with her

opinions. I'm not sure what I did to piss her off, but I really don't want her to hate me anymore."

"No offense, but why do you care? You're a pretty popular guy around here, and probably anywhere you go." Logan paused and examined Garrett closer. "Oh, dude, I get it. You like her!" Logan grinned and nodded, sending his dreads swaying.

"No! Why would you say that?"

Riley wasn't even close to his type. She didn't have the sophistication of the kind of girls he liked. She had that long ginger hair and was always running around in tennis shoes and jeans. However, he had noticed how well they fit her. What was he thinking? "No way. She's a know-it-all, full of attitude, and always seems pissed off about something."

Logan paused at the door to Studio C. "And you're always baiting her. It's like you're trying to get a rise out of her." He pushed the door open and entered. Garrett followed.

Logan was right. She was such an easy mark, but teasing was all he was doing. He liked to watch her get all steamed up. Her eyes would flash with irritation. She'd turn feisty and argue back. It was like fighting with his brothers, only better. Peter and Adam didn't flip their hair or purse their lips.

"Listen, here's the deal. The reason I'm at Sound Sync is to learn the ropes and start producing records. When I heard Riley sing, I knew she was something special. That girl has pipes. It's insane how good she is." Not to mention totally unfair that someone with her natural talent refused to use it.

"She blew me away, too. I can't believe she kept all that under wraps."

"Exactly. I really need to convince her to let me produce a record with her."

Logan tilted his head in skepticism. "Good luck with that."

"You two seem to be pretty good friends. Maybe you could give me some pointers on how to get back in her good graces."

"Seriously? Garrett Jamieson is asking me for girl help?"

"Hey, I can land any girl I want, but this is different. This is business."

Logan started flipping switches and powering up equipment. "Well, if you want her to stop hating you, you might want to lighten up. Seems to me that any chance you get, you're putting pressure on her or telling her how it is. Riley doesn't take well to that. You've got to finesse the situation. Have a couple of conversations where you aren't actually asking her for anything."

Garrett nodded and sat at the console. Easing up on the pressure was not his strong suit, but then again, he could finesse as well as the next guy. He had been pretty direct with Riley. He'd figured she'd jump at the chance to record. "I can do that. And if you could put in a good word for me, I'd really appreciate it."

"It shouldn't be that hard. She's a huge fan of Jamieson."

Garrett did a double take. "Are you sure? I didn't get that vibe."

"She keeps some things pretty close to the vest. Trust me, she just about lost it when she heard you were here."

"Funny, I thought she hated me from the moment I sat at the sound board." He remembered the death stares she gave him that day.

"She did; that is, once you took *her* seat at the board," Logan said.

"Oh shit."

"Bingo!"

"I didn't know it was hers. I thought Barry had been planning on me sitting in on the session. Well, I have an idea. Let me work out a couple of details and I'll get back to you." He stood.

"I'll be here," Logan said as Garrett walked away.

This was going to be fun. Sassy little Riley was a fangirl.

16

After leaving Barry's office, Riley checked her phone. Two more texts. Another from her mom and one with extra exclamation points from Britta, begging her to call home. She called her mom first.

"What's going on?" Riley asked when her mom answered on the second ring.

"Your brother has done something stupid again. I'm trying to get home, but my car won't start. Can you go deal with it and let me know how bad things are?"

"Mom, I'm at work. I can't leave."

"You know I wouldn't call you if it wasn't important. Britta said Matt's bleeding all over the apartment. You're close to the 'L,' so you can get there a lot faster than if I take a bus."

"What'd he do?"

"I'm not exactly sure. Something having to do with a crowbar and a storage unit."

Riley collected her bag from the break room, and slid the check and paperwork from Steven Hunter inside. "I'm on my way. I'll call you when I get there."

She ended the call and went in search of Ron, whose session she was supposed to work today. She found him listening to tracks in Studio D.

"Ron, I have a family emergency, and my mom can't get there. Is it okay if I take off for a while? I'm really sorry. I can work extra shifts this weekend to make up for it."

"That's fine. If we need anything I'll have Tara handle it. I hope everything's okay."

"Thanks." She hoped Matt was okay, too, so she could bawl him out. Whatever her brother had done, she was pretty sure it included breaking the law. As she walked to the "L" station, she texted Britta that she was on her way.

Maybe she should have been stressed out; instead she relaxed in her seat for the ride to the South Side, and smiled as the train rumbled and clacked along the rail. She had a five-thousand-dollar check in her bag. Despite all the crazy in her life, something special had happened. In Riley's experience, special didn't come around very often.

What should she do with her windfall? A year ago, she'd wanted to go to school. But now that she had her job at Sound Sync, her hands-on experience would probably get her a lot farther ahead than a degree in recording and music technology. She could certainly use a few things, and it would be nice not to worry about money. Making rent was always hard, so now she'd have an emergency cushion. She'd never had that before.

Her phone buzzed. She looked down to see a text from Jason Edgette, and immediately smiled.

It's nice to see you singing again, he texted with a link to the Steven Hunter video.

Riley laughed and texted back. *It was a bizarre fluke. Don't get your hopes up.*

The "L" reached her stop. She pocketed her phone and exited the nearly empty car and walked the final three blocks to the apartment, unprepared for what she found.

Blood dotted the creaking wooden steps leading to the apartment. Inside, more droplets splattered the floor like bright paint. Dish towels piled next to the sink were soaked red.

Britta came from the hall carrying more towels. "Riley, you're here!"

Riley saw the prone form of her brother on the couch with a yellow washcloth pressed against his face. "Matt, are you okay?" She tossed her purse on the kitchen table and ran to his side.

Blood stained the front of his T-shirt and more had splattered on his pants.

"I'm fine. I just can't get my nose to stop bleeding." He raised the towel enough to reveal a gaping cut on his upper forehead and a bruised nose that trickled blood as soon as the towel was removed.

"Oh my God," she uttered. "Who did this to you?" Her heart dropped to her shoes.

"I did." He grinned, revealing that half his front tooth was broken off.

"Your tooth!"

"Yeah, that's probably not so good."

"Britta, rinse some washcloths in cool water and bring the bag of frozen peas." She turned back to Matt. "And how did you manage to totally mangle your face?"

"I was trying to pry the lock off a storage unit door. The crowbar slipped and knocked me in the face."

She shook her head. "What is wrong with you?"

"It's no big deal. We were just screwing around."

"At least you didn't get caught. Did you?" She eyed him.

"Of course not. But I kind of left a trail. I hope it rains."

Britta returned with the washcloths. Riley removed Matt's bloody towel and dabbed his swollen face.

She cringed at the sight of the open cut. Riley was no doctor, but she was certain he needed stitches. The blood kept running from his swollen nose. She wasn't sure what to do. Even after banging the frozen veggies on the coffee table a couple times to loosen them up, the makeshift ice pack seemed too hard to put on his tender nose.

"Here, hold this wet washcloth to your nose. Try pinching it."

Britta perched on the arm of the couch. "Should I call 911?"

"No. This isn't an emergency, but he better see a doctor. I'll call Mom."

She wiped some of the blood off her hands and

retrieved her phone from her purse.

"Mom, he's cut his head really bad and I think his nose is broken. Oh, and he chipped off most of a tooth. We should take him to Urgent Care."

"No, go to the hospital emergency room."

"Why? Urgent Care is closer."

"I don't have health insurance right now, and the ER can't turn him away."

Riley sighed and held back her temper. "Fine. Meet us there."

Her mother paused. "It might be a little while."

"Mom! Your kid is going to the hospital. You better be there or I'll . . ." Riley didn't know what she'd do.

"Calm down. I'll get there as soon as I can," her mother said, sounding annoyed.

Riley was tired of being the grown-up in their family, but nothing she did seemed to convince her mom to grow up.

She turned to her siblings. "All right. We're going to the emergency room. Britta, grab Matt a clean shirt to wear."

"Why? I'm gonna get blood all over it anyway." Matt's voice sounded muffled under the washcloth.

"No cabdriver is going to let a kid covered in blood into his car."

Britta returned with a shirt. "We're going to take a cab?" She brightened.

"I'm not dragging him there by city bus." She tried to guess how much this was going to set her back.

Matt removed the towel and pulled off his blood-soaked

shirt. Riley pinched the shirt by the edge, took it to the kitchen, and dropped it into the sink. When she returned, Matt had pulled on the new one. Before he could return the towel back to his nose, a big drop of blood plopped onto the front. He smirked.

"Cover your nose," Riley snapped. "Britta, bring along two clean towels. One for him to sit on and the other for the front of him."

It took some maneuvering, but she managed to get them all to a busy intersection four blocks away and into a cab. The driver watched them with curious eyes and seemed eager to be rid of the ragtag group.

Inside the crowded emergency room waiting area, the intake nurse handed Riley a clipboard and gave Matt a box of tissues. Riley filled out what she could on the form, but beyond name, address, and parent's name, she really didn't know what to put.

"My mom is on her way. She'll have to fill out the rest," she said, handing the clipboard back to the nurse. Riley sat back down next to Britta and called her mom, but she didn't answer. So help her, if her mom blew them off, she'd . . . freak.

After an elderly man, a girl holding her arm, and a young mother with a screaming baby had all been taken back, Riley's mom finally walked in.

"Oh my God! Matthew, are you all right?" She flew to Matt's side like an adoring mother. "You're bleeding, oh, honey. How long have you been sitting here?"

"A half hour," he mumbled.

"Well, that's unacceptable."

Riley knew what was coming and prepared to sink into her chair.

Her mom stormed to the intake desk and pushed past a hacking middle-aged woman. "Excuse me, but my son has been sitting here for nearly an hour. Why hasn't he been seen?"

"Ma'am. Patients are seen based on level of emergency. Your son will be seen as soon as we're able. What's his name?"

"Matthew Parks. And he's bleeding. At this rate he's going to pass out from blood loss. I insist you take him back right now or I'll report you."

Annoyed, the nurse furrowed her brow. "Please calm down. As I said, he'll be seen as soon as possible. Could you please take a seat and complete the rest of this intake form?"

"I will not sit down until my son gets the care he deserves. Who's your supervisor? Who do I need to talk to?" she said loud enough to capture the attention of the entire waiting room.

Matt glanced at Riley and rolled his eyes. Mom wasn't around much, but when she was, it was always a show. Riley slouched down in her seat. This would be a good time to cut bait and run.

"Ma'am. If you don't calm down, I'll have to call security."

"My son is injured, he's probably hemorrhaging to death, and you're worried about forms and security!"

The people in the waiting room stared on uncomfortably.

The door opened and a woman in blue scrubs appeared. "Matthew Parks?"

The intake nurse raised an eyebrow. Riley's mother ignored her and helped Matt forward as if he were an invalid, not a foolish delinquent. Riley sighed in relief. At least now the drama would be in another room.

Two hours later, Matt was released with four stitches in his head and tape over his broken nose.

"You look like you were in a bar fight and lost," Riley said.

"I've gotta post this." Matt held his phone in front of himself. He grinned, revealing his broken-off front tooth, and took a picture. Riley cringed.

"What are you gonna do about your tooth?" Britta asked, staring at the hole in Matt's smile.

"We'll have to get him to a dentist, but it'll have to wait until I can save up some money. I don't get paid until next week, the rent is due, and the car won't start half the time," her mother said.

"Mom, you can't let him walk around like that indefinitely."

"Have you got a thousand dollars lying around to pay for a crown?" her mom asked.

Riley stood silent, but burned to say more.

Her mother huffed in satisfaction. "I didn't think so. Let's get out of here. I borrowed a car from a girl at work. I've gotta drop you guys off and get back." They left the hospital and headed for the parking ramp.

Riley mulled over what to do about the expensive crown. Why was she hesitating when she had a windfall in her bag? Of course she'd help out. "Mom. I can pay for it."

"What? How?"

"I just got a bonus at work."

Her mom stopped short. "You did? How much?"

"A thousand," she lied.

"That's incredible. What kind of company gives a new employee a bonus?"

There was no way she was telling her mom where the money really came from. "It's a probation thing. They give it to everyone who passes the three-month mark."

"Well, Matt. It looks like it's our lucky day. Riley, you hang on to that job, hear me?"

Riley bristled. "I plan to."

"What do you guys say we stop for ice cream on the way home?" her mom offered.

Riley wanted to feel good about sharing her money, but she didn't.

17

After her mom dropped them back at the apartment, Riley stopped by her bank and deposited the miracle check from Steven Hunter into her savings account. She kept out a little bit for herself then caught the "L" and returned to work. She braced for another onslaught of pressure from Garrett, but he only smiled and said hi as she passed.

"That was weird," she said to Logan in the records room. She peeked out the door and watched Garrett disappear down the hall.

"What's that?" he asked.

"Garrett said hi to me and he seemed genuine, not, not . . ."

Logan laughed, looking up from the file drawer. "Not what?"

"I don't know. Not like he was being a manipulative jerk for once."

"Maybe the guy likes you."

"Oh please. No way. He's always sniffing after anything with a pretty face and tight pants," she said.

"I don't know. I think he's got the hots for you."

What was she supposed to do with that bit of news? It couldn't be true. He liked sexy women who were confident and looking for action. Women like Candace Capri and even Tara. Riley was nothing like them.

The days flew by. Riley worked with the band Amnesia, running to Starbucks for coffee, taking Nuggett for walks, and looking the other way when the band snuck off to snort something illegal.

Garrett was becoming Mr. Popularity, bringing in treats every day. First came fresh doughnuts, then deep-dish pizza. The break room became a fun place to hang out. The bands would take breaks and everyone mingled freely, whether they be classical singer Mitchell Freeman, glam queen Candace Capri, the rock band Amnesia, or an indie rock group.

The only downside was that Riley seemed no closer to sitting in the assistant engineer's chair. She shouldn't expect so much so soon, but knew what she wanted, and it seemed so elusive.

The next day she arrived to work and discovered Logan and Garrett eating ice-cream cake in the break room.

"Hi, Riley," Logan said. Garrett smiled and nodded with his mouth full.

"Whose birthday is it?" she asked.

Garrett swallowed. "No one's. It's so hot out, ice cream seemed like a good idea. Want some?"

"It's really good," Logan added.

She put her bag away and grabbed a plate. "Sure. Why not."

Before long, Tara, Tim, and Nick joined them.

"You know what would be really fun?" Logan said.

"What?" Riley asked.

"A Cubs game. We should try to go sometime."

"That sounds great," Tim said.

"Why don't we go tomorrow? The studio is closed," Garrett suggested. "I bet I could get us into a box."

"Seriously? I'd love to," Tara cooed, still under the Garrett spell.

"What do you think, Riley? Up for a baseball game?" Garrett asked.

"Sure. Why not." She scraped the remains of melted ice cream off her paper plate and into her mouth. "I better start setting up before Amnesia gets here."

"I'll look into tickets right away and let you know what I find out," Garrett said.

"I sure hope you can get them." Logan smiled at Garrett in a conspiring way, causing Riley to wonder if something else was at play.

18

Riley's jaw dropped as Garrett pulled up in front of her apartment building the next day in a sporty silver convertible.

"Hop in." Dark sunglasses hid his eyes and any judgments he might be making over the shoddy appearance of her building.

"I see you're trying to keep a low profile." She opened the door and slid into the leather seat.

Garrett grinned. "I wanted to take you to the game in style. Nothing wrong with that."

"I can't believe you're even driving in downtown Chicago traffic. No local person even does that." She glanced at the empty backseat. "Where are the others?"

"On their way to the game, I assume. Why?"

"I figured you were picking them up, too."

"Nope. Just you." He relaxed his arm over the back of

her seat, and for a moment she thought it might drop to her shoulder. She chided herself for thinking that way.

He pulled out and hit the first red light. Cars, delivery trucks, and taxis were backed up in every direction.

"The heavy traffic is exactly why no sane person drives here." She bit back her smile, but still reveled in the fact she was sitting in a sports car with none other than Garrett Jamieson. Thank God her mom couldn't see her. She would flip out with jealousy.

Riley raised her face to the balmy sun of a gorgeous day. A light breeze wafted through the air. Garrett inched his way through downtown traffic to Wrigley Field.

They talked about the Cubs, her latest incident with Nuggett, the dog who loved to roll in anything smelly, and speculation at work that Beyoncé would record a gospel album.

When at last they approached the large red iconic sign that read WRIGLEY FIELD HOME OF THE CHICAGO CUBS, Garrett swung the car in front of the stadium and put it into Park.

"Ready?" he said, an eagerness to his voice.

"Yeah, but you can't park here. Don't you see the no-parking signs?"

A man wearing a chauffeur's uniform stepped up to the car.

"We're not parking." Garrett winked at her and stepped out of the car. He tossed the keys to the man, came around, and opened Riley's door before she could digest what was happening.

"You hired a driver to park your car?"

"Of course. There's no parking here. Let's go." He held out his hand and helped her out of the low vehicle.

They walked to the main entrance, and Riley was unsure how she felt about this polite, new and improved Garrett. "Where are we meeting everyone?"

"In the suite."

A group of four teenage guys approached them. "Hey Garrett, could we get a picture with you?" asked one of the guys, who wore a Led Zeppelin T-shirt.

Garrett stopped and smiled broadly. "Sure."

"I can't believe you're in Chicago, man. Are you performing somewhere?" he asked.

"No. I'm here working on a special project."

"That's great." The guy turned to Riley and held out his phone. "Would you mind taking the picture for us?"

"Not at all." She snapped a photo, and waited while Garrett signed their game tickets. More people approached. Five minutes later, Garrett finally escaped his adoring fans.

"Sorry about that," he apologized, still in a great mood.

"Does that happen to you very often?"

"Not as much anymore, but this is a pretty crowded place." Garrett checked the direction signs and led her to an elevator. A security guard sat to the side. Garrett showed their tickets and the man turned a key next to the elevator that opened the doors.

"Wow. I've never needed a security guard to get on an elevator before. What kind of seats do we have?"

"Only the best." He flashed his eyebrows at her and leaned against the back wall as the elevator rose. "Have you ever been to a Cubs game before?"

"A couple times we came on school field trips. You?"

"My first time for the Cubs, but I've been to a few Rangers games. I think you'll find this a little different than your school visits."

Once they reached their floor, Garrett checked their tickets again and led her down a wide concourse past numbered doors until they arrived at their suite. Inside she discovered a swanky room complete with bar, a blue leather couch, and seating inside and out. A spread of food covered a table against one wall. A large framed and matted picture of Wrigley Field adorned another, and a large flat-screen TV occupied the third.

The room opened up to outdoor stadium-style seating where Logan, Tara, and several others from work hung out drinking beer.

"Hey, Garrett, great tickets, dude," said Tim, one of the runners.

"No problem. Want a beer?" he asked Riley.

"Sure."

"What took you so long?" Logan asked, joining them.

"Garrett decided to drive."

"You came together?" He smirked. "I told you," he said in Riley's ear as Garrett stepped away to fetch the beers.

123

"Shut up. It doesn't mean anything."

"Sure it doesn't," Logan said.

Garrett returned, twisted the cap off a beer, and handed it to her. Riley had consumed plenty of beers in her day. Living with her mom, not to mention above a bar, it was only natural. But usually she drank with other under-aged kids, not coworkers who were all over twenty-one. She took a sip of the cold ale.

She joined the others checking out the awesome view from their luxury box. The lush green grass contrasted against bright white lines of the diamond. The clear blue sky made the stadium look like a photograph.

Usually the artists recording at the studio didn't include the staff in special social events, but then again, Garrett was one of them now. Sort of. She looked up and noticed him watching her. He smiled and raised his bottle in salute.

A short while later, Garrett touched Riley's arm. "I'd like to show you something special. Want to see?"

She looked at him with unguarded eyes, and her diamond nose stud sparkled. "Sure."

Perfect.

He took her beer and set it on the counter, then held the door open. They walked down the concourse back to the elevator. He liked how she had dressed in little navy shorts and a bright yellow top. Very Cubs baseball. "Having fun?"

"Yeah. I've never seen the stadium from a luxury suite. I'll never forget it. Thanks."

They stepped into the elevator and Garrett pressed the button for the lower level. He shrugged off a brief jitter of nerves. Should he tell Riley what was in store? No. Better to surprise her. "I hope you like it. So you're feeling good today?"

"Of course. Why do you ask?"

"No reason." He slid his hands into his pockets and watched the numbered lights on the elevator change as they descended.

"So where are we going?"

"To a part of Wrigley Field that not many people get to see." He smiled.

"You sure you don't want to bring the rest of the group?"

"No. This part is just for you." She'd be mad at first, but once she did this, she'd have the confidence to do anything.

Riley glowed with happiness and smiled sweetly. Nice change from a few days ago when she'd as soon bite his head off than spend more than two seconds with him.

They reached the lower level, the elevator doors opened, and they stepped out to another security guard.

"Hi, I'm Garrett Jamieson and this is Riley Parks. We're here to see Anita Wacha."

"Sure. One moment please." The security guy radioed in the message. "She should be right out."

"Great. Thanks," he said.

"Garrett, what's going on?"

"You'll see. Only a couple more minutes." He tried to act casual, but his heart raced. A minute later, a thirty-something woman came around the corner with a radio in one hand and a clipboard in the crook of her arm.

"Hi, you must be Garrett. It's so nice to meet you. I'm Anita, we spoke on the phone."

"Hi, Anita. This is Riley Parks, who I was telling you about. I promise you, she won't disappoint."

"Such a pleasure to meet you, Riley. You must be excited," Anita welcomed.

"Um, sure," Riley said, then glanced at Garrett, her eyes losing the sparkle from moments ago, now replaced with a trace of confusion.

"This way, please." Anita led them down the corridor.

"What's going on?" Riley asked under her breath. He ignored her and followed Anita.

"Here we are." Anita opened a door and they followed her into a holding room with a linen-covered table containing water, tea, and soda. A love seat and soft chairs created a seating area.

Garrett noticed Riley's eyes settle on a piano in the corner.

"You can wait in here until it's time. I'll come get you about ten minutes before, so you can warm up, relax, or whatever you need. There's a bathroom through those doors as well. Please let me know if there's anything you need."

"Actually, I'm confused." Riley looked from Anita to Garrett and back. "What are we doing here?"

"Excuse me?" Anita asked, and then looked at Garrett.

"Haven't you guessed?" Garrett asked. "You're singing the national anthem." He smiled.

His words hit like a sucker punch to the gut. "Uh, no. I'm not," she snapped, and took a step backward.

"I'm sorry, is there a problem?" Anita asked, checking her watch as if she had no time for problems.

"She'll be fine. Could you give us a minute?"

Anita looked at them with concern, but left without another word. The moment the door closed, Riley turned on him.

"Are you out of your freakin' mind? I am not singing the national anthem. Why would she think that? Why would *you* think that?"

"Calm down. It's going to be fine." Garrett reached for her arm, but she jerked away.

"It'll be fine because you're going to clear this up and tell her that you made a monumental mistake." Riley's hands trembled and her face flushed with anger.

He experienced a twinge of guilt but brushed it away. "Riley, you need to overcome your fear, or whatever it is that's been keeping you from singing in public."

"And your solution is to put me in a public venue in

front of thousands of people and television cameras with absolutely no warning?" she shouted.

"Keep your voice down. Sometimes it's best to just jump in and not look back."

"No! It's not!" This time she whispered, but still shot daggers with her eyes. "I'm not sure if I even remember all the words right."

She stalked to the other side of the room.

"It's a cinch. It'll all come back to you."

She paced back and forth. "What is wrong with you? You can't force me to get out there and sing."

Garrett took a breath to give himself the patience to deal with her. "You had no preparation or warm-up when you sang with Steven Hunter, and look how great you were. That YouTube video has exploded. Everyone is wondering about you again. You're relevant. This is the perfect chance for you to get more exposure."

"You are seriously warped. What part of you can possibly think this is a good idea?"

"Riley, you need to learn to work under pressure, to be able to do the unexpected. That's how artists get noticed."

Garrett crossed to the piano. "Why don't you warm up? There's a copy of the song right here."

A soft knock sounded at the door.

"Come in," he called.

Anita entered with concern etched on her face, or maybe it was annoyance. "How's everyone doing in here?"

He could handle Anita. He'd dealt with hundreds of venue managers, promoters, and publicists in his time. He donned a relaxed smile.

"We're doing great. Riley's—"

Riley stepped forward. "Actually, Anita, there has been a huge misunderstanding. I won't be singing the national anthem today or any other day."

The room went morbidly silent.

Anita's jaw clenched. "I don't know what's going on with the two of you, but I need someone to sing the national anthem in exactly five minutes." She crossed her arms and stood in the doorway, effectively blocking Riley's exit.

"And you'll have someone," Riley said. "Garrett regrets the confusion and has volunteered for the honor. He's a big star and much better suited for this gig anyway."

Damn her. Riley was going to sing the song one way or another.

Riley turned to him. "Garrett, it's been a day I'll never forget. How can you ever top this? Wow. Anita, it's been a pleasure meeting you, but it's time for me to go."

Riley headed for the door.

Garrett caught her by the arm before she escaped. "You can't go. You need to get out there and sing the damn song."

She looked at his hand holding her arm and then into his eyes. "No, Garrett. I don't. You do." She shrugged out of his grasp, slipped past Anita, and disappeared into the corridor.

He turned to Anita. "Hang on a sec while I get her back."

"No! We now have four minutes. You convinced me to bump our scheduled singer for you. Well, I bumped them, and now I need a body to get out there and sing. I don't know who that girl was, but it's pretty clear she knew nothing about this. You, however, the crowd knows. You will be singing today." She crossed her arms and held her radio as if it were a weapon.

"But—"

She held up a hand to stop him from saying more and raised an eyebrow.

Damn it! He looked at the TV monitors, showing the ball players finishing their warm-up and running toward the dugout. He couldn't go out there by himself. He wasn't a soloist, for Pete's sake. He was part of a group. A now defunct group.

"Three minutes," Anita said, pursing her lips.

"Shit." He looked around the room like a trapped wild animal. He couldn't do this. But he also couldn't go back on his word. He wanted to punch something. "Fine."

"Good. Follow me, please."

He followed Anita from the holding room toward the field. He could wring Riley's neck.

19

Riley stormed away from Wrigley Field. She couldn't believe Garrett was still pulling this crap. If anything, his antics were getting worse. Although he'd been acting friendly the last few days, she should have known it was to lure her into trusting him.

Logan was so far off base with his "I think Garrett likes you" line of bull. And to think that she had actually started to believe it.

And what was with that wink Garrett gave her when they arrived at Wrigley Field? At least she hadn't done anything stupid in response. Plus, if she was honest with herself, there was no reason on the planet that a guy like Garrett would like a girl like her anyway.

Her phone buzzed. A text from her mom.

Come to dinner.

That was odd. Her mom hadn't invited her for dinner,

let alone made dinner in, well, forever.

What's up? Riley texted back.

We're celebrating. It's a surprise. Be here by 5.

Considering her plans of spending the day at the Cubs game had turned into an epic fail, she texted back: *OK.*

Two hours later, Riley showed up at the apartment to find her mom using a dishcloth to pull a pan of cupcakes out of the oven.

"Hi, Mom," Riley said, closing the oven door. "Baking. This must be big news."

"The best." Her mom beamed and leaned in for a quick hug.

"Hi, Riley," Britta said as she trotted into the room carrying an old tablecloth.

"Hi, Britta. Wow, a tablecloth and everything." They didn't celebrate much in the Parks household. She couldn't imagine what could be such a big deal. Maybe Mom won the lottery. She played it often enough that her number was due to come up.

Riley scooped a pile of gossip magazines and junk mail off the kitchen table. As she set the items onto the coffee table, a piece of paper slipped to the floor. Riley picked it up. The words RENT PAST DUE jumped out at her. She walked over to her mother, showed her the letter, and gave her a pointed look.

Her mom sighed and mouthed, "Shh. Not in front of Britta."

Riley shook her head. She slipped the letter beneath the pile of papers, then helped Britta spread the faded floral tablecloth.

"So, any new guys in your life?" her mom asked cheerfully as she fetched things from the fridge and piled them on the counter.

"Nope. But Erika's seeing a new guy. She met him at work. He actually has potential." She handed Britta four dinner plates.

"How about your job? Any cute guys there?"

Garrett, with his clever smile and perfect hair, popped into her mind. She pushed the image away. How could he be so hot and yet detestable? "Not really."

"How's your job going?" her mom asked. "It's an insurance company, right?"

Riley pulled some mismatched silverware from the drawer and set it on the table for Britta, who fussed over making it look nice.

"Yeah, it's fine." Riley could never let her mom know that she worked at a recording studio. She'd only start harping on how it was another chance for a recording contract. God, her mom and Garrett had a lot in common.

"I'd say it's far more than fine. They gave you a bonus after only three months. That's huge. You be sure not to mess that job up."

Riley almost said, "You mean like you do?" but didn't. Instead she replied, "I'll try not to. What's for dinner?"

"Breakfast!" she said with an overly bright smile.

"Seriously?"

"Eggs are cheap," her mom said under her breath.

"Riley, want to see the basket I wove at summer school?"

"Sure." She followed Britta into the small bedroom the two used to share. Riley's old bed was now home to a grand display of every stuffed animal Britta owned. On the bookcase Britta had arranged her doll collection.

Britta pulled out the crudely woven pink-and-yellow basket.

"That's really nice. What are you going to keep in it?"

"I don't know. Maybe hair ties?"

"Good idea." Riley ran her finger along the basket's ridges. "So what's Mom's big surprise?"

"I don't know. Do you think it's a trip to Disney? She always said we'd go."

Britta's face was so hopeful. It broke Riley's heart to know her sister would be disappointed. "Probably not," she said.

"Well, I'm sure it's something wonderful," Britta said, picking up a doll and smoothing down its hair.

"Dinner's ready," their mom called in a cheery voice.

Riley felt like she was living in the Twilight Zone. Her mom placed the frying pan full of cheesy scrambled eggs in the center of the table, and lined sausage patties around the edge of the pan.

Britta took her seat, looking so excited for a home-cooked meal and the pretense of family time.

"Riley, would you bring the jelly over?" her mom asked as she dished eggs onto Britta's plate.

"Sure. Where's Matt?" She set the jelly next to a plate of dark toast and took her seat.

"God only knows. I told him not to be late, but your brother and time aren't exactly in sync."

They dug into the hot food. Riley took a cheesy bite and it tasted exactly as she remembered. While it wasn't Riley's idea of dinner, if there was one thing her mom could cook, it was scrambled eggs. Britta ate happily, humming a tune.

Her brother chose that moment to appear.

"Matt, you're late," her mom said.

"Smells great. Did Riley cook?" He ducked as their mom took a fake swipe at him. He grinned, revealing his broken tooth.

"Mom! You didn't get his tooth fixed yet?"

"I'm taking him tomorrow. I'll need you to get me the money for the dentist."

Matt plopped into his chair and heaped food onto his plate.

"I can go to the bank in the morning. I don't have to be at work until tomorrow afternoon."

"His appointment is at ten. I can swing by the bank with you in the morning and you can give me the cash."

Riley choked down her mouthful of eggs. "That's the opposite direction of the dentist's office. I'll bring it straight there."

She avoided letting her mom see the distrust in her

eyes. That money was going for Matt's tooth and nothing else. Not even the late rent payment.

"That'll be fine," her mother said stiffly.

"Mom, now will you tell us what your news is?" Britta pleaded.

"All right." She wiped her mouth with a paper towel.

Matt glanced at Britta and rolled his eyes. They'd been down this road before. Mom's surprises were never really good news.

"You guys are not going to believe this, but . . ." She paused for effect. "I got a new job!"

Matt continued shoveling eggs in his mouth.

"That's great, Mom, but what about your job at the nail salon?" Riley asked.

"My supervisor was a real witch. Plus the fumes from all the acrylic nails gave me headaches. It's a good thing I got out when I could."

Most likely she'd been let go, but Riley didn't say it. "So where's the new job?"

"I'll be working as a receptionist at a hotel."

"Really?"

"Don't look so surprised."

"It's just a lot different than your other jobs." Her mom usually took jobs as a cocktail waitress, a hostess at a diner, or maybe a grocery store checker. "You've never worked in a clerical job before, have you?"

"For your information, when I was in high school I

worked in the office of a furniture store. It's where I met your dad." She aimed a pointed look at Riley.

And that worked out real well. Her dad, just out of high school, was hired to deliver furniture. He hooked up with her mom and got her pregnant. "Has he sent you any child support recently?"

"Why do you always have to be so negative? This is a party." Her mom frowned.

Britta begged with her eyes for Riley to stop.

Riley took a drink of water and set her glass down. "I'm sorry. It's great that you got a new job. I'm happy for you."

"Thank you. I can't wait to start. There's so much to do. I need to get some new clothes."

"Does this mean we get to go to Disney now that you have a new job?" Britta asked.

"Not right away, but maybe after a few months. Before that, I need to get a new car."

"What do you need a new car for?" Matt asked.

"My car is officially dead. Okay, not totally, but I can't afford to fix it, and something else is going to break on it any minute. I stopped by the used car lot yesterday and there is a great little Mazda. It's only six years old."

"How are you going to pay for a car? You can't even make rent!" Riley's stomach turned sour.

"I'm doing the best I can. It's not easy being a single mom," she snapped.

"You guys, don't fight," Britta pleaded, her worried

eyes watering with emotion.

"I'm sorry, Britta," Riley said. "But Mom, I don't see how you can possibly get a car loan right now." She took a bite of sausage and willed herself not to say more.

"Actually, I need your help with that." Her mom's voice turned soft and friendly again. Too friendly.

Riley froze. A sense of dread crept over her. She forced herself to swallow the food.

"All you have to do is sign the loan papers," her mom said in a rush.

"Why does Riley have to sign them?" Britta asked.

"Because Mom's credit is crap," Matt answered.

"Matt. Language!" her mom snapped.

Riley wanted to cry. Why couldn't her mother behave like a normal grown-up? Couldn't she be responsible? Ever?

"Riley, you don't have to pay a thing. I'll make the car payments once I start my new job. I just need the loan and you're eighteen now. You have perfect credit and a steady job. They won't turn you down."

"Why can't you take the 'L' like everyone else?" Riley desperately grasped for a way out of this.

"Because the hotel isn't on the 'L' route, or the train, or bus. And this job pays two dollars more an hour than my old job. It's the luckiest break I've had in a long time."

"Please, Riley. Sign the paper for Mom," Britta begged, hating the confrontation.

Riley's gut twisted and a heavy weight descended over

her. She looked at her mom and felt all the agony and hurt her mom had inflicted throughout the years. Riley did not want to be dragged back into her messed-up world.

"It's only a formality, honey. I'll make all the payments. I promise."

"What will you use for a down payment?"

"They'll take my old car. They're knocking five hundred dollars off the price." Her mom hopped up and brought over a large envelope. "Here's the paperwork. You just need to fill in your employment info and sign it. The dealership will take it from there."

At that moment Riley loathed her mother. "Fine," she said flatly, and took the envelope.

"Oh thank you!" Her mom leaned over for a hug.

"Don't!" Riley pushed back her chair. Her mom's face fell.

"I only wanted to thank you," she said softly.

Riley stood. "I have to go."

She grabbed her bag on the way out, slamming the door behind her. When she reached the street, she leaned against the scratchy brick wall and closed her eyes.

She hated her mother.

20

Garrett knocked back another beer, but no amount of alcohol would wash away the memory of walking onto Wrigley Field by himself and trying to pull off the national anthem. He should have run, not that he had the chance.

His phone rang. His brother Peter's number popped up. *Shit.*

"Yeah," he answered.

"Why didn't you tell me you were going solo? I would have flown in for your debut."

"Screw you."

"You're all over the internet. Nice save after you forgot the words." Peter cracked up on the other end.

Garrett tore at the paper label on his bottle. "You done yet?"

"Heck, no. I think I'll get some posters made of you standing there all alone holding the mic. I've never seen someone look so uncomfortable."

And Garrett had never been so uncomfortable. He didn't do solo. None of this would have happened if his brothers hadn't crapped out on the band.

"What were you doing singing at a Cubs game anyway? I thought you wanted to try producing."

"I am. Let's say it was a bit of a misfire." He hadn't spoken to Peter since his mother's birthday dinner, and he didn't really want to now either. Garrett would never forgive his brothers for throwing in the towel. Still, alcohol had loosened his tongue and he couldn't help but share his troubles.

"There's this girl that works at Sound Sync. Her voice is crazy brilliant, but she's the most stubborn person I've ever met."

"Sounds like she's your twin."

"She's a pain in the ass. Doesn't listen to a damn thing I say."

"Are you playing nice with her?"

"I always play nice," he said, raising his bottle to his lips, but Peter responded with silence.

"What?" Garrett said.

"Let's just say not everyone on the planet is willing to put up with your methods of persuasion like I did."

"What's that supposed to mean?"

"Oh come on, Garrett. You're not happy unless you're calling all the shots. Admit it."

"You're talking out of your ass."

"Oh really? How long have you been in Chicago? A couple weeks? And you've already pissed this girl off so much you got stuck singing solo on national TV?"

The door of the condo opened. Brad entered, back from his concert in Reno. He nodded his greeting and set down his bags.

"You don't know Jack about what's going on here."

"No, but I have a pretty good idea. You sleep with her already? Is that why she hates you?"

"On that note, go to hell." Garrett ended the call and tossed his phone on the table.

Brad took a look at the empty bottles. "Having a good day, I see."

"It's one for the record books. I'm working on wiping clean the memory banks."

"I'm good at that. I'll take one." Brad snatched a beer from the fridge and collapsed on the couch.

Several hours later they were on the patio, high above the city, surrounded by empty bottles and a half-eaten pizza. Garrett looked out at the city lights.

"You'd think that reaching the kind of success we've had would eliminate all the bullshit in life. I mean, aren't we supposed to be happy?"

"I'm happy," Brad said.

"Well, congratulations on living the dream."

"When I'm onstage, when I'm in the studio, and when

I get to meet fans. Unless, that is, I haven't had a decent night's sleep in a week. Or there's a power outage during a concert. Or the label has booked me to do twelve radio interviews every day during the morning drive."

"Or your band goes behind your back and decides they don't like world tours or sold-out concerts anymore," Garrett said.

"Or your publicist thinks it's a good idea to appear on *Sesame Street* and sing to a puppet." Brad frowned.

"Or the one person you're trying to help refuses to let you."

"Or you fall off the stage and need two pins in your ankle." Brad lifted his leg in the air.

"Or the most aggravating girl on the planet has fiery red hair and stubborn blue eyes that call you out on all your shit."

"Women. Don't get me started."

"I need a new life." Garrett stood and moved to the railing.

"I thought you were getting a new life. You're not going to jump, are you?"

"Not at this moment, but my life is a mess. I want to be someone new."

"Who do you want to be?"

"I don't know. Maybe a superhero."

Brad joined him at the railing. "I always wanted special powers, like Spider-Man."

"I could be Spider-Man," Garrett said.

"We could scale tall buildings."

They looked at the crescent-shaped balconies all protruding around the octagon-shaped building like orange wedges.

"You ever thought about climbing down the side of the tower? I mean, the balconies are so close together and the slats on the railings would be easy to grab."

Brad grinned. "I've always wanted to try it."

Garrett looked out at the distant street and the Chicago River bridge. "It would be a nasty fall from fifty-two stories up."

"Even if you went in the river, you probably wouldn't survive."

"Definitely not."

"A hundred bucks says you won't do it," Brad taunted.

Garrett looked at his friend and grinned. "You're on!"

21

Garrett dangled from the lower railing of the fifty-second floor. His foot flailed until it hit the edge of the balcony railing below. Once he had his footing, he held his breath until he found his nerve. Then he released the railing above, and slid to the balcony below.

"Woohoo!" he called to Brad. Looking around the patio, he saw a couple of white plastic lawn chairs and a small gas grill. No lights shone from the condo.

Brad's legs dropped into view, swinging erratically in the evening breeze until he too found his footing and popped down next to Garrett.

"That's freakin' dope!" He high-fived Garrett and they looked out over the lights of the Chicago skyline. "Okay, I'm going first this time."

Brad climbed over the railing, clinging to the outside of the balcony. "See you on the dark side." He grinned and lowered himself until he hung only by the metal slats. His hands were all Garrett could see and then suddenly they disappeared.

Garrett looked for Brad over the edge.

"Houston, we have landed," Brad called from below.

Garrett laughed and followed over the edge. Once his feet were secure, standing on the next railing, he let go and jumped onto the patio below. "And he sticks the landing!" Garrett held up his arms like an Olympic gymnast.

"You know what would be really cool?" Brad asked, sitting on the floor of the bare patio.

"A beer?"

"No. Filming a music video about climbing the tower."

"I like how you think. Might have trouble getting your label to sign off on it, though. Okay, my turn."

Garrett grabbed the railing and swung first one, then his other leg over, careful to slide his feet under the railing as he moved his hands to grip the slats from the outside.

"See ya!" He was really getting the hang of this. He lowered one leg and then the other, hanging in the air for a few seconds, enjoying the sensation of hanging free and being in charge of his own destiny.

His feet found the rail below. As he secured his footing, something caught on his shoe. Something on the railing kept him from getting a sure grip, and his other foot was having the same problem.

He couldn't really pull himself up, so he gingerly

released the upper railing, one hand and then the other, placing his hand on the wall of the building. He leaned into the wall for dear life and then slid his way onto the railing below.

"Umph." He landed on something and fell to the balcony floor.

"What's the matter?" Brad called.

Garrett sat up amidst a large potted plant that he'd upended and a balcony chair he tipped over. He discovered twinkle lights wrapped around the rail.

"There's lights on the railing, I couldn't get very good footing, and then I landed on top of a pot of flowers."

He heard Brad laughing.

"Ready or not, here I come!" Brad yelled.

Garrett scrambled up to help guide Brad. As soon as his legs touched the railing, Garrett reached around and grabbed him mid-thigh. "I've got you."

"Gee, Garrett, I don't really like you that way." Brad laughed.

"Dude, I'm trying to save your life."

Brad reached for the wall and Garrett tried to step back to lower Brad, but he tripped on the flowerpot.

"Hang on!"

Garrett fell backward, pulling his friend to safety. Brad kneed him in the gut on impact.

"Ugh." Garrett pushed Brad off of him and rolled to his side, holding his aching stomach.

"Sorry, man. I had it. You didn't need to play Superman." Brad crawled to a sitting position and leaned against the balcony railing.

Garrett grabbed one of the loose plants and threw it at Brad. "Nice thanks I get for saving your life."

Brad spat dirt from his mouth and tossed the plant over the railing.

"Litter bug."

Brad looked over the side at the falling plant. "Look, there's something going on down there."

Garrett crawled to the edge and looked out. Sure enough, three cop cars, with lights flashing, were parked at the base of the tower. A small crowd of people had gathered, and they all seemed to be looking up.

Garrett waved at them. From fifty stories up, the people looked like tiny toy figures. "You don't think the cops are here for us, do you?"

Brad looked at him. "Busted!"

They laughed.

"The cops can't possibly be here for us. We're too high up for anyone to even notice," Garrett said.

"I don't know." Brad pointed to the sky. "Do you think that helicopter is a coincidence, too?"

Garrett looked up. A news helicopter hovered in the distance with a spotlight roaming the building looking for something or someone.

"We've gotta get outta here." Garrett scanned the patio, suddenly feeling like a caged animal.

"We sure do, 'cause I've got to take a leak," Brad said.

Garrett tried the balcony door to the dark condo. "Locked."

"Now what? Keep going down?"

Garrett looked at the balcony straight across and below. He didn't relish the idea of trying to make it across now that he'd taken a moment to consider what they were doing.

"Someone's got to be home around here. Maybe if we make enough racket, someone will come and help us get out of here."

Brad leaned over the railing where it attached to the building and tried to touch the next railing over. Suddenly, they heard what sounded like a voice amplified through a megaphone from below, but it was too far away to make out the words.

"Um, Brad. Maybe you better not. I have a feeling someone is on their way."

Brad started to laugh again. "Well, this ought to be good. We might as well enjoy the show. Think we'll make *TMZ*?" He took a seat in one of the chairs. Garrett picked up the other one and sat next to him. "It's looking that way."

"Beautiful night. Too bad there isn't a cooler of beer here."

Less than five minutes later, the balcony door of the unit next to them opened and two police officers appeared, along with building security.

"Police! Stand slowly and put your hands in the air!"

said an officer with short buzzed hair and a solid frame.

"Don't shoot!" Brad jumped out of his lawn chair.

"Sir, please put your hands in the air," the cop repeated, his hand near his sidearm. His partner aimed what looked like a Taser at them.

Brad's hands shot up. Garrett couldn't help himself and laughed.

"Garrett, get your ass off that chair and put your hands up. I don't want to die on this balcony."

Garrett rose. The officers remained in an aggressive stance. Garrett raised his hands high enough to show he would cooperate.

"Sorry, officers. We didn't mean any harm," Brad said.

"Stay away from the balcony railing," the second, taller officer barked.

Garrett laughed, but it sounded more like a giggle. "We're not going to jump. We were just having fun."

"That's good to hear. Now move slowly toward the door and reenter the building," the first cop ordered.

"That's the point. We can't get inside. We're locked out," Garrett explained.

"And I've really gotta go. Could you get the door open for us?" Brad asked.

The tall officer looked at Brad as he came closer. "Are you Brad Stone of the Jade Monkeys?"

"Guilty as charged," Brad answered, his hands still raised.

Both cops seemed to relax a little. "What were you doing climbing down the side of a skyscraper?"

"I think it had something to do with Spider-Man," Brad said.

"I hope you're done playing superhero. People have died falling from balconies. Plus, I think you'd have a lot of very unhappy fans. Please stay put."

"I have fans, too," Garrett said, swaying slightly. Keeping his hands in the air and trying to keep his balance at the same time wasn't the easiest feat.

The officers ignored Garrett. "We'll have you back in the building in a moment. So when does your next album come out?" the cop asked Brad.

"Don't you recognize me?" Garrett interrupted.

The police studied him.

"No, sir, can't say that I do."

Brad laughed.

"Jerk," Garrett muttered to Brad. Unbelievable. Could this day get any worse?

"Have you ever heard of Jamieson?" Brad asked the cops.

"Of course, who hasn't?"

"That's Garrett Jamieson," Brad said.

"Really? I didn't recognize you," the shorter cop said. "Didn't Jamieson break up?"

Garrett clenched his jaw and felt about two inches high. His star power was fleeting.

Suddenly the balcony door opened. Strong hands grabbed him from behind and yanked him into the condo. Before he could react, his hands were pulled behind his back and cuffed.

"Sir, you are under arrest for criminal trespass and recklessly endangering safety."

22

Riley arrived at the dentist's office the next morning, a few minutes after ten. A bell on the door dinged as she entered. Her mom paged through a *People* magazine in the waiting area. Riley took a seat next to her.

"Hi, Riley. Matt is back with the dentist. We'll get an estimate once he takes a look at the tooth."

"Okay." Riley still hated that she was giving away so much of her own money, but she couldn't let her little brother go through life with a broken front tooth.

She opened her bag and pulled out the envelope of documents her mom had given her last night. "Here's the paperwork back for your car loan."

Riley resented being the person in charge of bailing the family out of financial trouble when she barely got by on her own.

"I knew you'd come through for me," her mom gushed.

Riley wanted to retort that it'd be nice if her mom came through for her once in a while.

"Mrs. Parks," the receptionist called.

Riley and her mom stepped up to the desk.

"Here's what Matt's procedure will cost today."

Riley looked at the invoice: $843. At least it wasn't the whole thousand. Her mom looked at her expectantly. Riley pulled out the bank envelope and counted out nine one-hundred-dollar bills.

"Isn't it crazy when your own daughter has to float you the money until payday?" her mom said to the receptionist. "Don't worry, Riley, I'll pay you back on Friday."

Riley tried to ignore her mother's lie, but it was still a sting to the heart. She handed over the money.

The receptionist looked at Riley with sympathy. "One moment while I get you some change." She disappeared around the corner.

"Look at all that money. You must feel pretty rich," her mom said.

"Not anymore," Riley snapped.

Her mother frowned.

"Here's your change." The receptionist put the bills in Riley's hand. "Matt should be done in about two hours."

"Thank you." Riley tucked the money into her wallet and slipped it back into her bag. They stepped away from the desk. Riley wanted to make a quick getaway.

"Two hours is perfect," her mom said. "It'll give us

plenty of time to hit the car lot and be back before Matt is finished."

"Why do I have to go to the car lot? I signed your papers."

"I'm not sure if they'll accept the papers without you there. They'll want to check your employment. Just a couple of hoops to jump through. It's easier this way, and you said you don't work until this afternoon."

Riley huffed. "Fine."

They hopped on the "L" and exited three stops later, walking the last couple of blocks to a small used car lot tucked next to a liquor store. Inside, the scent of burnt coffee permeated the office. A balding man with stained teeth greeted them.

"I told you I'd be back for the car," she said. "This is my daughter, Riley. She has the paperwork all ready to go."

Riley handed over the documents. He glanced at them. "Very good. I see you've been employed for over three months."

"Yes." Suddenly Riley realized that she'd put down Sound Sync Studios as her employer. Would he out her and say the name out loud? Her mom thought she worked for an insurance company. She did not want to deal with her mom's third degree about her working in the music industry. That was a door Riley would just as soon keep closed.

"Hey, Mom, why don't you show me the new car?"

"That's fine. I'll take the loan papers and have a couple

of things verified," the salesman said.

"Perfect," her mom said. "My car is the cute little red Mazda over there."

They exited the building and for once Riley was happy her mom kept blabbing incessantly. Riley smiled and nodded, mostly ignoring her as she poured out the details about leather interior and gas mileage. All Riley saw was a ball and chain weighing her down and keeping her from escaping the insanity of her mom.

After a few minutes, she noticed the sales guy waving. "He's ready for us."

Back in the office they sat before his cluttered desk as he explained the various papers.

"Everything here looks good. Your employer checks out, and you have a healthy bank account. I wish my kids were as responsible as you are."

"Riley has always been a good girl." Her mom leaned over to brush back a lock of Riley's hair. Riley leaned away and gave her a halting glare.

"Only a couple more signatures." He held out the papers and Riley signed her name. "Great. That'll do it. Here are the keys." He held the keys out, unsure if he should give them to her mom or the actual owner of the car, Riley.

Her mom snatched them.

"Enjoy your new car," he said as they all stood.

Riley nodded and escaped the stifling office as fast as she could. Her mom caught up. "Oh honey, thank you!"

she squealed. "This is the nicest car I've ever owned." She threw her arms around Riley.

"Mom! You better make every single payment. You can't miss one. Ever! And get it insured. Today!"

"Calm down."

"No. This is nonnegotiable. You get insurance."

"Look at you, Miss Know-It-All, now that you work for an insurance company. There's nothing to worry about. I have everything under control. You're such a drama queen."

"How can you say that? Everything you touch is drama."

Her mother curled her lip. "You know, I put up with a hell of a lot of your attitude. For once, you could act a little supportive."

She stared at her in disbelief. "Mom! I just signed loan papers for you to get a car! I paid for Matt's dentist bill. I don't think I can be much more supportive than that!"

Her mom sniffed. "Come hop in the car. We'll take it for a spin before I drop you at your apartment."

Riley took a step backward. There was no way she could stand another minute of her mother gloating about a car that literally belonged to Riley. "No, thanks. I'll walk."

For a moment her mom looked annoyed, but then she smiled. "Suit yourself."

Riley turned the opposite direction and started walking before she said or did something she'd regret. A minute later she heard tires squealing away.

23

The next day, after sleeping until almost noon, Garrett rolled out of bed and pulled on cargo shorts and a plain green T-shirt. He needed air. The walls of Brad's condo seemed to press in on him, and he didn't know why. Spending most of the night in jail hadn't made him claustrophobic, but in the light of day, the reality of his life did.

He stepped onto the balcony of the condo. Warm, humid air blasted him. He leaned his elbows on the railing and looked to the street below.

Climbing down the side of the building was a dumbass thing to do. What the hell had he been thinking? Something needed to change, and soon. He needed a fresh perspective on life. Maybe getting arrested, again, was the sign he needed.

He returned to the cool air of the condo and slipped on some shoes. With it being Sunday, there was nowhere he had to be. He grabbed his phone, wallet, and sunglasses. At the last second he pulled on a baseball cap.

Outside in the oppressive heat, he walked past the House of Blues. Jamieson had performed there a handful of times before they hit it big and needed arenas to accommodate fans.

Would he ever walk through the stage door again instead of the front doors as a patron? Not at the rate things were going.

He hooked a right onto State Street and crossed over the Chicago River, pausing to look down at the murky water. Boats filled with tourists motored past, and the sound of the guide's voice crackled through the air, mingling with the buzz of traffic. He pushed off and continued on, weaving his way over to Grant Park.

People bustled everywhere, but no one paid him any attention. He was still getting used to that. Couples with young children wheeled past with helium balloons tied to the strollers and ice cream smeared on the toddlers' cheeks. Bikers whizzed by and joggers dodged people walking their dogs. Everyone seemed so happy and content. Why couldn't he be?

He came upon Buckingham Fountain, a granite structure in the middle of the park with water spraying in a festive pattern. Tourists gathered around the edge, some tossing in coins and making wishes. He should try. Nothing else seemed to be working, so what the hell? But what should he wish for? The band to get back together? For Riley to record with him? Both seemed impossible at this point.

Garrett reached into his pocket for a coin, but found none. He didn't even have a damn nickel in his pocket, and tossing in a five-dollar bill wasn't exactly appropriate. He kicked the edge of the fountain and moved on.

The humidity in the air grew heavier, but the strong breeze off the lake refreshed him. Above, the overcast sky blocked the sun. Leaving the park, he crossed Lake Shore Drive and followed the breakfront along Lake Michigan.

It was barely four months ago that he'd been touring with his brothers, each day packed with interviews, meet-and-greets, and sound checks. The demand for his attention was at an all-time high, but now, nothing. His own brothers had rejected him, opting for an ordinary life rather than to make music together.

He came to the Shedd Aquarium, but followed the lakefront sidewalk away from the building, avoiding all the tourists on a mission to see exotic fish. The walkway jetted out into the lake; the planetarium sat at the end. Stretching his legs had been a good idea. He may not have any answers, but at least he had fresh air in his lungs.

The ring of his cell phone interrupted his thoughts. He pulled it from his pocket and groaned.

"Hey, Dad."

"Climbing the side of a skyscraper! What the hell is wrong with you?"

Garrett held the phone away to save his eardrum.

"I told you to get a new dream, not give your mother a heart attack, not to mention giving me one, too."

"I'm sorry, Dad. I wasn't thinking."

"That's perfectly evident. Your grandmother is the one who alerted me to this mess. How do you think she feels?"

Talk about a guilt trip.

"I thought you were out there working on contacts and learning a new craft, not finding ways to ruin your reputation and that of the band. Who do you think will want to work with you now?"

Garrett looked out across the choppy waves of Lake Michigan. There was no response that could possibly satisfy his father.

"What do you have to say for yourself?"

"I messed up big time."

"Damn right you did!" he barked, reminding Garrett of all the times his father chewed him out as a kid when he got caught throwing stones at the river taxis near their childhood home in San Antonio or some equally bad scrape.

"Your mother wants me to ship you back here to Boston, but you're no longer a child, Garrett, and you need to handle this one on your own."

Garrett didn't need to be parented at his age, but he'd disappointed his mom and grandmother. Ashamed, he hung his head. He'd let his dad down when he wanted more than anything to show him he could be a success.

"Pull yourself together."

"I will."

"What did you say?"

"Yes, sir. I will."

24

Riley grinned at Erika and tapped her red plastic cup to hers. "I can't think of a better way to spend the Fourth of July." After all the mama drama, she needed to let off some steam.

The music blared at the rooftop party in Wrigleyville. Red, white, and blue pennants waved in the evening breeze, and the scent of cold beer and warm bodies filled the air.

"I think it just got better." Riley tilted her head toward the blond, dreamy-eyed Chad as he worked his way toward them.

"Looks like he brought a friend," Erika said, spotting a guy with shaggy dark hair following behind, a full pitcher of beer in hand.

"Hi, Erika. You made it," Chad said with an eager smile. Erika grinned back.

"Hi, Riley," he said. "You guys, this is my friend, Bennett."

"How ya doing?" Bennett stood slightly shorter than Chad and possessed an infectious smile and warm eyes. "I brought beer." He held up the pitcher he'd nabbed from next to the keg.

"Bennett, I like you already." Erika held out her cup, and he filled it.

"Hi." Riley held out her cup for a top-off, and smiled.

"I hear you're kind of famous," he said with a playful glint in his eyes as he poured.

Riley lost her smile and turned to Erika.

"It came up, okay?" Erika said. "I mean Chad found the YouTube video, so it's not like it wasn't already public knowledge. I guess he told Bennett."

"I'm sorry. Did I say something wrong?" Bennett looked from Riley to Erika and back again.

"No. It's fine. You just caught me off guard. Trust me. I'm not famous." She offered a tentative smile. She hadn't meant to scare the guy away. He was awfully cute.

"Are you kidding? You were singing with Steven Hunter. That's epic!" Bennett said, so full of excitement.

"Is it okay if we don't talk about that?" Riley asked.

Bennett seemed taken aback, but recovered quickly. "Sure. If you don't want to talk about yourself, I guess we'll have to talk about me."

Riley relaxed. "I'd be a lot more comfortable with that."

"Riley, we're gonna go find the food table. Back in a few." Erika and Chad wandered off.

Riley let Bennett do most of the talking, and the

evening flew by as they laughed at each other's stories. At dusk, a fireworks display lit the night over Wrigley Field. Bennett slipped his arm around her waist, and Riley didn't mind a bit. She relaxed into him as a new display sounded and a huge burst of colorful lights filled the night sky. She could get used to this.

Between the oohs and the ahhs, her phone vibrated in her back pocket. She didn't want to interrupt her perfect night, but it might be Britta. She hated to leave her sister to fend for herself if there was a problem.

Riley reached for her phone. It wasn't Britta at all, but Matt.

"Excuse me, it's my brother. I've got to take this."

Bennett smiled and released her. She felt a chill where his warm arm had been.

"Hello," she answered, trying to make sure she didn't slur her words.

"Hey, Riley. I'm calling because I know Mom won't."

"Is everything okay?"

"Not for you. Mom's car was stolen."

"What!" She moved away from her friends and stepped into the stairwell where she could hear better.

"Mom was at the bar with her friend Tess. They were playing darts and she left her purse at the table. When it was time to go, she couldn't find it. And when she went outside, her car was gone."

Riley couldn't believe her ears. It wasn't possible her

mother could be that stupid. "Do you think maybe it was one of her friends just borrowing the car? Or maybe they were pulling a prank? Maybe they'll bring it back tomorrow."

"I wouldn't count on it. It happened two days ago. The only reason I found out is my friend Steve's brother works at the Alibi Room and told him."

"Oh my God." She pressed her hand to her head. "This can't be happening."

"Well, it did, and I figured you'd want to know since she made you sign those loan papers."

"Where the hell is she? I want to talk to her."

"She's out somewhere with Tess and Sue."

"Thanks." She hung up on Matt and called her mom, pacing in the small stairwell while the phone rang and rang and then went to voice mail. She called again, and this time her mom answered. Riley heard laughter in the background.

"Hi, Riley, what's up?" she said as if she hadn't a care in the world.

"Mom! Did someone steal the car?"

"What? Where did you hear that?" she asked, but her voice wavered.

"Matt told me."

"He shouldn't have done that."

"Please tell me you insured the car."

There was silence.

"Answer me, and don't lie. You know I'll find out."

"I was going to tell you. But with the holiday coming up and my new job, I didn't get a chance."

"How could you do that?" Riley yelled. "I never ask you for anything. Ever. And the one time I need you to do something, you don't."

"Riley, we can talk about this later. I'm in the middle of something."

"No, we're going to talk about it now. Did you call the police and report it?"

"They never find stolen cars. They take the report and then make you feel like an idiot because it was stolen. I'll figure out a way to buy another car."

"Oh my God, Mother! My name is on those loan papers. I'm liable for those monthly payments. I can't afford that." The walls of the stairwell started to close in, trapping her. Tears filled her eyes.

"It'll work out. It always does. Just don't make the payments. What are they going to do?"

"It'll ruin my credit for life!" she cried.

"I'm not going to talk about this anymore tonight. I've got to go." Her mom hung up.

Riley fell against the wall, the phone dead in her hand, tears streaming down her face.

The door to the stairwell opened. Erika peeked in. "Oh no! What's wrong?"

"The car my mom had me sign the loan papers for was stolen. And she never insured it."

"What do you need me to do?" Erika asked, always the loyal friend.

"I want to be very, very drunk. Can you help me with that?"

Erika took her by the arm. "I can do that." She led her back to the rooftop and over to the guys.

"Is everything okay?" Bennett asked.

"No. But I don't want to talk about it."

"You say that a lot, don't you?" he teased.

"I do. Can I get something stronger than beer?"

"Uh, sure." Bennett looked to Erika for permission. She nodded.

25

"*Riley,* wake up."

Riley's brain ached and the inside of her mouth felt fuzzy.

"You have to wake up, right now!" Erika's urgent voice sounded in her ear.

"Go away," she moaned, clinging to her pillow.

Erika shook her shoulder. "The police are at the door. Get up!"

Her eyes popped open. "What! Why?"

"I don't know. Hurry. They're waiting."

Riley sat up, the motion causing her head to swirl. She braced her hands on the bed to stay upright.

"Here are some shorts." Erika tossed them onto Riley's lap.

She took a slow breath to steady herself and slipped her legs into the shorts she'd worn last night. She stood slowly and buttoned them. Erika handed her a fresh top. She pulled it on over the cami she slept in.

Why would the police be here? She hadn't done anything wrong. Matt! What had her brother done? But why would they come here? Her mind raced with possible scenarios. She glanced in the mirror at her pale face and messy hair. She smoothed it as she made her way through the living room.

Two ominous-looking police officers stood larger than life on the other side of the open door.

"Um, hi. Can I help you?"

"Are you Riley Parks?" one officer asked.

"Yes." She held the doorframe for support.

"Your vehicle was located crashed into a bagel shop on Halstead Street at four o'clock this morning."

"What?" Her mind swirled as she tried to make sense of things.

"Yes. It's a 2009 Mazda registered in your name."

Her heart sank. "It's not actually my car. I mean, my name is on the paperwork, but it's really my mom's. It was stolen a couple of days ago."

The officers exchanged a doubtful glance.

"Miss, there is no stolen vehicle report on file for this car. May I remind you that lying to the police is considered obstructing, and that you need to be truthful from this point forward."

"I'm not lying. I promise," she pleaded.

"I suggest you speak to your mother and see if you can determine who may have stolen the car and been driving at the time of the crash."

"I talked to her last night, and she has no idea who stole it."

"In that case I will be issuing you a ticket for Owner Liability Hit and Run." He pulled out his pad and began writing.

"But I didn't do it," she said in almost a whisper.

The officer glanced up. "Miss. It's your vehicle and your responsibility. If you had reported the vehicle stolen before the time of the crash, it would be a different situation." He resumed scribbling.

How could this be happening? Her stomach churned with turmoil.

"What is your phone number?" he asked.

She recited the number. He jotted it down and tore off the slip of paper.

"Here you are." He held out the ticket.

Riley didn't want to touch the thing but had no choice.

"There is a court date listed for a month from now."

She accepted the ticket.

"Also, your vehicle has been towed, and it's in pretty bad condition. Here's the address." He handed over another slip. "Do you have any questions?"

Her pounding head swam with details. "No. I don't think so."

"All right then, good day." He turned and left her standing alone in the open doorway, with the ticket in hand.

"It's a little late for that," she mumbled, staring at the citation. She closed the door and leaned against it. Thank God she had all that money from Steven Hunter, but at this rate, she wouldn't have enough left to do her laundry.

Erika joined her. "That's a crime. You've never even driven the car."

"And now I have to pay to get it out of hock, and then make payments on a car that doesn't even run. I don't have that much money."

"What are you going to do?" Erika asked.

Her stomach rolled. "I'm going to be sick."

Riley ran to the bathroom, slamming the door behind her. She heaved into the toilet. Her hair hung around the porcelain bowl, creating a red curtain, a pathetic veil of privacy to her shame.

When her stomach finally stopped churning, she lay on the bathroom floor. She gripped a bath towel and willed her head to stop spinning.

She tried to make sense of everything the police officer had said. Someone crashed her mom's car, and yet Riley had to pay for it all. She pressed her flushed face to the cool tiles.

How could she come up with money to pay for a car that she no longer owned and damage to a building she'd never been to?

26

Whoever decided July fifth should be a workday had never been to a decent Fourth of July celebration. Riley couldn't imagine what artists would be recording today. Despite her pounding head, she pushed through the front doors and was greeted by a fake silver Christmas tree glittering in the lobby. She turned her weary eyes on Tara.

"It's Jamie Halloway. She's working on a Christmas album and wants to set the mood," Tara explained as she taped tiny stockings to the edge of her desk.

"Lord save me," Riley mumbled. She entered the break room and headed straight for the ibuprofen. The two she took after the police left weren't working. She forced herself to drink an entire glass of water, even though her stomach wasn't happy about it.

Logan found her a few minutes later, scrounging through the cupboards.

"How was your Fourth?" he asked in far too chipper of a voice.

"Rainbows and unicorns. You?"

Logan laughed and leaned against the counter. "Low key. My girlfriend and I went to my uncle's place for an annual picnic. Lots of family, potato salad, and sparklers."

"Aha!" She found a box of crackers and seized it.

"So what did you do, beyond drinking a whole lot of alcohol?"

Riley leaned against the counter and dug into the box. "Well, I met a nice guy who seemed to like me up until the moment I turned into a sloppy drunk and wiped out the snack table, and cried over spilled salsa." She wished she could delete that memory.

Logan cringed.

"And my mom has probably ruined my credit for the rest of my life, not to mention saddled me with debt."

Logan's eyes widened and he nodded. "Fun times."

"The only good thing is that I've got that money from Steven Hunter, so at least I can use that to make the payments for a while. After that, I'm not sure what I'll do."

"That really sucks."

Garrett strode in. "What sucks?" He stared at her with too many unspoken words between them. She hadn't seen him since he tried to railroad her into singing at the Cubs game, and she wasn't especially happy to see him now.

"Nothing." Riley forced a carefree smile.

"Garrett, I'm surprised to see you here. I thought you might still be on lockdown," Logan joked.

"Huh?" She'd been so wrapped up in her own drama. Had Garrett been arrested?

Garrett poured himself coffee. "Nope. I'm out and I've turned over a new leaf."

"Out from where?" Riley asked, but neither guy was talking. "Okay, someone has to catch me up."

"Oh, Garrett and Brad made the news when he was arrested at the Marina Towers the other night after his performance at Wrigley Field." Logan grinned.

Riley almost wished she'd been there to see it, but she'd been so mad at the time and had left. At least Logan enjoyed it. "So, what was the arrest for, a drug bust or soliciting a prostitute?" She smirked. Logan blurted out a laugh.

Garrett slid the coffeepot back into place. "Nice to see you have such a high opinion of me."

"Come on. Tell me," Riley urged, happy to focus on someone else's problems.

"Tell you what?" Tara asked, strolling in, clutching a bag.

"What Garrett and Brad were arrested for," Riley answered.

"Where've you been? It's in the *Tribune*, on *TMZ*, there's even a YouTube video of their walk of shame. I have the paper at my desk with the picture. It's kind of cute," Tara said, tossing an affectionate smile Garrett's way.

"And?" Riley asked.

"He and Brad were climbing down the Marina Towers. From the outside."

Riley gaped at Garrett. "Seriously? You did that?"

He grimaced the affirmative and took a sip of his coffee.

"Are you nuts?" she asked.

"Apparently so."

"Look, here's the pic on *TMZ*." Logan held out his phone. Riley took it and saw a grainy picture of the two guys walking with their hands cuffed behind their backs, staring at the camera, their faces lit by the flash.

"You're looking straight at the camera. Oh my God. This is so adorable." Nothing like Garrett getting arrested to cheer her up.

Garrett rolled his eyes. He didn't storm out of the room, so he must not be too embarrassed.

"You shouldn't make fun of him," Tara said.

"Why not? It's not every day I get to see Mr. Big Shot here taking the walk of shame."

"Because you're working with Jamie Halloway on her Christmas album, and she bought sweaters for everyone on her team." Tara held the bag out to Riley and struggled to keep a straight face.

"She didn't," Riley said, afraid of what it contained.

"Oh yes, she did." Tara seemed too eager to hand over the bag.

"No," Riley whined. She accepted it, reached in, and pulled out a red sweater with a huge Christmas tree complete with garland and embroidered ornaments appliquéd to the front.

Her good mood evaporated. "She doesn't expect me to actually wear this, does she?"

"Pretty sure she does. Be glad you didn't get the one with dancing reindeer with little pompoms where their boy parts are."

Garrett smiled broadly. "Now I can die happy. Mind putting that on so I can get a picture of you?"

"Not on your life." Riley stuffed the sweater back in the bag and stomped off.

27

$Riley$ entered the control room of Studio D. A blast of cool air greeted her. A woman in red skinny jeans and stylish black boots was sliding a fake fireplace against the wall next to the sound board. Beside it, a box overflowed with fake greenery.

"Hello," Riley called, rubbing her arms against the chill.

The woman turned, swinging her silky black hair over her shoulder. She wore a cream-colored cable-knit sweater.

"Oh, hi. I'm just setting up this fireplace. I couldn't find one in Chicago, so my grandmother sent me hers. I'm Jamie. I see you got the sweater, so you must be on my team."

Riley looked down at the bag and fought back a grimace over the ugly sweater. "Yes, ah, thanks. I'm Riley. Can I help you, maybe turn up the heat? It must be sixty degrees in here."

Jamie laughed, setting her red Christmas ball earrings swinging. "Oh, that's on purpose. I'm turning the studio into a holiday winter wonderland to put us all in the mood to record Christmas music in July. And sorry about the sweater. They're hard to find this time of year, but don't worry. You didn't get the worst one."

Riley smiled. "What can I help you with?"

"A lot, actually. I want this room and the live room oozing with Christmas spirit. Let's put up what we have and then I'll send you on a run for what we're missing. But first, put on your sweater. It's cold in here."

Riley hesitated.

Jamie grinned. "Come on, we're going to have a blast. I promise."

Riley pulled the obnoxious sweater on over her T-shirt and laughed. This day might turn out well after all.

An hour later, a wreath hung from the door, the fake fireplace burned bright, and twinkle-light garland swooped from the door and the window to the live room.

Jamie surveyed their work. "That's most of it. You'll need to go out in search of more supplies. See if you can find some tinsel, maybe some candy canes, and definitely more white lights. I want to lower these glaring fluorescents and create a mood."

"All right," Riley said, although she had no idea where she'd find such items this time of year.

"You can put it all on this card. Anything you find

that's Christmassy, go ahead and buy."

"I'll do my best." As soon as Riley stepped out of the control room, she slipped off the sweater. No reason to set herself up for ridicule.

She retrieved keys to the company errand car, a slightly dented blue Impala, from Tara at the front desk, and headed out in search of Christmas. Was it only a week ago that her mother drove off in the car Riley had stupidly bought? Her Christmas cheer evaporated in an instant.

Where the heck was she supposed to find Christmas decor? No regular store would carry decorations this time of year. Maybe a discount dollar store would.

She pulled into a strip mall and parked. Once inside the bargain store, and with a basket over her arm, Riley perused the shelves for any held-over holiday supplies, finally finding Christmas stuff in a back corner. She passed on ugly stiff ribbons stapled flat to cardboard, but put the plastic silver ornaments shaped like icicles into her basket. As she squatted next to a box of mostly chipped Christmas mugs, her phone rang. She didn't recognize the number.

"Hello."

"Is this Riley Parks?" an unfamiliar voice asked.

"Yes."

"This is Hank Schmelzer from Radial Insurance. I'm calling to verify that you are the owner of a 2009 Mazda?"

Crud. Her shoulders tensed, she set down a reindeer mug and stood.

"Yes."

"I represent the owner of the Bokorski Bagel shop. Are you aware that your vehicle crashed into the building?"

"Yes." She sighed. "It wasn't me. The car was stolen. I've already talked to the police."

"My company insures the bagel shop and will be compensating the owner for damages. However, we will now be seeking reimbursement for damages from the liable party, which in this case would be the vehicle's owner, you."

"I didn't do it. Honestly. The car was stolen."

"But it was your vehicle that struck the building, so that makes you liable." He went on to confirm her mailing address. "You'll receive legal documents in the mail in the next several days."

"For how much?"

"I haven't received the damage estimates yet, but I'd assume it's north of ten thousand dollars."

"I don't have that kind of money."

"As I said, you'll receive more exact information via the mail. Thank you for your time."

The phone went dead.

28

That night, Riley tossed and turned in bed, unable to stop thinking about her financial disaster. She had the police ticket, a monthly car payment due soon, and now bills for the damn bagel shop. It was too much.

Somehow she needed to take control of this insane situation. The first step would be to disown her mother. Next, she could pay the police ticket. The sooner it was off her pile of debt, the better. At least that she could afford. Before she caught the "L" to work, she stopped by the bank.

"What do you mean there's not enough money in the account?" Riley asked the bank teller in disbelief.

"According to our records, all but two hundred dollars was withdrawn a few days ago."

"But I should have almost four thousand dollars in my account."

The teller clicked a few keys on the keyboard, her brow

knit. "You did, until it was withdrawn. Hang on a second, let me check something."

Riley shifted from one foot to the other. How could her money be gone? Could it be stolen? Did someone steal her identity?

"I see that this is a custodial account with your mother as custodian and you as the beneficiary. Maybe she made the withdrawal?"

Riley's heart and soul fell from her body like a trapdoor had opened up and swallowed them into no-man's-land. "How could she do that? I'm eighteen. She shouldn't be able to touch my account."

The teller grimaced. "Unless you both come in and sign off to change the account, it remains as a custodial account."

Riley rubbed her forehead and fought back the tears that welled in her eyes. "I didn't know. I never would have put money in my account if I knew that."

"Hold on and I'll pull the slips from the date of the withdrawal." The teller left her alone.

Riley should have told her not to bother checking. It had to be her mom. Riley had mentioned a bonus, the loan guy had complimented her on good money management. Her mom must have figured out she'd been saving money. She covered her mouth to prevent a sob from coming.

What was she going to do? Not only could she not make the car payments for the crashed car, but she couldn't even begin to pay the insurance company back for the bagel shop damage. Looking around the bank, she wondered if anyone else could see her world crumbling, but they all went about their business without a care in the world.

The teller returned with a piece of paper. "Here is the withdrawal slip. Is this your mother's signature?"

Riley nodded, anger and despair burning through her.

"I'm sorry, but she was within her legal rights to the money."

Riley swiped at her eyes. "I understand. Could I withdraw the rest of the money?" No reason to let her mom come back for the last little bit.

"Of course." The teller nodded in sympathy.

Outside, with the two hundred dollars in her wallet, Riley walked in a daze. What had she done to make her mother act so cruel?

Riley sniffed and refused to let her mother hurt her anymore. If she didn't let her in, she couldn't cause her pain.

She called Erika. "My mom took all my money."

"No!"

"I'm not even shocked anymore. I'm a fool for not thinking it was a possibility."

"Oh, Riley, I'm so sorry. What are you going to do? Are you going to go ask for it back?"

"It wouldn't do any good. I'm sure she already spent it.

I need to cut her out of my life. All she does is hurt me over and over, and I let her."

"I'm so sorry. I wish there was something I could do."

"Having you to talk to helps. Thanks for dealing with me and my constant drama."

"I was supposed to go out with Chad tonight, but I can cancel and we can binge on ice cream and pizza. His friend Bennett keeps asking about you."

"He does? That's surprising considering the lousy first impression I made. Thanks, but I have to work late tonight. Jamie Halloway keeps late hours. I have to go celebrate frickin' Christmas every day for the next month. Any idea where I can find poinsettias in July?"

"No. God, this sucks so bad."

"Yeah, but what is it they say? What doesn't kill you makes you stronger."

"Well, you're the strongest person I know."

Riley frowned. "I don't feel strong. I feel like the world's biggest idiot."

"Stop it. As soon as you have time off, I'm taking you somewhere to cheer you up. How about the Navy Pier? We'll get the funnel cake with the whipped cream, chocolate sauce, and peanuts on top."

A smile tugged at Riley's mouth. "You're the best. Thanks."

"Wait a minute. I have an idea! I don't know why I didn't think of this before. But I think there is some rule

.about your old insurance carrying over for a new car."

"What do you mean?"

"My uncle bought a new car last year and then got in a fender bender before he called his insurance agent to switch over the insurance. The insurance company covered it. There's some rule, I don't exactly know, but it's worth checking out. If the car is still insured, then maybe that would cover the building damages, too."

"Thank you! I love you! I'll call you later."

Finally, the break she needed.

29

As soon as Riley arrived at work, she borrowed the dented company car. She used the excuse that she was shopping for more Christmas decor for Jamie, but instead drove straight to the hotel where her mom worked.

Her mom had better be there and have the answers Riley needed. Her hands began to sweat as she entered the chain hotel.

She walked up to the marble reception counter. A large bowl of shiny green apples sat on top, making her suddenly hungry. A guy with a large forehead and sporting a navy jacket greeted her.

"Good afternoon, may I help you?"

"Hi, I'm looking for Shelly Parks. She's my mom." Her heart pounded with anger and adrenaline. Her mom was the last person she wanted to see right now, but she was the only person who might be able to save her.

"Oh sure, I should have recognized you by your hair. I'll get her. Hang on a sec."

Riley forced a flat smile as high-forehead dude disappeared around the corner. Her eyes traveled over the gleaming hotel logo on the wall behind the counter, and the ice water with cucumbers floating in it on a table nearby. Her stomach growled.

"Hi, honey, what are you doing here?" Her mom appeared from around the corner wearing a brilliant smile, and a jacket similar to the guy's. Her name tag was pinned to the front. Apparently Mom didn't need new clothes for this job after all. The guy returned to his station.

Riley approached the counter, her eyes never leaving her mother's. She meant to ask about the insurance but instead said in a quiet voice, "You took all my money." Tears of hurt and defeat threatened, but she forced them back.

Her mother's smile dimmed. "That's not true. I left some."

Her coworker's eyes darted uncomfortably. He disappeared into the back.

Riley stared at her mom, waiting for her explanation.

"I had to. My purse was stolen, the rent was overdue, and I didn't have a car. You can imagine my surprise when I found out that you had all that money stashed. You always were such a good saver."

Riley refused to speak, afraid of what she might say.

Her mother shifted uncomfortably. "I was only checking your account for enough to help with the rent, but when I saw how much you had, I borrowed some to get a new car. Well, not a new car. Not even a nice car for that little money, but now I have wheels again. Yay!" she said enthusiastically. "I'll pay it back starting with my next paycheck."

"Stop lying," Riley said in a steely voice.

"Listen," her mother said in a quiet voice, matching Riley's. "You cannot come into my work and talk to me like this. I will not allow it."

"I just need to know one thing. Did you have insurance on your old car? The one that you traded in?" Riley held her breath, waiting for her answer.

"Why would I insure a car that wasn't worth anything?"

"But the other kind. The kind of insurance in case you get into an accident and someone has to go to the hospital. Or to pay for damage to a building if your car is stolen and someone drives it into a bagel shop at four a.m. on July fifth."

"What are you saying? Was there some kind of accident?"

"Tell me, Mom. Did your old car have insurance?"

Her mother looked at her with disdain. "No."

Why wasn't Riley surprised? She had known the answer before she drove all the way over here. What a waste of time. She left the lobby and climbed into the car, noticing an old beater in the spot next to her. That was probably the car her mother bought with the stolen money.

Why did her mother hate her so much? As Riley started the car another idea popped into her head, like a tiny flicker of light in a dark tunnel. It made her stomach tighten into a big knot, but it was her only option left.

30

Riley found Garrett alone in Studio D, listening to tracks. Was she really going to do this? She had to. She didn't know where else to turn.

"Did you need something?" he asked, distracted.

This was a bad idea.

"It's okay. I can wait." She backed away.

"Are you okay? You look upset." Garrett stood and came toward her.

Upset didn't begin to explain her complicated emotions. She thought about what she needed to ask him and changed her mind.

"You know what? I'll figure something out. Don't worry about it." She opened the outer door.

"Wait. Don't go. Come in and let's talk."

This was new. She was used to his combative side that always led to an ulterior motive. "I don't know. You look busy."

He guided her over to the sound board, held out the producer's chair for her, and then sat next to it. She sat down hesitantly. This chair was for the producer, the person in charge of a studio album.

"So what did you want to talk to me about?"

She sighed. "It's dumb. No. It's more than dumb. It's the stupidest problem on the planet and I can't believe it's my problem. And I can't believe I'm actually asking you for this favor. But it's more than a favor. It's huge. It's saving my life."

He raised his eyebrows. "Sounds important."

"It is." She stared at her shoes, and her stomach churned again.

"Are you going to tell me or make me guess?"

"I don't think you'd ever guess this."

"Unless you're asking me for money, you're right. I have no idea."

Her face fell, and she saw the realization dawn on Garrett's face.

"You *are* asking for money?"

She sensed his disappointment and flushed with guilt. "You know what, never mind. I'll figure something out." She stood to leave.

"Wait." He captured her hand, preventing her from running away. "Sit down and tell me what's going on. It must be bad if you're coming to me."

Her heart raced. She didn't know if it was from the warm strength of his hand or her fear of asking for help.

More than anything, she wanted to evaporate into thin air from the shame of it all.

She sucked in a breath and explained it in the plainest terms possible, including the stolen car, the crash into the bagel shop, and her lack of insurance.

Garrett stared at her, dumbstruck. "Your mom had you take out a loan on a car she couldn't afford?"

"That's what you got from all that? I thought for sure you'd be more weirded out by someone not insuring their car and then having it stolen."

"That's pretty bad, too." He shook his head. "That sucks. What about the money you got from the Graphite Angels?"

"I used a bunch of it so my brother could get a broken tooth fixed. Helped pay some back rent. It's all gone. I'm going to have to pay for damages to the bagel shop, and there's no way I can pay for that by myself. Plus, I have the ticket to pay."

He stared at her. "I still can't believe your mom would do that to you."

Tears brimmed in her eyes, but she dashed them away. "That's what my mom does. She's not exactly Mother of the Year."

"So, how much do you need?"

"I haven't gotten the final bill yet, but at least ten grand."

Garrett whistled low.

"I know. I'm so sorry to even ask, but I didn't know who else might have that kind of money. I'll pay it all back. I promise."

"You don't have any other family you can go to? Your dad, maybe?"

"No. He's been out of the picture since my sister was little. I wouldn't know how to find him even if I wanted to. There's my grandma, my mom's mom, but she wouldn't have anything and even if she did, she'd never help. She's more of a figure-it-out-yourself kinda person."

"I see." He leaned back and stared at the wall.

"I'm so sorry to ask." She really wanted to curl up and die rather than ask him for help, but it had to be done.

"No, I understand why you'd think to ask me." He blew out his breath and leaned forward, his elbows on his knees as if he didn't want anyone else to hear, despite the fact that they were alone. "But I don't give people money."

Riley's heart froze in her chest. He wasn't going to help.

Garrett looked straight into her eyes and she wished he hadn't. She wanted to forget the whole thing, but she'd put him on the spot and now she had to listen to him make excuses about why he wouldn't help her.

"I wish I could, but my brothers and I came up with a strict policy a long time ago not to casually give away money. Not unless it was for a charity or non-profit for needy or ill children, an organization with a proven track record for making a difference in helping the less fortunate."

Couldn't he see her desperation? If he wouldn't help her, who would? And why wouldn't he look away?

"You see, we get asked for handouts constantly. Our manager, Mom, and Dad screen them for us."

"I understand. It's fine. Really. Don't worry about it." She stood to flee and hide, but he stood, too. The mistletoe hung directly above them. She looked away.

"Don't go. Maybe there's another way we can work this out," he said.

"Really?"

"Of course. I want to help, I do. You'd have to earn the money."

"Doing what? Cleaning your apartment or something? Do you even have an apartment?"

"That's not what I had in mind." Garrett laughed, and it reached all the way to his eyes, making him appear relaxed and unguarded. He slid a hand in his front pocket. "I was thinking you could sign a contract with me to record an album."

Of course, it always came back to that. Hadn't he figured out yet that singing was the last thing she planned to do with her life? No. He'd want to take full advantage of her need for cash to get what he wanted.

"You asshole."

"What? You came to me asking for more than ten thousand dollars. You think I'd just hand it over? Here you go, have a nice day? You want money from me, and I want you to record. It's a pretty obvious trade-off."

She looked at the candy canes taped around the control room window. There was no escape from her bizarre world. He was offering an out. It came at a huge cost, but it would save her from all her legal woes. "You love this, don't you? Me having to beg?"

"No. I'm offering you a deal. Did I ever imagine things would work out so nicely? No. But your situation sure is convenient."

"I hate you. You do know that."

He smiled, showing off a dimple in his cheek, and his eyes glittered. "Yeah, and I'm okay with that."

Could she do it? Record with Garrett, work with him, and even worse, let him make the decisions? Put herself out there again to be judged by the public? God, with every fiber of her being she didn't want to.

"So do we have a deal?" he asked with a smug look.

Riley glared at him. She either had to face years of legal problems and bad credit, or make a deal with the devil.

She weighed her options. If she recorded with him, that was it. It would be painful, but if she sucked it up, she could find a way to suffer through and get it over with quickly.

Then again, could she even trust Garrett after the episode at Wrigley Field?

He stood and walked to the door to leave. "I've got other issues to deal with. I'm not going to wait around all day for you to make up your mind."

"Wait," she called out.

He turned.

"I'll do it."

31

"Can I borrow Riley for a bit?" Garrett asked Ron later that day.

Riley looked up from recording notes for Jamie Halloway's Christmas album. So this was it.

"Sure. We're good for a while," Ron said.

Riley blew out a breath and followed Garrett. He stopped outside Barry's office, where prestigious gold records and recording awards were prominently displayed on the wall.

"Before we go any further, I want to know if you're sure about our deal. About recording an album," Garrett asked with a businesslike tone.

His personal consideration caught her off guard. She expected him to be gloating that he won. Instead a flicker of humanity shone in his eyes.

"I told you I am."

"No. I want you to take a minute and be sure you know what you're doing. Up until this morning, you were adamant that you were done singing. I don't want you making a rash decision and regretting it later."

"I'm not," she said, praying it was true.

Garrett looked her straight in the eye. "Recording an album is a huge decision. Once you do this, you can't change your mind."

"It'll be fine." She looked away, her eyes landing on a gold record for Jamieson's *Triple Threat* album. And here was one of the band members wanting to record her.

He dipped his head and recaptured her gaze. Flecks of light in his gray eyes caught her attention. "This is going to be a lot of hard work and long hours."

Riley swallowed and nodded. She had no other choice. She couldn't live buried by all this debt. She'd worked hard and for so long to avoid singing again. There had been so much criticism from the judges and producers on the show, and ridicule from the kids at school, that singing professionally had been ruined for her. She prayed this time would be different.

"I'm good. Let's do this." She offered a brief smile.

Garrett grinned. "Now that that's settled, come into Barry's office. I want you to meet someone."

She took a deep breath and followed. *Here we go.*

"Riley, I'd like you to meet Craig Johnston. He's an entertainment lawyer who specializes in the music industry. I've been meeting with Craig since I first arrived in Chicago."

Craig stood and shook her hand. "Nice to meet you, Riley." He wore a dark business suit, his dark brown hair neatly trimmed and his sideburns graying. His handshake was firm and formal.

"Nice to meet you, too, Mr. Johnston," she said, suddenly out of her league. "I didn't expect a lawyer and everything."

"Call me Craig. Please take a seat."

Once they were all seated, Garrett said, "You told me to give you a contract. I would never enter into a contract without a lawyer drawing it up."

"That's right. Working by only a handshake is always a bad idea." Craig smiled.

"Okay, where do I sign?" Riley asked.

Craig opened a folder and started pulling out papers. "Here you go. This is a general music recording contract."

She stared at the thick packet.

"This covers all the basics. Each party's name, where the recording will take place, start and end dates."

Riley looked to Garrett, who nodded encouragement.

"It includes who has control over recording quality, the minimum number of tracks to be recorded, and their duration," he continued.

"I thought the contract was about the money," Riley said.

"We'll get to that section in a minute. This contract also includes an exclusivity clause, which states that you cannot record elsewhere while under contract with Garrett and his production company."

"Trust me, that won't be a problem." She didn't want to record with him, let alone someone else.

"No, I don't think it will be. As I said, all of this is standard language. Now under compensation and royalties, it states you are receiving this amount." He showed her the number on the page.

"Twenty thousand dollars!" She turned to Garrett. "That's a lot more than what I asked for."

"The number you asked for wasn't enough. I wasn't going to take advantage of you."

True, but this was more money than she'd ever dreamed of earning. It would solve a lot of problems. Maybe Garrett was a good guy after all. She couldn't wait to tell Erika and see her reaction.

Craig interrupted her thoughts. "This is an advance to work against future royalty earnings that are fifteen percent, based on . . ." He paused to see if she was paying attention.

"Industry standards," Riley answered.

"Exactly. This next section is about termination, disputes, and breach of contract."

All the monotonous legal talk made her head swirl in confusion. "Excuse me, do we have to go through all this?

Can I just sign it? You said it's all standard anyway." She needed to get out of there and find someplace to either do a happy dance, or throw up as she realized what a big deal she was about to sign.

"Certainly, but it's always in your best interest to read a contract before signing. There is one section I must address. Do you wish to have independent counsel in regards to this contract?" he asked.

"Wouldn't that cost more money?"

"Yes, it would. So if you wish to decline independent counsel, please check and initial here." The lawyer indicated the box.

Riley took the pen, checked the box, and initialed. Each page he turned in the contract made her squirm in her seat.

"If you'll excuse me for a moment, I'm going to bring Tara in to witness the signatures." Craig left for a moment.

"I thought we were just going to throw together a record and see if it stuck or not," she said to Garrett.

"If we're going to make a record, we're going to do it right. This isn't some garage band putting out a cobbled YouTube video. We're going to make a high-quality record."

Mr. Johnston returned with Tara. "Tara is here only as witness to the contract signing and will sign off as such."

"This is so exciting," Tara said. "You have no idea how lucky you are."

Riley forced a smile. "Okay, where do I sign?"

After signing her name several more times, she passed

the pages to Garrett for his signature, and Tara signed the last page.

"Thank you, Tara, you're free to go," the lawyer said.

Tara grinned at Riley before leaving and closing the door behind her.

"Congratulations!" Craig said. "And here is the check that serves as your advance." He handed her an envelope.

She peeked inside at the twenty-thousand-dollar check. First Steven Hunter and now Garrett Jamieson. What bizarre dimension was she living in?

"If I were you, I'd put that in the bank and be careful not to spend it too quick. It could be a very long time before you earn royalties, if ever," Mr. Johnston said.

"I will." She would open a new bank account at a different bank, where her mother could never touch it.

Mr. Johnston stood. "I'll get copies of the contract made and ready for you in a few minutes. In the meantime, congratulations to you both." He shook hands with both of them.

"So what happens next?" she asked Garrett, once the lawyer left the room.

"We start working," Garrett said.

"Already?"

"What did you think was going to happen? We need to move fast. I'd like to put out a demo track as soon as possible. There's still buzz about you from your video with Steven Hunter. We've got to ride that wave."

Craig opened the office door. Barry Goldwin and nearly the entire staff entered. Tara pushed a cart containing a bottle of champagne and clinking glasses.

"Congratulations!" they yelled, stunning Riley.

"Let's get a picture," Logan said.

Garrett put his arm around her and smiled. Riley gave a strained smile as Logan captured the moment.

What had she gotten herself into?

32

After their impromptu celebration, Garrett raced back to Brad's condo. There was so much to do, and he couldn't wait to get started. But first, a phone call.

"Hey, Dad. I got her to sign!" He waved his way past the doorman of the Marina Towers and entered the elevator.

"No kidding? That's great. I never had any doubt."

Garrett wasn't about to confess that the only reason Riley surrendered was her need for insta-cash. The reason she signed didn't really matter. Hearing the approval in his father's voice was exactly what he needed.

"It's great to see things coming together for you. Your mother will be so happy, too. So when do you start working?"

"I already have. I've reserved a studio to record in next week. I'm reaching out to some studio musicians to lay down tracks. Now I've got to find the perfect song. I only have one debut as a music producer and I want to do this right."

"Excellent attitude, and finding the perfect song is always the biggest problem."

Garrett juggled his phone and messenger bag as he unlocked the apartment door. "Yeah, I've got calls out to a couple of songwriters. Barry even offered to call in a couple favors if I need him to."

"That's one way to go. But consider this. You have access to an extremely talented songwriter with an encyclopedia of songs waiting to be recorded."

Garrett paused in the entryway. He knew who his father meant, but refused to ask for any favors. Not now, not ever. "Forget it, Dad. I'm not calling him."

"For God's sake, he's your brother."

"And he's been acting like a little diva the past four months."

"Is this how you're going to run your career? Letting personal issues interfere with making smart business decisions?"

"Dad, he broke up the band!" Garrett tossed his keys on the entry table, crossed the apartment, and laid his bag on the glass-topped dining room table.

"Garrett, you know it was a lot more complicated than just quitting the band. What are you going to put first? Business? Or your personal feelings?"

"Fine. I'll think about it. Listen, I'm home and I've got a ton to do, so . . ."

"I'll let you go. And son, I'm proud of you."

"Thanks, Dad." Garrett hung up and smiled.

He set up his laptop and pulled a legal pad out of his messenger bag. There were about two dozen items to add to his to-do list. He needed to start thinking about publicity, album covers, marketing, and appearances. There was so much to do and he couldn't dive in fast enough. In the old recording mold, they'd take months to complete all this, but with YouTube, he could move as quickly as he wanted.

His father's words echoed in his mind, and as much as he didn't want to admit it, he was right.

Garrett picked up his phone and dialed his brother.

"So how's the Windy City?" Peter answered.

"Pretty damn awesome," Garrett said, looking out the windows and across the city.

"I hear you've taken up climbing." Peter chuckled.

He was confused for a second but then realized Peter was talking about his most recent arrest. "At least I'm living life to the fullest."

"Yeah, until you kill yourself. Are you doing okay, or was it a cry for help? Do you want me to call the guys in the little white coats to come get you?"

Garrett turned his back on the massive windows and sank into the leather couch. "Give it a break. I was only having a little fun."

"The kind that gives Mom a stroke."

"And how's the life of a reclusive singer songwriter who sneaks into open-mic nights to get his performance fix?"

"Incredibly well. It's so nice of you to ask," Peter answered, unruffled by Garrett's jab.

"I give you six months and you'll be begging to crawl back on any stage that's bigger than a postage stamp."

"Is there a reason you called, or did you miss treating me like a human punching bag?"

"Actually there is." Garrett hesitated, not sure how to proceed without sounding like a dick. "Can you send me some of your songs?"

"What songs?" Peter sounded confused.

"Some of the better ones that we never recorded."

"Why?"

"Never mind why. I need them, and only send the good ones. None of the shitty rejects from three years ago."

"Oh my God. You're going solo, aren't you?"

"No. I'm not going solo. You knew I came out here to produce records. I've found the perfect artist, but now I need material, and it's got to be great."

"And you want my songs."

"Theoretically they belong to Jamieson, not you."

"Which is another reason that you can't just give away my music."

"You aren't seriously going to fight me on this?" Garrett growled, ready to battle.

"No, I only wanted to yank your chain. It's fun to make

you squirm." Peter laughed.

"Asshole."

"So who'd you find willing to record with you? They must be really desperate. That or they've never actually met you."

"You ever hear of Riley Parks?"

"Doesn't ring a bell."

"Well, it will. Are you near your computer? Go to YouTube and type in Riley Parks and Steven Hunter."

"Hang on."

"This girl was on *Chart Toppers* a few years back. She works at Sound Sync."

"Got it. She's pretty, but not really your type."

"Shut up and listen." Garrett heard the video playing in the background and pictured Riley baring her heart and soul in that song. He waited for her to hit the big notes.

"Wow! And she's agreed to let you produce her record? Does she know you don't have a clue what you're doing?"

"Sure I do. I've put out four albums. How hard can it be?"

"What's she like?"

"She's strong and funny and everyone loves her. You saw her stand toe-to-toe with Steven Hunter. But she's kind too, and not arrogant."

"I'm impressed. Has the cold, heartless Garrett Jamieson finally found love?"

"What? No! I worked hard to land her."

"Don't you mean land her in bed?"

"It's not like that. It's business."

Peter laughed. "Sure it is. I give you three weeks. Bet you can't hold off that long."

"Just send me the songs. Tonight." He hung up and tried to clear his mind of the image of Riley in his bed.

After the contract signing and impromptu party, Riley returned to work only to find they'd wrapped up early for the night. Still in a surreal daze, she headed back to her apartment, trying to digest the horrible steps she'd taken to fix her life.

"You're home early," Erika commented while staring at the TV. "Hey, you never called me back about the insurance."

Riley pushed the door shut and dropped next to her on the battered couch.

"Oh no. What now?" Erika asked.

Riley pulled a large manila envelope from her bag that contained the weight of the world. She tossed it to her friend. Erika scrambled to pull out the documents.

"What are these?" Her eyes scanned the pages. "Is this saying . . . ?"

"Yup." Riley stared at a crack in the wall on the other side of the room.

"Riley, are you okay with this?"

"Nope."

"You're going to record, like, for real?"

"What is there to say? My life sucks." She pictured herself spiraling down a drain.

"It does not. This might be exactly what you need to turn it all around."

"I know this sounds really lame, but," she hesitated then whispered, "I'm afraid."

"You don't have to be afraid. Listen to me." Erika scooched closer and faced her. "Garrett wouldn't have pushed you so hard to do this if he didn't think you could."

Riley grabbed a sofa pillow and hugged it. "But what if I'm really bad? You're not the one who has to stand up in front of the world and expose your heart. I was so scared when I sang with Steven Hunter. You didn't see me. My legs were shaking, my hands were sweating. It was bad."

"Don't be so dramatic. I've seen the video and you were amazing, and you did that on the spur of the moment. Imagine what you can do after a little rehearsal."

Riley laid her head back against the couch. "I don't want to think about it. It makes me ill."

"Okay, we need to do some serious cheering up. I know the perfect thing to get you out of your funk." Erika sprang off the couch.

"What?" Riley lolled her head toward Erika.

"Come on. You're going to love it." She pulled Riley to her feet.

"I really don't feel like going to Navy Pier."

"This is way better than going to the pier. Trust me. Now grab your bag. We're going out."

Riley shook her head, but followed.

33

The next day, Riley pushed through the front door of the studio, bracing herself for the new direction her life was taking. When she'd woken this morning, for a second she thought maybe it had all been a bad dream, but, no, Garrett had already texted her to meet for a late breakfast. She hadn't responded. He couldn't wait to talk about recording together, and she wanted to talk about anything but.

"Morning, Tara," she said, passing through the reception area.

"Stop! Don't move! Did you dye your hair?"

Riley's hand flew to a chunk of hair that Erika had dyed a brilliant blond. She grinned. "I did."

Last night, Erika had dragged her to a corner drugstore where they picked out a blond highlighting kit. They spent the night eating pizza and turning several huge chunks of Riley's hair from dark red to glossy blond.

"Let me see." Tara came out from behind the counter.

Riley shook her head so Tara could see the blond chunks strategically mixed in with her red hair. "What do you think?"

"It looks great."

"Thanks." She pushed her hair behind an ear, glad to know Tara, who possessed a great sense of style, approved.

"It's very rock and roll. Did Garrett tell you to do that?"

"Nope. It was my friend Erika's idea. She did it for me."

"I can't believe how cool you are about this whole recording contract. If it were me, I'd be screaming through the studio and telling everyone who'd listen. You do know how lucky you are, don't you? I mean, Garrett Jamieson? You and him, working alone all the time." She wiggled her eyebrows suggestively.

Riley didn't want to seem ungrateful, and Tara wouldn't understand her reservations. "It's great. I'm excited on the inside. And we won't really be alone much; there's always a crowd around in this business." A crowd telling her what she was doing wrong, most likely.

"You could show some excitement once in a while," Tara suggested.

"I'll work on it. Catch you later." Riley passed through to the break room. She fished out her phone and called Garrett. Within ten minutes she was at the restaurant at the end of the block, as Tara predicted, alone with Garrett.

"Hi." He welcomed her in an eager voice as she slid into

the booth, and then his next words were lost as he noticed her hair.

"You like it?" She proudly turned her head each way, hoping he did.

"What have you done?"

He didn't seem nearly as happy about her hair as Tara.

"I think it's pretty obvious. I added highlights."

"You can't color your hair."

"Of course I can," she said, her good mood fading. "So what did you want to talk about? I'm supposed to be at work. We're adding the string tracks to Jamie's album today. I've got a lot to do."

"No. Your contract says that you can't change your hair."

"Seriously? That's the dumbest thing I've ever heard."

A waitress appeared and placed a plate of steaming scrambled eggs, buttered toast, and delicious-smelling bacon in front of each of them.

"I didn't order this," Riley said.

"I ordered for you. I figured everyone likes scrambled eggs," Garrett said.

"Thank you," Riley said to the waitress.

"Coffee?" the waitress asked.

"No thanks."

"And I'm dead serious," Garrett said. "You can't go changing your look. Thank God we haven't done the photo shoot for your cover yet."

Riley fought the unease the thought of a photo shoot gave her. "There is a whole lot wrong with what you just said, but I'd rather not get into it." She unrolled her paper napkin, spread it across her lap, and picked up her fork. "So what's this little meeting about?"

Garrett sighed. "I wanted to set up a tentative schedule for the next week. I know this is an aggressive plan, but I'd like to get to work as soon as possible." He stabbed at his eggs and ate.

"Whoa! Slow down. I only agreed to this thing yesterday." Riley took a bite of greasy bacon and savored the flavor.

"That was the whole point of signing you. To record."

"Yeah, and I have a full-time job, so you can redo your schedule right now." She didn't care who he was, or what contract she signed, he didn't get to run her life.

"About that. You need to put in your two weeks' notice." He took a sip of his black coffee.

She stared at him in shock, tempted to knock the cup right out of his hand and onto his overpriced jeans.

"Don't worry. Barry will understand."

"I'm not quitting my job. I love my job." She took a bite of eggs. They weren't as good as her mom's.

"You don't love your job."

"Yes. I do," she said with her mouth full.

Garrett spread grape jelly on his toast. "You love running around town searching for Christmas ornaments in July?"

"Actually, I do. Plus, I need my paycheck. I have bills."

"And you were given a check for twenty grand yesterday. So unless you have an addiction to online shopping or have suddenly started doing crystal, the money should tide you over for a while."

She set her fork down. "I am not quitting my job."

He ignored her and bit into his toast.

"Is quitting my job in the contract, too?"

"No, but I see now that it should have been."

"Good. Because I'm not going to." She resumed eating.

"You're killing me here."

"You think I'm enjoying this? Hardly." But she did like beating him at his own game. She covered her smile by taking a drink of water.

"Okay, but would you agree to cut back your hours?"

"I'll have to talk to Barry."

"Don't worry. I'll handle it."

She slammed her glass down a little too hard, and water sloshed out. "No! You are not interfering. I'll talk to him and if he's okay with me working less, I'll let you know. If he's not, then we'll have to work early in the day and on the weekends. It's not like this needs to take that much time."

"What planet have you been living on? The recording process takes forever."

"Not for me it won't."

He rubbed his forehead. "Could you please be a little more cooperative?"

"Hey, I'm here. You should be happy with that." How

much more could he expect from her? She was already practically prostituting herself.

"Fine. Listen up. I've started going over potential songs. I'd like to get together in a couple days and work through a few that I'll have selected, to see if they work."

"How can you have songs picked that soon?"

"I work fast. You keep underestimating me, and you shouldn't." He set his gray eyes on her.

Riley tried not to squirm under his piercing gaze. How could she not like him, and yet be so affected by his attention? She shook off the feeling. "Well, I want to pick the songs."

"No."

"And why not?"

"Because I can pick a hit better than you," he said with that irritating, cocky set to his mouth that she hated.

"I'm not singing a song I don't love." Memories of the disasters on *Chart Toppers* raced across her mind.

He pointed at her with his fork. "You'll sing whatever I tell you to."

Riley laughed. "Don't bother going there. It's a dead-end street."

He sighed again. "I've reserved a studio starting next week."

Already? She had hoped getting started would take longer than he predicted and that she'd have a few weeks to get used to the idea of recording with him.

"There are some excellent studio musicians I plan to hire. In the meantime I want to set up a photo shoot. We better do it fast before you go dying your hair blue or some other idiot thing."

"Hey, if I want to shave my head, I'll do it. You don't get to tell me what I can do with my hair."

"Actually, I do. So lay off any other forms of personal expression you might be thinking about, and that includes piercings and tattoos. I'm trying to create an image here and I don't want you to ruin it."

The waitress appeared and topped off his coffee.

"Darn, and I was planning to get a tattoo of your face on my ass."

The waitress startled and over-poured his cup.

"You wouldn't be the first," he said.

The waitress turned and left, her face contorted with laughter.

"Really?"

He nodded.

"That's just sick."

Her phone buzzed. She read the text and said, "Sorry. That's work. I've got to run. The musicians are arriving and I have to make sure they get their presents from Jamie."

"You can't love a job where your primary objective is to hand out Christmas mugs stuffed with candy canes and hot chocolate packets."

"You don't know me."

"Well, by the time we get through this album, I guarantee we'll both know a whole lot more about each other," he said.

Riley wiped her mouth and stood, pretending she wasn't a little bit nervous and maybe excited about that.

34

Riley spent the rest of her day listening to the gorgeous strains of violins, violas, and cellos. As bizarre as spending a July day surrounded by holiday music was, it coaxed her into a relaxed mood, which was a miracle considering all the crazy in her world.

As the instrumentals lulled her into a place of childhood comfort, her mind drifted back to when her musical journey began on *Chart Toppers*, when she first met the judges.

Riley's knees shook so violently, she was afraid they might buckle. This was her third and final audition in Chicago to make the show, but none of the others mattered.

This was the big one. These were the real judges, not unknown assistants or entry-level producers. The judges today would make or break the rest of her life.

Her mother picked at her shirt. "Why did you insist on this horrible blue top? You'd look much better in the pink. And don't chew on your fingernails." She slapped Riley's hand away from her mouth and then fussed with her hair.

"Mom, stop."

"You need to relax. Don't worry about the lights or the cameras. Play to the audience. Be sure to look the judges in the eye. And smile, don't forget to smile."

Riley stepped out of her mother's reach.

"I should have taken you for highlights. Your hair would look so much better." She took Riley by the shoulders and looked her in the eyes. "Remember to take deep breaths. You know you can nail it. You're better than everyone here. I don't care if you're only thirteen. Oh no, I can still see your freckles. Hold on while I put more powder on your face."

"Mom! You're making it worse. How can I relax with you in my face? I can't even breathe."

Riley's stomach churned with anxiety. Four thousand people would be watching, not to mention the judges. She rubbed her clammy palms on her jeans.

Her mom stopped fussing and instead looked into a mirror at herself, fluffing her hair. Her mom wanted to be the one on camera. She'd acted overly clingy and dramatic all day.

"You could be a little nicer. I took off work to be here

for you," she said, reapplying lip gloss.

Riley rolled her eyes. "You always have Tuesdays off."

"You don't have to say it so loud. They don't know that," she said, referring to the producers who wandered around backstage, making sure everyone was set.

A young woman named Wendy approached. "Riley, you're next. This way, please."

Suddenly, the waiting was over. It all came down to this moment. Riley turned to her mom, suddenly terrified to go out onstage. "I think I'm going to throw up."

"No, you're not. You're only nervous. It's all in your head."

Perspiration collected on her brow. "No, I'm going to be sick." Riley rushed off in search of a wastebasket and found one just in time near a tech table. She fell to her knees and unleashed the contents of her stomach.

The cameras better not film her vomiting into the trash. Her carefully styled hair hung around her like a curtain. Her mom had spent an hour taming her unruly red hair. Now Riley needed to check it for hurl.

"Riley, how you doing?" Wendy asked, holding a box of tissues at arm's length.

Riley grabbed a couple and wiped her mouth, dropping the soiled wipes into the trash, covering up the unfortunate contents. "I'll be fine in a second."

"Honey, you need to get up. It's your turn and you're creating a scene." Her mother's voice sounded in her ear.

Riley sat back and took a breath. She pushed the hair out of her face.

"Here's a bottle of water. Do you need more time?" Wendy asked.

"No. I feel better now." Somehow hurling cleared away her nerves. She stood and looked in the mirror of the makeup table. She looked a little flushed, but no one should be able to tell she'd just lost her lunch.

"All right. Makeup, give her a quick touchup and then you're on."

A minute later Riley stood in the wings off the mammoth stage as her name was called. Her mom had been corralled to watch from a monitor.

"Our next contestant is Riley Parks," sounded a booming voice over the speakers.

The stage director smiled and nodded. "Good luck."

"Thanks." She took a breath, smiled, and walked onto the brightly lit stage. A thunderous roar greeted her. Riley had dreamt of this moment her whole life, and now she had a shot.

It took a moment for her eyes to adjust. There before her at the judges' table sat Morton King, a famous record producer; Jason Edgette, a chart-topping singer; and Desiree Diamond, a former teen sensation and well-documented diva.

Suddenly Riley relaxed; she waved at them.

"Oh, she's so cute," Desiree said.

Morton King smiled. "Hi, what's your name?"

"Riley Parks."

"How old are you?" Jason Edgette asked.

"Thirteen," she said, loving that she owned the massive stage and the spotlights shined on her.

"And why do you want to win *Chart Toppers*?" Morton asked.

"Because I love to sing more than pretty much anything." She blushed and for once didn't even care. The judges all chuckled.

"Nice answer. What are you going to sing for us?" Morton asked.

"'Eclipse' by the Graphite Angels."

"Wow, big song for a little girl," he said. "Whenever you're ready. The stage is yours."

The panel went into judge mode with contemplative expressions. Desiree looked hard to please, but Jason offered an encouraging smile.

The lights on the judges dimmed. She gripped the microphone. Her knees started to shake again, but she willed it away.

Don't screw up, don't screw up.

The intro played, Riley sang, and her voice rang out strong and true. She put every ounce of her heart into the performance, losing herself to the music just like she did at home when she sang with a hairbrush for a microphone in her bedroom.

When she finished, the audience roared their approval. Riley's eyes widened in surprise. Each of the judges smiled.

"Riley, you have a gift that would please God," Morton said.

"He's the one who gave it to me," she answered, and the audience applauded more.

Jason Edgette spoke next. "Little girl. I've never heard a voice like that from someone so young. You are exactly what we're looking for, and I wouldn't be surprised if you were opening for me someday."

Riley's heart soared. "I'd really like that!"

"Congratulations. You've left me speechless," Desiree Diamond said.

Riley jumped up and down, unable to contain her excitement. The judges laughed.

"That's three thumbs up. Great way to finish off the day," Morton said.

"Thank you!" She ran offstage and into her mom's arms.

"You did it, baby! They loved you. You're going to be a star."

"Riley? Riley?" Ron kept calling.

She startled out of her fog. "Yes?"

"Can you make reservations for the musicians? Jamie wants to treat them to a late dinner."

"Of course, I'm on it." She stepped out of the room

and back to the present from that long-forgotten memory. Would her next experience singing go so well? Probably not. She'd been an innocent kid back then, living out her greatest dreams. What she was going to do now was cold hard reality.

35

Garrett spent the rest of the day at the apartment poring over the old recordings of Jamieson songs that he, Peter, and Adam had rejected for one reason or another. He finally selected a few songs that they had liked and almost recorded, but either the songs didn't fit with the overall theme of the album, or they seemed better suited for a female voice, which turned out to be perfect for scoring songs for Riley.

Satisfied that he was on the right track, he set up a meeting with the music arranger that Jamieson had used on their last two albums. The man promised to get straight to work and deliver the first song in a few days. Damn, it was good to know people in the business. His dad was right again. Jamieson still carried a lot of clout, and Garrett planned to use it to succeed.

He stretched and looked at the time. Eleven o'clock

already? Where had the day gone? His stomach rumbled, reminding him he hadn't eaten since his late breakfast with Riley. She had to be the most stubborn girl he'd ever dealt with.

A vision of her with those bright streaks of blond hair mixed in with her dark red filled his mind. It looked terrific and gave her a nice edge, not that he'd ever admit it to her. She was hard enough to deal with, without pumping up her confidence even more.

He closed his laptop for the day and headed for the elevator. Time to find a bite to eat and celebrate all that he'd accomplished today. A night on the town was just what he needed.

Two days later, rock music blared as Riley danced her way from the stove to the counter carrying a pan of fresh-from-the-oven cutout cookies. Her hair up in a ponytail, and wearing old shorts and a tank top, she plopped the pan onto hot pads to cool. She spun to the beat, opened the oven door, and tossed the next pan of trees, stars, and bells into the oven. The kitchen window was open to let in some cooler air; the apartment was a hot box.

"Smells like my grandma's house. What are you making?" Erika asked.

"Christmas cookies." She grinned. "Want to help?"

"Only if I get to eat some, too."

"Help yourself." She pointed with her spatula to the

cookies cooling on paper towels.

Erika hitched her hip against the counter. "I take it these are for Jamie Halloway and her mission to turn July into December."

"Yup. I couldn't find a bakery to make Christmas cookies this time of year, so I'm making them myself. I hope they're edible."

Erika broke the head off a Santa cookie and popped it in her mouth. "Tastes good to me. Where'd you find cookie cutters?"

"At my mom's place."

"And how'd that go?" she asked with slow caution.

"Perfectly fine. I went while she was at work." And that's the only way Riley would have gone over after all the horrible things her mom had done.

"Have you talked to her at all since the whole car accident news?"

"Only once, and I'll be fine if I don't talk to her again until . . ." She waved her spatula in the air. "Christmas."

"Good. Your life is much calmer when your mom stays away. What do you want me to do?"

"You can start frosting." She handed Erika a bowl filled with frosting the color of a Shamrock Shake.

"You're in a good mood lately. That must mean things are either going very well with Mr. Jamieson or you're giving him a lot of shit."

Riley couldn't suppress her grin. "A little bit of both."

Riley picked up a tree cookie and carefully frosted it. "I try to avoid getting together to go over songs, and he's always finding ways to rope me in and force me to learn them. In return, I tell him how bad his taste is and that he's wrong about what key they should be in."

She should be nicer to Garrett, since he basically bailed her out of financial trouble, but she enjoyed irritating him.

"You are so evil."

"I know, right?" She slid the spatula under a bell-shaped cookie and dropped it onto the paper towels. "But he deserves it for being such a jerk all the time. I must say though that pretty much all of Jamieson's music is really good. I mean these are songs his brother wrote, and then yesterday he played a few songs that I loved." She had started to enjoy their sessions together.

"That is so cool. You're singing songs that Peter Jamieson wrote."

"What's even weirder is seeing this new side of Garrett. I'm used to him walking around like he knows everything and practically owns the place, but you should have seen him sitting there with his guitar."

Erika put down her cookie and propped her chin on her hands to listen.

"It's like he was a different person. Sort of a softer version of himself."

"How so?"

She had met with him in a control room at the studio,

facing each other on the couch, with music spread out between them, and his guitar rested on his leg.

It was the most honest time she'd ever spent with him. "I don't know. It's like he was in his true comfort zone. He strummed his guitar and sang in this low, rich voice, like it was no big deal. He wasn't singing loud like in a performance, just soft and personal. It was . . . nice."

"Are you falling under his spell?"

"What? No! I mean, yeah, it was fun and I got to see a new side of him, but that's it. It's not like he's going to ask me to dinner or something." She stacked cool cookies onto a platter. Her heart was melting where Garrett was concerned, and she wasn't sure what to think about it.

"And if he did, would you go?"

"Trust me. He has no interest in me. It's strictly business." And if it were ever more than that, she had no idea what she'd do.

"Okay." Erika smirked. "But you sure seem happier these past few days. You were dancing in the kitchen just now, and I heard you singing in the shower the last two mornings. You never used to do that."

"I guess maybe I am. Huh?" She smiled.

The timer on the oven dinged. She pulled out the hot pan and set it on the counter.

"By the way, you sounded really good."

Riley ignored her and transferred cookies to the paper towels.

"You never told me about being on *Chart Toppers*. I mean, I heard rumors flying around school when I first started, but I never watched the show. I didn't know you during that time, and when we first met, I was so wrapped up with my parents' divorce and trying to survive at a new school that I never bothered to check it out online."

With her head low and eyes averted, Riley said softly, "I always figured you did, but never said anything, to be nice."

"Nope. The one time I asked you what the kids were talking about when they called you a reject, you said you didn't want to talk about it. I guess I was pretty self-absorbed back then."

"You were exactly what I needed. Someone who didn't pry into my life."

Riley brought the plate of cookies and a bowl of frosting to their tiny kitchen table. Erika followed and they sat.

"The show was a disaster. I went in there with all these bright hopes and dreams. I used to sing all the time. Ever since I was a little girl. My mom would go to the bar. She'd bring me along sometimes and when the band took a break, she'd put me on the little stage to sing. I guess I sounded pretty good to all those drunks."

"I bet you did," Erika commented.

"So when we heard that *Chart Toppers* was holding auditions in Chicago, my mom signed me up. You can't help but get all wrapped up in the excitement of it. I never expected to go very far. But I kept getting further in the competition. It was crazy. And the further I got, the more pressure there was. My mom started freaking out because she was so sure I'd win the whole thing and we could move to Los Angeles and I'd tour the country. There was so much pressure from the people with the show. I started to get so freaked out, and by the end I knew I was going to get kicked off. When I did, I cried." She closed her eyes and shuddered. It had been so embarrassing. She had ruined everything.

"I looked like this big crybaby who got sent home. And I totally deserved it."

"I'm sure it wasn't like that," Erika said.

"It felt like it, and then back at home, the kids were so cruel. They'd hum my last song whenever I'd walk by. I started wearing earbuds and pretending I couldn't hear them, but I did. They assumed I thought I was better than them. But I never thought that."

Granted, she'd seen a new type of life that she really liked. The idea of living in a nice place that wasn't above a bar or in a crime-ridden neighborhood was very appealing.

"I wanted to quit school, but my mom made me go. She was so mad I didn't make it further on the show. So I quit everything else, including choir. I stopped hanging out with my friends when I found a couple of them making snide comments about me behind my back. And I stopped singing. It took until the next fall when I started high school and met you before things calmed down."

"One misfit finds another," Erika offered.

"No. You were my salvation. I don't think I could have gotten through high school without you."

"Aw, thanks. Here, have a cookie."

Riley took the cookie and smiled through a bite. She knew Erika was a true friend—one who wouldn't let her down.

36

Later that night, after Riley made sure that Jamie Halloway and her band members and team were fed dinner and had oohed and aahed over her cookies, she got the okay to leave.

She couldn't wait to meet up with Garrett and see what tonight might bring. But every studio she checked was occupied with an artist or group working.

Finally, she found Garrett and Tara in the reception area. Tara should have gone home by now, but instead she lounged on the couch, leaning into every word Garrett said.

"There you are," Riley said.

Tara frowned at her arrival.

"I'm sorry, did I interrupt anything?" Riley asked, 'cause it sure looked like she had, and this was supposed to be her time with Garrett.

"Nope. Just waiting for you," he replied, apparently clueless to Tara's signals.

"Sorry it took me so long; I was looking for you everywhere but here."

"You gonna wear that all night?" Tara asked, indicating Riley's ridiculous Christmas tree sweater. Garrett chuckled.

"Oh God, no. I'm so used to wearing this thing, I forget I have it on." She pulled the sweater off over her head and dropped it on the couch.

"It's a full house tonight. What do you want to do?" Garrett asked.

"I was wondering about that. I'm not sure."

"You could work here in the reception area," Tara offered. "I'd love to listen in and watch a music producer at work."

Did Tara not realize how obvious she was? But who was Riley to stand in Tara's way of hitting on Garrett?

"No, we need privacy." He tapped on his guitar case, thinking. "Does this place have a rooftop?"

"Yeah," Tara answered. "But it's an ugly flat roof with utility boxes."

"How do I get up there? I want to check it out."

"It's this way. I'll show you." Tara popped to her feet.

"While you do that, I'll go put this away," Riley said, picking up the sweater.

By the time Riley returned with her handbag, Tara was

back in the lobby holding her purse.

"Garrett said you should join him on the roof. He just took some folding chairs up." She looked at Riley as if she wanted to say more.

"Thanks. See you tomorrow," Riley called, kind of happy to see her go.

Riley climbed the dusty stairwell to the roof. Sound Sync Studio was a mile west of downtown, and the buildings were a lot smaller. The rooftop of the three-story building was flat, with some huge gray mechanical boxes humming loudly. The edge of the building was framed by a brick facade.

She spotted Garrett at the far corner, pulling his guitar out of its case. The rooftop was illuminated by the glow of nearby neon street signs, along with the full moon.

"Interesting place to work." She slid a folding chair closer.

"I picked the furthest spot from the noise of the air-conditioning unit." He strummed a tune she recognized from the night before. "You wouldn't believe some of the places we would warm up or meet when we were on the road. When it got too hard to go to any place public, we visited many a rooftop, basement, or equipment room."

"I would have thought it was all VIP rooms with champagne and fancy hors d'oeuvres."

He laughed. "Not usually. Our tour rider included things like pizza rolls, Mountain Dew, and Cheez Whiz.

Of course, my mom always insisted on a veggie and fruit tray, but I was more of a red licorice guy."

She tried to imagine Garrett with his brothers, so young and yet so hugely successful. "Sounds like fun."

"It was," he said thoughtfully.

"Do you miss it?"

"Every day." He looked down at the gritty texture of the roof, as if talking about the past caused him pain.

"So why did the band break up?"

His jaw clenched. He didn't answer right away.

"I'm sorry. It's none of my business. I shouldn't have asked."

"I assumed you already checked the internet for that answer."

Riley cringed, guilty as charged. "I did. But there were a few different theories. I wondered which one was true."

"Bottom line, Peter and Adam wanted a break. They said they were tired of all the constant travel and lack of free time. They wanted to live their lives, which is what I thought we'd been doing," he said, his tone cynical. He sighed and looked dejected.

"I'm sorry. You didn't get a choice in the matter?"

"No, not really. I mean, they called a band meeting and laid everything out. I argued all the reasons we needed to keep going, like the fans, the commitments, the love of the tour, but it was two against one."

"That sucks."

"Yes, it does."

His fingers picked out a tune she hadn't heard before. The lyrical music filled the late summer night. She watched, mesmerized, as he lost himself in the piece, and transported her to a beautiful place.

He ended the song. Riley wished they could hang out all night so she could listen to him play.

"So why did *you* quit?" he asked, startling her back to reality. "You asked why I stopped performing. It's only fair I ask you why you did."

"I got voted off the show. You know that."

"That's a copout, and you know it."

"Um, no. It's not." Why did she suddenly feel on the defense?

"But that was five years ago. Clearly you have a natural talent, you spend your days surrounded by music. What's the deal?"

Riley sighed. First Erika and now Garrett. This was entirely too much talking about her past for one day.

"Being on the show was really hard for me. I wasn't prepared for the stress and criticism. Week after week it wore me down. And my mentor, Desiree Diamond, was neurotic and controlling. One day she'd be all helpful and reassuring, then the next she'd criticize everything I did from the way I sang to how I smiled."

"I heard she's been in rehab three times," he said.

"I wouldn't doubt it. I loved classic rock like the

Graphite Angels, the Stones, and Aerosmith, but the producers wouldn't let me sing any of those songs. Instead Desiree picked out these stupid outdated pop songs, most of which I'd never heard of. A choreographer tried to teach me dance moves. That was a joke. It was like teaching a giraffe how to roller skate."

Garrett laughed and she smiled despite herself.

"Well, I failed, that's for sure. Basically I had a nervous breakdown on live TV."

"You were too young," he said matter-of-factly.

"That's what Jason Edgette said, too. That I was too young and wasn't ready yet. I was so mad, because I really wanted to perform, but looking back, he was totally right."

At the time it broke her heart.

"It was the hardest, most embarrassing time of my life. The press went crazy. My picture was in magazines and all over the net. Here I was, this middle school kid who wanted to follow her dream and instead, I crushed it to smithereens on national TV."

"Sounds like you have a classic case of post-traumatic stress syndrome. And now you've got yourself stuck recording with me," he said.

"Pretty much sums it up."

"You must hate me," he said as if realizing it for the first time.

She smiled weakly, but didn't say anything.

"You're not even going to deny it?"

"I like to see you suffer." She grinned.

"Yeah, I've figured that one out." He laughed. "I'll help you get back your courage little by little." He strummed his guitar again, sending low hollow notes into the air.

"I don't think I'll ever get over it."

"It's just stage fright."

"*Just* stage fright?" She glared.

"That's right. It's mind over matter."

"I don't think it's that simple."

37

A couple days later, Riley stepped off the Marina Towers elevator onto the fifty-second floor to meet with Garrett at Brad Stone's condo. She'd gazed up at these two unusual towers her entire life. They anchored the edge of State Street and the Chicago River like old-fashioned beacons, or giant corncobs, as she'd always thought. She followed the oddly curved hallway, passing door after door until suddenly she spotted Garrett standing in an open doorway, barefoot, wearing jeans and a simple white T-shirt.

"You found it," he said with a relaxed smile.

"This is really cool up here."

"Wait till you see the inside." He stepped aside to allow her entry.

The first thing she noticed was the gleaming marble floor; the second, a baby grand in the corner by a massive bank of windows. "Wow, this is Brad Stone's place? Not bad!" She ran her hand over a granite table in the entryway. She noticed a coffee table with papers strewn across it and Garrett's guitar on a leather couch in the living room as if he'd laid it down as she arrived.

"Want to see the view?"

"Yeah."

They stepped outside onto a crescent-shaped balcony overlooking the city. A warm breeze blew and the sun shined bright. Riley could see for miles in each direction. She held on to the railing and looked straight down to the street.

"Is this where you and Brad climbed?"

Garrett nodded.

"You are nuts."

"It's definitely not a trick I plan to repeat."

She took in the view for a minute. She had to admit that the idea of being totally alone with Garrett in his apartment unnerved her a little bit. It took private to a new level. "Why are we meeting here?"

"Two reasons." He opened the door and they went back inside. "One, there was no available rehearsal space at the studio, and, two, I thought it was time we brought in a vocal coach."

Her head snapped around. "I thought I was doing fine."

"You are, but you can do a lot better. Recording these songs isn't like sitting around with a guitar for a sing-a-long. It's about nailing every single note."

How many times had she heard those words, *you can do better,* back on *Chart Toppers*? They'd analyzed and criticized every detail about her from where she took a breath, to how much mascara to put on a young girl.

"I know what it takes. If you don't think I'm good enough, why did you pressure me so much to record?"

"Relax, would you? Don't you want to put out a great record?"

"Of course."

But if she had her way, she wouldn't put out any record. They might have started to get along better, but her feelings on the topic hadn't changed. She was tolerating this process only because she needed the money. As soon as the record was done, so was she. Maybe having the experience of recording would be enough to finally get her a seat at the control board at work.

"Then stop fighting me at every turn and get to work."

Her jaw clenched. All the progress they'd made in the friendship department went right out the window.

"I've been working my ass off seven days a week if you include all my hours at Sound Sync."

"And you're going to need to work even harder, because this is just the beginning."

A knock sounded at the door. They glared at each other.

"Fine. Bring in your snotty know-it-all voice coach, but don't expect me to like it." Riley headed for the balcony door.

"And where do you think you're going?"

"What? Afraid I'm going to jump? 'Cause it's tempting."

The knock sounded again.

"You better go answer the door!" she called, and escaped to the privacy of the balcony.

Why did he have to be such a jerk all the time? She could picture Garrett and his crony dissecting her and every little thing she did.

She remembered those sessions on *Chart Toppers* like it was yesterday. Every week she'd meet with Desiree Diamond and one of the show's vocal coaches, and it was always the same thing.

"You're too timid."

"You have to step it up."

"Each performance you need to be better."

Desiree would perch on a stool, with her thick makeup and arrogant attitude, drumming her clawlike nails on the piano. Riley could never satisfy the woman. If Riley sang out, they told her to hold back. If she sang softly, they said she lacked emotion.

The vocal coach preached at her and she'd try to do everything he said, but on performance day, Desiree would contradict everything Riley'd been taught.

She gripped the balcony wishing she could fly away. Maybe that's why Garrett climbed it. He was trying to escape his life. But what he had to escape from, she couldn't imagine.

Garrett opened the door and peeked out. "You ready to play nice?"

"As long as you do." She stepped past him into the condo.

A fortyish-looking woman with her messy brown hair clipped on top of her head and dangling earrings set her bag next to the piano. She glanced up as Riley appeared.

"Hi, you must be Riley," she welcomed, not looking nearly as terrorizing as Riley imagined. "I'm Ginny Potts."

"Nice to meet you."

"I understand that you're Garrett's guinea pig on his first attempt at record producing."

Riley frowned. She hadn't thought of it that way before. Heck, he didn't know what he was doing any more than she did, so why was she allowing him so much power over her?

"You don't have to make it sound so bad," Garrett said. "And I wouldn't exactly call it my first attempt at producing. I do have a couple of gold records under my belt."

Ginny raised an eyebrow.

"Fine. It's my first time producing."

Ginny grunted with satisfaction.

"I've worked with Garrett and his brothers on all their albums. You could say I've known him since he was a snot-nosed kid, except that he's still kind of a snot."

Riley liked Ginny better all the time.

Garrett rolled his eyes. "Ginny has worked with all kinds of successful artists, including Jason Edgette."

"You know Jason?" Riley asked.

"I sure do. He's a great guy and an amazing artist."

"He was my favorite when I was on *Chart Toppers*. He's always been so nice to me."

"I called Jason and told him I was meeting with you today. He had only good things to say. Right now he's on tour in Europe with his wife. He says hi."

"You're still in contact with Jason Edgette?" Garrett asked Riley in disbelief.

"He calls every few months to catch up."

Garrett's eyes bugged out. He shook his head. "Geez, you're well connected for a nobody."

"Excuse me?" Riley and Ginny said at the same time.

"You know what I mean. You're not exactly on anyone's radar."

Riley wanted to sink into the floor or maybe toss Garrett off the balcony. It was one thing for her to want to stay unknown, but the way he said it hurt. She really did know Jason. Why was that so hard to believe? He even gave her tickets to his concert in Chicago a couple years ago. She had brought Erika and they got to visit him backstage. Her mom had been so mad that Riley hadn't taken her.

"Garrett, I see you're still as charming as ever. Didn't you mean to say that Riley's not on anybody's radar *yet*?" Ginny drilled him with a stare.

"You know what I mean." He shifted his feet.

Riley had never seen anyone stand up to Garrett

before. It was a nice development.

"Garrett, how about you run out and do something while Riley and I work."

"No. I'm fine staying here. That way I can add my input."

Ginny stared him down.

"You're serious? You want me to leave?"

"That's right."

"Unbelievable." He huffed, then gathered his papers and laptop, muttering, "Kicked out of my own place."

"Don't worry, we'll give you a little listen when we're done." Ginny winked at Riley.

As soon as Garrett closed the door behind him, Ginny said, "Much better. Let's enjoy a little bit of this beautiful day." She headed for the balcony. Riley followed. "Now that we've got the place to ourselves, tell me about yourself."

"Well. There's not that much to tell. I'm pretty boring."

"Don't be so modest. Everyone's got a story." Ginny sat on one of the cushioned deck chairs, and indicated the other for Riley. "Jason speaks very highly of you. You've landed a job at Sound Sync Studio working with Barry Goldwin, and now you're recording a record with Garrett Jamieson as your producer. How does that work?"

"Luck, I guess. I met Jason when I was on *Chart Toppers* a long time ago."

"That must have been exciting."

"It was at first. Jason was one of the best parts. I couldn't believe it when he first called me after the show was over. Maybe he thought I was going to slit my wrists or something."

"Was your experience that bad?"

Riley nodded. "It was humiliating. I stopped singing after that. I guess I don't take criticism very well."

"That's terrible. Who was your mentor on the show?"

"Desiree Diamond."

"Ah. That explains a lot. Desiree is a very insecure woman who builds herself up by putting others down. She was a terrible judge on the show. They replaced her after only one season."

Riley had never considered there might be more to the criticism than was warranted.

"I know it's a gorgeous day, but I think we better get to work. If Garrett gets back and we're still out here sunning ourselves, then we'll be in big trouble."

Riley followed Ginny into the apartment, her nerves jumpy that she wouldn't live up to this woman's expectations.

Ginny sat behind the piano and ran Riley through some vocal warm-ups. "Very good. Garrett gave me several songs for us to work on today. Now let's run through the first one and see where we're at."

Riley squeezed and flexed her hands, trying to throw off her jitters. She sang through the song that she now knew by heart.

"Very nice," Ginny said, seeming impressed. "I can see why Garrett raved so much about you."

Riley wrinkled her nose.

Ginny laughed. "You don't believe me?"

"Garrett's not much into handing out praise."

"No, I suppose he's not. Guys can be pretty dense when it comes to things like that. Be sure you guard your heart. He's quite the ladies' man, and I would hate for you to get hurt."

"Trust me. It's not like that. We can barely stand each other."

"Ha! That's what they all say."

How many girls were there? Well, she didn't plan to be one of them, except that Riley knew a part of her was falling for him. She shook off her thoughts and got back to business. "So can you teach me to sing better?"

"You already have an amazing voice. I'm here to help you give each song all the nuances it needs. Where to play with the melody, or pull back. And how to put your heart and soul into each song, so that your audience believes every word you sing. Lots of people sing well, but only artists with star quality make it."

"And you think I have that?"

"I do." She smiled and Riley smiled nervously back. What if Ginny was right and she did have what it takes? Did she want that anymore?

They worked for over two hours. For one song, Ginny

raised the key so that Riley struggled to hit the high notes.

"The lower key was too easy for you. If you work for it, it sounds more impassioned, and listeners will appreciate the emotion you're giving them."

In other spots, Ginny shortened notes, or elongated them, adding dimension and depth.

"Use your gift to take people on a ride. Each song is a story, and your job is to pull them in. There's a natural rasp to your voice. It's incredible and carries such honesty in your tone. Not many people have that. Who taught you voice before this?"

"No one. I mean, I had choir in middle school, but then I quit in high school."

Ginny shook her head. "I wish I was you. I worked my tail off my whole life, and while I can do some impressive things with my voice, I have to work extra hard. My voice will never have the distinctive sound and character of yours. Now I understand Desiree's behavior. She was afraid of you, and for good reason."

Riley laughed. Desiree Diamond afraid of her? Impossible to imagine. She didn't know if what Ginny told her was a bunch of hooey, but it warmed her insides and gave her a new confidence.

Over the past five years Riley had been afraid to sing in front of people because she wasn't good enough, but now she realized that wasn't the case. She might actually be able to do this.

Garrett returned a few hours later. "So how'd it go?" he asked right away, pretending to be casual. Riley held back her grin over his frustration at being left out.

"I think Riley is amazingly talented and should dump you to find better representation."

"Ha! Not going to happen, she's under contract."

"In that case, I think if you both do things right, and can find a way to get air play in this saturated market, she has a real chance."

"That's what I was hoping."

"Riley, should we give him a little sample?"

"Sure."

Ginny played the intro. Riley took a deep breath, focused on the things Ginny had taught her, and pretended no one else was in the room. She'd forgotten how much she loved to sing, to lose herself in a song and become someone else entirely.

"Damn," Garrett said with an astonished look on his face. "Why weren't we recording that?"

Ginny smiled proudly.

Riley's heart swelled. "That was fun!"

"She's ready to record the first two. Let me know when you want to work on some of the others."

The door opened and Brad walked in with a huge duffle bag on wheels and his guitar case.

"Looks like a party going on." He greeted everyone with a smile.

"Hi," Riley said, glad they'd finished. An audience of two had been plenty.

"Hey man, hope you don't mind I had Riley and Ginny over to work for a bit."

"The more the merrier. How you doing, Ginny?"

"Good to see you, Brad. I wish I could stay and catch up, but I'm already late to a meeting." She gathered her things and left.

"Gee, was it something I said?" Brad joked.

"I think we went a little long today. You just missed Riley practicing a couple songs we're going to record," Garrett explained.

"Congratulations," Brad said. "I heard you were recording with Garrett. If someone with the name Jamieson has anything to do with your album, it's bound to be a hit."

"We'll see. I should get going, too." Riley felt awkward being left alone with the two superstars.

"Now I am definitely getting a complex. I did shower today."

Riley laughed. "I need to do some things at work. Nice to see you."

"You too," he said.

"I'll call you tomorrow," Garrett said.

"Okay." She made her way to the door, but before she was out, she overheard Brad. "Hey Jamieson, you want to hit the town tonight? There's a new club open, and I bet it'll be filled with hot girls."

"Sounds perfect. Exactly what I need right now."

The door closed and Riley stood alone in the curved hallway. Garrett was going out to pick up girls. Paired with Brad, that ought to be quite the scene. She wasn't even old enough to step foot in a bar. At least not legally.

She hit the elevator button and imagined what kind of girl he'd end up with.

38

Garrett's phone buzzed like an annoying gnat in his ear. Streaks of early-morning light streamed into the room through the edges of the window shades. He fumbled for the phone on the unfamiliar nightstand. Opening one eye, he silenced the irritant, but not before noticing the caller was his dad. He groaned.

Rolling over, he saw the form of his sleeping bedmate, a leggy brunette with an annoying giggle. Why had he gone home with her? He wasn't even all that attracted to her.

He eased out of bed, careful not to tug on the sheets, collected his clothes, and snuck out into the living room to dress. He heard movement in the bathroom, but dashed out the door before having to make any awkward morning-after small talk.

Outside of the apartment building the morning was crisp and bright. He wished for his sunglasses as he headed toward a stoplight a few blocks east. Garrett wasn't actually sure where he was, but a cab would deliver him home.

He returned his dad's call as he walked. "Hi. What's up?"

"Did I wake you?"

Garrett ran a hand over his face. "Yeah. It's only eight o'clock here."

"So it is. I always forget that you boys sleep in now that you're not on tour."

"It's a perk I enjoy since I don't have to worry about early-morning radio interviews."

"I'm glad you're finding the silver lining."

"Remember that girl I was telling you about, Riley Parks?" He smiled as he pictured her. "Yesterday I had her work with Ginny."

"Smart move to bring Ginny in."

"Afterward, Riley sang through the songs I've picked, and she sounds amazing."

"I'm glad to hear it. I know you'll do well producing."

"Thanks. I'm giving it my all." Garrett spotted a Starbucks at the corner and swung in. He nodded to the barista, covered his phone with his hand, and said, "A two-shot espresso on ice."

He returned to his dad. "We start laying down vocals in a couple of days. I'll send you the tracks as soon as they're ready."

"I'd love to hear them. By the way, your mother and I are finally taking that trip to Tuscany that I've always promised her."

Garrett paid the cashier and dropped a buck in the tip

jar. "Good job, Dad. Nice sucking up now that the kids are gone."

"I'm actually looking forward to it. When we were in Milan during the last tour, we spent more time at the hotel and concert venue than we did seeing the city."

"Honestly, I don't even remember. All those concerts blended together."

"It's been nice to stay put for a while."

"When are you going?"

"In a little over a week. We'll be in Paris for our twenty-fifth anniversary. Your mother is over the moon."

"Nice." He picked up his iced coffee and took a sip.

"But that's not actually why I was calling. I'm glad that producing is working out. But don't let a few good things let your guard down."

"What do you mean?" Garrett turned right at the corner and hailed a cab.

"You need to get serious and stay serious—no more silly stunts or poor choices. Understand?"

He looked back in the direction of the apartment he'd just escaped from and realized he knew nothing about that girl.

"I do," Garrett said, and climbed into the cab.

39

Riley waited inside the small vocal recording booth with its spongy, padded walls. She rubbed her sweaty hands on her jeans.

The instrumental tracks for her first song had been recorded. She'd been present for most of it, and knew every nuance of the song, yet she still didn't feel ready. Her stomach tightened.

One saving grace was the closet-sized booth. Sound-absorbing foam tiles provided some needed security, but also reminded her she was literally in a padded room with a single window. All she needed now was a straitjacket and a lock on the door to be officially committed for this insane situation.

"Let's get this party started." Garrett's excited voice sounded over the talk-back. His body practically bounced from all the coffee she'd watched him down. Seeing him in the producer's seat unnerved her. He had so much power over her.

A freelance engineer, Darren, occupied the middle seat, and Logan served as assistant engineer. Riley had demanded Garrett give Logan a chance at the control board. Behind them stood Tim, her runner, as well as Tara, Nick, and a couple of sound guys who'd showed up uninvited to hear her sing.

"Check, check, check," she said, testing the mic, but heard nothing through her headphones. "Is the mic on?"

"Logan, would you please connect sound to Riley's headphones so she can hear herself," Garrett said.

"Oops, sorry about that." Logan quickly fixed the issue.

Riley bit back her smile at his rookie mistake.

Now that she could hear herself, she tried again. "Check, check, check. One, two, three." The sound of her own voice unnerved her more.

"Sounds good." Garrett's voice sounded strong and steady. "Logan, cue up the track and let's give this a shot."

She wiped her hands on her pants again, praying she wouldn't miss her entrance or crack on the high notes in front of everyone.

Riley avoided looking at the room packed with people and focused instead on the nubs of the acoustical foam walls.

The intro started.

Her heart raced.

She missed her cue.

"Shoot. I'm sorry." Everyone in the control room shared a laugh. Her face flamed with embarrassment.

"No problem. Here we go again," Garrett said.

Don't screw up, don't screw up, she pleaded with herself.

The intro began. This time she hit her entrance, but stumbled over the words.

"Crap," she muttered under her breath, and shook out her hands, trying to let go of her nerves. Tim and Tara laughed. At least Garrett didn't.

"Don't worry about it. We've got all night," he said. Then she heard someone in the background say, "Yeah, and you're gonna need it."

How long before Garrett grew annoyed with her, too? Riley chewed at her lower lip. She bet he never froze up when he was in the studio recording.

"Here we go," he said.

Music sounded in her ears. She took a breath, ready to come in, but a quick glance at the control room critics caused her to go blank.

She stared at the ceiling and willed her tears not to come.

"Riley, what's the problem?" Garrett's voice sounded in her headphones.

"Could we talk in private, please?" she asked softly.

He headed in her direction, while Logan and Darren

leaned back in their chairs and chatted with the rest of the group.

Garrett entered the small booth. Suddenly the air seemed warmer with him so close.

"What's going on?" He tried to mask his impatience. It was his job to keep her calm.

Another glance at the control room revealed everyone waiting to hear what she had to say.

"Don't look at them. Talk to me," Garrett said.

She reached down and pulled the mic cord from the wall, preventing their conversation from broadcasting to the groupies.

"Okay, should I be worried?" he asked with a disheartened grimace.

Riley crossed her arms and hugged herself. "Do all those people need to be in there . . . watching . . . judging?" She hated how paranoid she sounded.

"They're excited and want to be a part of this. They are all friends and coworkers."

"I can't relax with everyone staring and laughing at everything I do." She rubbed her furrowed brow.

Garrett sighed. "You know that's part of the recording process, having more than one set of ears, so we can make the best record possible."

"I know that. But I feel like I'm back on *Chart Toppers* and everyone in that booth is a judge, getting ready to rip me apart."

"You were fine singing in front of Ginny and me."

"That was different. You're in this with me. They aren't." She motioned to the control room.

Garrett paused, considering something. "Let's take a quick break."

"I'm sorry. I know that I should do something like imagine everyone in their underwear or something, but I, I don't know. This just isn't working."

"Hang on. Take five and I'll be right back." He left her alone and returned to the control room.

Riley perched on the stool in the corner and shuffled through her music, trying to appear busy. She didn't need it, but having the sheet music nearby saved her from another level of panic.

She saw Garrett talking to everyone. They all looked at Riley, and their faces fell in disappointment like little kids being shooed from the room while the grown-ups watched an R-rated movie.

She turned away and drank from her water bottle. This was going to be a long night.

When she turned back again, Garrett was ushering everyone out of the control room, except for Logan and Darren.

A minute later Garrett returned.

"Okay, they're gone, and I promise they won't be back."

"I'm sorry I'm such a drama queen," she said, her eyes

downcast, embarrassed at needing everyone to leave. She couldn't win.

"You're fine. I should have anticipated this. I've got Tim sitting outside the control room, so the only people in there will be your crew. Are you okay with that?"

She rubbed her hands on her pants again. "I feel like such an idiot."

Garrett reached out and touched her arm. "Don't. You haven't done this in a long time. You've put in a ton of work." His gray eyes settled on hers. "Riley, you have no idea how much I believe in you. You have an enormous talent, you're beautiful, and everyone wants to be around you."

Her breath caught. He called her beautiful. Did that mean he thought so, too? But she didn't care what he thought, she reminded herself.

"I know you can do this, and even though the process can be grueling at times, I'm positive it will come out great."

She looked away, unsure how to respond to his generous words. He lifted her chin.

"I mean it. Whatever it takes to help you relax, we'll do. If you need anything at all, you tell me."

She nodded, wanting to hug him for understanding her psycho freak-out.

"Now, if it's okay with you, can I plug the mic back in, so we can work?" He smiled.

"Yes." She laughed, liking this new side to him.

As Garrett returned to the control room, she took

a couple of deep breaths to let off some stress and let go of the jumbled emotions Garrett had just stirred up. She wasn't used to compliments and support from him. What the heck was she supposed to do with it? She slipped the headphones back on.

Garrett's voice sounded in her ears. "All right. We've cleared out the place and now we can relax and have some fun. Let's start again, and this time we'll play all the way through just for a warm-up. I don't care if you make up lyrics about watermelons and warthogs or sing with a French accent."

Riley giggled. Darren and Logan smiled. Garrett had successfully washed away most of her anxiety.

Logan cued the music, and she sang the whole thing through. It was far from perfect, but she loved the song and the beat, and felt much better about the whole process.

"That was great. We're going to start from the beginning and work through it phrase by phrase."

Now the real work began. Most people didn't realize it, but music was rarely recorded start to finish. They worked through the song trying one line or phrase several different ways so that Garrett would have a variety of options when mixing the final song.

They worked for three hours and took one half-hour break to eat burgers that Tim brought in. A few hours later, when her throat began to tire, Garrett called it a night.

"Great work, Riley. You gave us some awesome stuff,"

he said with satisfaction, leaning back in his chair and smiling at her.

Logan gave her a thumbs-up.

She sighed in relief at his compliment and felt a shift in her heart, as if something was now there that wasn't before.

40

Garrett had to give Riley credit. The girl worked like a dog and never complained. That was unless she disagreed with him, which happened constantly. But if it came to long hours, or dozens of takes, she didn't comment. Considering she was pulling double duty working on the Christmas album for half the night and then switching over to work with him, she must be exhausted. He wondered how long she could keep up this pace.

Every time she entered the room wearing her corny Christmas sweater he smiled. Luckily, Jamie Halloway had taken a week off for a family event, which opened up Riley's schedule and made their lives simpler.

Riley was in the booth laying down tracks for the third song on the album. After her first-day jitters, Logan brought in a picture of a kitten and pinned it to the wall of her sound booth to cheer her up. Ever since then, everyone started bringing in different forms of distraction, from pin-up pictures of male models to a giant inflatable dinosaur. Garrett's least favorite item was a life-size cutout of the Jamieson brothers, but Riley laughed so hard he let it stay.

Riley was turning into a great partner. She was humble and funny, with an inner beauty he hadn't noticed before. Everyone she worked with seemed to fall in love with her. It's as if she wove some spell that drew people to her. Each day he looked forward to their banter. Riley was quickly turning into the most interesting girl he'd ever known.

"Was that take better?" she asked after singing a phrase for the umpteenth time.

"That's exactly what we were going for. Nice job," he said over the talk-back speaker.

A soft knock sounded at the door. He looked to see Tara with a group of people. Tim, their runner, who Riley had allowed back in the room, opened the door.

"Guests here to see Riley," Tara said.

"Riley doesn't want outsiders watching," Tim responded.

"We're friends of Riley's. I'm her roommate," said a girl with curly dark hair.

"It's fine. We were about to take a break anyway," Garrett said, curious to meet Riley's friends.

In filed the girl and two guys. He had expected a group of girls. The presence of guys caught him off guard.

The newcomers scanned the room, the high-tech

equipment, and then stared through the window at Riley in the sound booth. Before Garrett could introduce himself, Riley spotted her friends and squealed, the sound amplified into the control room.

"I think she's glad to see you," Garrett said to her roommate.

Riley whipped off her headphones and flew out of the sound booth, past the dinosaur, and into the control room like a flash.

"Erika, you're here!"

"You said you might not hate me if I came by, so I took a chance and brought backup protection."

"Hi guys." Riley smiled, and hugged them all.

Garrett wondered who they were and what their connection was to Riley.

"You want a tour?" she asked.

They all nodded eagerly.

"Oh, I should introduce everyone," she said. "This is Erika, her boyfriend Chad, and his friend Bennett. Meet Tim, he takes care of us, brings me caffeine, and does late-night nacho runs." They smiled in greeting.

"Logan, he's working the control board for the first time." He nodded his greeting.

"Darren is our engineer."

"Nice to meet you," Darren said. "I think I'll step out and catch a smoke while we're taking a break."

"And this is Garrett. He's producing the album."

Their eyes widened.

"Hi, nice to meet you," Garrett said, standing to shake each of their hands, and sizing up Bennett, who couldn't take his eyes off of Riley.

"I've heard so much about you, I think I could write a whole piece for the *Inquirer*," Erika said. Riley elbowed her in the side.

He raised an eyebrow. What exactly had Riley said to her friend?

"She's kidding. I've barely mentioned you," Riley said.

Garrett laughed at her discomfort. "I'll take that as my cue to leave. Nice to meet you all." He was so used to having Riley all to himself that it was odd to see her with friends. He stepped out of the room, followed by Logan.

"Do you think she's dating that Bennett dude?" Logan asked.

"I have no idea. He doesn't really look like her type." At least Garrett hoped he wasn't. He didn't like the idea of Riley hanging with some other guy, and it had never occurred to him before that she would, which was stupid, because she was pretty, smart, and a ton of fun.

"If she's not, it's not because he doesn't want to. Did you see how he was looking at her?"

Garrett grunted. "We're back in ten minutes. Be sure to tell Riley."

"Will do." Logan went back to break the news to Riley's clan.

Garrett didn't want them getting too comfortable. He had an album to make.

He took the opportunity to step outside and call his dad with an update. It was almost like having him here for the whole process.

Fifteen minutes later, Garrett stepped back inside. Riley and company were in the reception area saying their good-byes. Bennett gave her a hug that seemed way too familiar for just friends. Garrett overheard Bennett talking to Riley.

"I was wondering if you'd like to go out one night this week."

Garrett didn't wait around to hear the answer. Why should he care what Riley did with her free time? But he did, and it didn't sit well with him. Not that she had much time off. In fact, he could make sure she didn't have any extra time in the next few weeks to meet with Bennett or any other guy.

Several hours later Garrett glanced at Riley, relaxed on the couch in the control room, listening while he and the guys at the board did their thing. They had finished up with a studio musician laying tracks for the next song.

After the bass guitarist packed up, Logan struck the minimal set in the recording studio and left to put the mics and equipment in storage.

"See you tomorrow." Darren waved as he and the guitar player took off.

Garrett joined Riley on the couch, stretching his long legs out in front of him and leaning his head back with his hands behind his head. "It feels great to get out of that chair after so many hours."

Riley sat with her legs curled under her and her head resting comfortably on the couch. "Is it hard for you, not to be recording?"

"Hmm?" He rolled his head in her direction.

"You've recorded what? Four albums? That's a lot. And now you're not singing or playing at all."

"But I get to call the shots. I have total control over this album."

"Which I imagine is your perfect world. Controlling everything." Her grin reached all the way to her eyes and lit up her face.

"Of course." He laughed to himself.

"But what about performing? Why aren't you playing guitar instead of hiring studio musicians? If nothing else, it would save money."

"Mostly because I want to concentrate on making the best album we can. I want to separate what's business and what's personal."

"That sounds like such a clinical approach. You've played guitar your whole life. Isn't it strange not to?"

He pictured all the hours he'd spent with his brothers and experienced a pang to his heart. "You know, I've only ever really played with them. Playing on anything other than a Jamieson album wouldn't feel right."

"I think it would be awesome if you played guitar on my album. I mean, it sounds like you really miss it."

He sighed, reminded of the complicated relationship that he had with his brothers now. "I do miss it, but that's my past. This is my future." He waved his arm to indicate the studio. It had taken a while, but Sound Sync was beginning to feel like a place he belonged.

"Do you talk to your brothers much?"

"Nah. Adam's traipsing through some jungle in Tanzania taking pictures, not that he'd call anyway. And Peter knows I'm still pissed at him for ending the best thing we ever had."

"That's so weird that they would break up the band so suddenly."

"There was a little more to it than that. Peter developed vocal nodes. He even had to have surgery."

That was the first time Garrett had actually admitted there was more to the band's breakup than just Peter and Adam acting like brats who wanted to quit playing Monopoly. It was such a relief to say the words. A heavy weight he hadn't realized he carried seemed to lift away.

Riley sat up. "That's terrible. Is he okay?"

"Peter's fine now and can sing anytime, but he doesn't want to. Says he's tired of the breakneck speed we were working at, but in this biz you have to strike while you're hot."

"Were you close with Peter and Adam?" She pushed a fallen lock of hair out of her face.

"Yes and no. We spent practically every minute together for the past five years, and I mean every minute. We clashed a lot, probably because we never had much time to be ourselves. I'm a lot closer to my dad. I talk to him all the time. He's the one constant I could always rely on."

"That's nice. I wish I had that."

"Yeah, my dad gets me. He and I think alike." Unlike his brothers, who complained that Garrett was an inflexible micromanager.

"I think having control issues is an oldest child thing," Riley said. "When you're the oldest, you're in charge of the younger kids. My younger brother's always off creating a mess of his life, and my little sister is a sensitive dreamer who needs emotional support."

"I didn't know you had sibs. Do they have ginger hair, too?" He took a lock of her hair between his fingers. He rolled its softness between his thumb and forefinger, and the strands caught the low light, glistening like spun gold. She didn't pull away.

"My sister's hair is like mine, but not my brother's. He's lucky."

"I love the color of your hair. It's so radical, especially now with your rocker stripes." He released her hair, and it spilled over her shoulder.

"You hated that I dyed my hair." She pushed the stray locks behind her ear.

"No, I was only trying to make a point."

"Don't you mean, acting like a control freak?"

"I wasn't acting like . . . fine. I'll let you have that one." He laughed. Riley sure called things as she saw them. "Are you getting used to being back behind the mic?"

She looked toward the sound booth. "I'll confess, it was really hard to start singing after so much time, but it didn't take long for me to love it again. And working in such an isolated way, without tons of people watching, and not having to worry that I'll be sent home, actually makes the experience fun."

"I'm glad." Watching Riley live up to her potential was intoxicating. So much talent in this average girl, who, he was quickly learning, wasn't so average after all.

"It's kind of insane watching all these people come together to create music that will be my record. I'm a teeny bit sorry I gave you such a hard time about it." She gave him a half-guilty, shy smile.

"Aw, the chase was half the fun of it. Now that I have you, I expect we'll do great things together."

And without thinking, he leaned forward and kissed her.

41

At first Riley seemed startled, but then she returned his kiss, igniting a flame inside him. He slipped his hand through her silky hair and cupped the back of her head. He paused and her breath warmed his cheek. Her blue eyes opened. Was it wonder he read in their depths, caution, or desire? He lowered his lips to hers once more.

Logan burst through the door. "Hey, Garrett, you have a message—"

Riley sprung away from Garrett's arms, and into the far side of the couch, as if scorched.

"Oh shit!" Logan looked away.

Garrett wanted to tell him to get the hell out, but one glance at Riley's embarrassed blush proved their private moment had passed. He rubbed his temple. "What is it, Logan?"

"Geez, sorry, man." Logan shifted on his feet and held out a pink slip of paper. "I found this phone message taped to the door. Something about the opening act at House of Blues is all yours for Thursday night."

"Are you performing at the House of Blues?" Riley asked, having found her voice.

"Of course not," he replied.

"Well, if you're not opening, who is?" Logan asked, then realization dawned on his face. "Oh."

Garrett silently swore at Logan's disastrous timing. They both turned to Riley.

"What?" She looked at him.

He'd planned on telling her soon, just not right after she'd enchanted him into kissing her. Now was as good a time as any. He cocked his head. "It's your stage debut."

"No! You did *not* do this to me again!"

"It's exactly what you need right now. You're ready."

Riley popped off the couch, putting distance between them. "Spill it. I want all the details." She crossed her arms defiantly.

"I've been working with House of Blues to get you back onstage. You're only performing two songs. No big deal. You're the opening act for Amnesia."

"No!"

He loved how her cute little nostrils flared when she was mad. "I know you're nervous, but trust me, you're ready."

"Are you out of your freakin' mind? I'm not ready, and I'm not doing it."

Garrett stood. "Yes, you are. We have the next few

days to rehearse, but think about it. You've basically been rehearsing for the past week. You know the songs inside and out."

"I don't care. I didn't sign up for this. I signed up to record an album, nothing more."

He slid his hands in his pockets and leaned against the edge of the control board. "That's not exactly true. You signed a contract to record an album, promote it, and tour."

"What!"

"It's all in the contract."

Logan whispered to her, "You didn't read the contract?"

"No. I didn't read it. It was twenty pages long. The attorney guy said that everything was standard."

"And it is. Promoting a record and a tour are standard. It doesn't do much good to make a record and then walk away."

Riley stared at him, her stubborn chin set. He felt a twinge of regret at the timing, but it couldn't be helped. "Jamie Halloway is out of town for the next few days, so your schedule is wide open."

Silence filled the room. Logan looked everywhere but at Garrett or Riley. Garrett wished Logan would go away so he could talk privately with her.

"You are horrible." Riley turned to leave.

Garrett caught her by the arm, but her dark, angry eyes warned him to release her.

She left in a flash, and he already missed her.

* * *

Riley unlocked her apartment. Erika sat up as she walked through the door.

"What's up? You send me this cryptic text and don't give me any details."

Riley dropped next to her on the couch. "Garrett kissed me."

Erika gasped. "I told you!"

Riley pounded her head against the back of the couch. Her mind flashed back to the kiss that turned her world upside down and inside out. She hadn't expected it, or thought she'd enjoy it so much.

"What? Garrett Jamieson kissing you is bad?"

"We were interrupted by Logan. He had news for Garrett that the House of Blues has a spot for an opening act on Thursday night." Riley waited for Erika to catch on.

Surprise lit Erika's eyes. "You're singing at the House of Blues?"

Riley grimaced. "Not because I want to. Apparently it's in the contract that I didn't read."

"You're singing at House of Blues and Garrett kissed you! This is so exciting! I guess this means you're not interested in Bennett anymore."

"I don't know what I think. Why did Garrett kiss me in the first place?" The two of them had been getting along so well lately, but the kiss came so unexpectedly.

"Because you're a totally hot rocker chick and he wants to get in your pants."

"Great, just what I don't need. Or more likely, did he

kiss me because he was trying to soften me up so I'd go along with his House of Blues gig?" Was he that manipulative? And if he was, she'd fallen for it like the groupie she didn't want to be.

"I guess that's possible."

"He's such a snake. I knew better than to trust him."

"But he's a totally hot snake. So, is he a good kisser?"

Riley leaned her head back, remembering the touch of his lips on hers and the way he held her close, their bodies fitting together. "Yeah, he's really great."

"I knew it!" she squealed.

"Except that he's a snake who can't be trusted. Remember?"

"Got it. Snake. Bad. But kissing, good."

"I don't want to be the stupid girl who is used by a well-known man whore."

"You don't know that for sure. Has he been sleazing around while he's been in Chicago?"

"Not that I know of. I mean, he hasn't mentioned anyone or brought anyone around." Tara sniffed around him a lot, but from what she'd seen, Garrett didn't seem interested.

"It's because he likes you!"

"Oh lord, save me."

42

"*Two* minutes," the producer called.

Riley was back on Chart Toppers. What had begun as the most exciting time of her life was turning into the biggest disaster. Every week the judges picked apart her performance more. She'd become frazzled, her initial confidence shattered.

Riley was going home soon. The other kids were better, older, and more experienced. Her mom grew more jittery, worried that Riley would blow it, which wasn't helping matters.

"Are you ready?" her mother asked.

No, she wasn't ready. Desiree had given her this song only four days ago and she'd never heard it before. She could barely remember the words, and the song was too high for her range. Would anyone notice if she ran?

Her mom looked in the mirror and adjusted her collar. She bought herself a new outfit for each week.

"Do you remember your words? Don't forget them like that last guy did. They'll knock you off immediately. And smile more. Make people like you."

"I'm trying, Mom."

"Well, try harder."

"Mom, I'm really nervous," she confessed.

Her mom looked away from her own reflection to face Riley. "You better get over it, and fast."

"I know they're going to hate me. They want Kylie to win."

"So get out there and show them that you're better than that little twit."

But she wasn't. Not by a long shot. And she knew it. Tears welled in her eyes.

"Oh good lord. You're not crying at a time like this, are you?" her mother warned.

Riley swiped her eyes with her arm.

"Look what you've done. You smeared your makeup."

Her mom grabbed her chin, pinching Riley's skin as she used her thumb to wipe away the smudge.

"Now listen to me. This is our big chance. You need to win this thing. For all of us. Because if you do, it means no more crappy apartment, no more thrift store clothes. Hell, we can go to Disney World. Now, get out there and sing your little ass off." She released Riley's chin.

"But Mom, I don't think I can do it anymore." Her voice trembled.

Her mother delivered a quick stinging slap across her cheek.

"You disappoint me. Now fix your attitude and go do what we came here for."

The producer appeared, shocked at Riley's red cheek and stricken face. He glared at her mother.

"Riley's just so nervous tonight. I don't know what's gotten into her," she gushed.

The producer took Riley gently by the shoulders and guided her away. "Are you all right?"

Riley sniffled but nodded.

"Makeup!" he called, and a woman appeared to tone down the color on her face. A moment later Riley stepped onstage.

Riley woke in a sweat. If she weren't in her tiny bedroom, she would have sworn she was actually back on that stage. What was happening to her world? Was she having a nervous breakdown? She had been right back in that horrible situation from five years ago.

She never planned to perform onstage again. Ever. But how could she not have realized this would happen? Normally she thought of herself as pretty smart, but she'd been an idiot not to foresee the need to get back up onstage.

But by trying to help her mom, she'd ended up taking on problems her mother should have dealt with.

Riley rolled over to go back to sleep and try to forget

what lay ahead. Her phone beeped. She blindly reached for it and looked at the message.

Are you up? It was Garrett.

She ignored the text and dropped her phone onto the bed next to her and closed her eyes. The kiss!

Her eyes popped open. It had been so out of the blue. And she'd really liked it. So much nicer than the simple good-bye kiss from Bennett yesterday. If only Logan hadn't walked in. But then again, why the heck was Garrett kissing her?

A minute later her phone beeped again. She read the screen.

I know you're awake. Want me to come over and prove it?

"Go away!" She yelled at her phone, then texted back, *No.*

Meet me downtown. Clothes shopping always cheers girls up, doesn't it?

So he wanted to buy her off for springing the House of Blues thing on her? Predictable. *I don't need any clothes,* she texted back.

Yes, you do, for House of Blues.

She refused to respond. He deserved a little cyber silence.

But he responded anyway, with an address and a time.

An hour later, Riley trudged up to a shop located downtown, a block off State Street. The window display included heavy metal T-shirts, chains with emblems on them, leather boots, and pants with spikes coming out of the side.

Great. This would be *Chart Toppers* all over again, but instead of wearing flouncy cotton-candy dresses, she'd be a goth, heavy metal girl. She sighed and pushed into the store.

"There she is," Garrett said with a lazy smile, leaning against the checkout counter as if he didn't have a care in the world. He looked great and Riley hated that she noticed. Her mind immediately flashed to their kiss, but she pushed it away so she wouldn't be so flustered.

He turned to the clerk, a tall, skinny woman with a lip ring and eye makeup that matched her black hair. "Viv, this is Riley, the girl I've been telling you about. We need a kick-ass outfit for her to wear Thursday night."

"I'm sure we can fix her up right." Viv looked Riley up and down, then headed off to the racks.

Riley played with the tassel hanging from her purse, unsure where to look. She glanced at Garrett, and all she could think of was the sexy touch of his lips on hers. He studied her and shot her a quirky smile.

"What?" she asked.

"You look uncomfortable."

"Well, I'm still recovering from the news that you're forcing me to perform." And the fact that she never knew what was going through his mind. Was he thinking about their kiss last night, too?

"Like a sacrificial lamb?"

"You said it, not me," she said, browsing the T-shirts, clinking hangers together as she pretended to study each graphic tee.

He came up next to her and put his arm on the rack. The scent of his aftershave tickled her nose. "Don't act naïve. You had to know you'd be performing."

She meant to glare at him, but the sight of his face and lips distracted her. "Well, you could have told me sooner instead of springing it on me." She moved to the next rack.

"I didn't know if it would happen until Logan came in with the message. And sometimes, an element of surprise makes a performance better, more urgent and exciting."

Riley licked her lips and tried to clear her head.

Garrett pulled a pair of black leather pants from the rack. The sides laced up and would expose a whole lot of skin. "How about these?"

"On what planet do you think I'd wear those?"

"I think they look hot." He grinned.

"Then you wear them." She slid hangers on the rack because she didn't know what else to do.

"I've grabbed a few things. Let me know what you like," Viv said. She held up a tiny black stretchy dress that would wear Riley like shrink wrap.

"No," Riley said.

"How about this?" She held up black pants with rivets along the waistband and spikes down the side.

"Not bad," Garrett said.

"No."

Viv held up a leather bustier with zippers.

"Definitely," Garrett said eagerly.

"Not! Does everything have to be black leather with rivets and spikes?"

"You want to make a statement," Viv said.

"Of what? That I'm a slutty, goth, metal rocker, biker chick? I am not wearing any of this."

Garrett sighed and turned to Viv. "How about something with a little less edge? Riley has enough edge in her shining personality without needing any help."

Riley shot him a dirty look as Viv went off for more goodies. "You can't seriously think I'd wear anything like that."

"We're just getting started. Stop acting so prickly." He reached out and gently touched the top of her hand with his. Their eyes met.

She froze. What was he doing? Was he about to kiss her again?

Viv called out. "Riley, I put a few things in the dressing room for you to try."

"Coming." She reluctantly eased her hand away and followed Viv's voice to the dressing room created by a canvas curtain.

Inside, several T-shirts, pants, and skirts awaited. She quickly dismissed the backless shirt, the super low-rise pants, and anything with spikes, the devil, or crosses.

She tried on a racer-back tank with a red graphic on the front, then slipped into a pair of black acid-wash skinny jeans.

"Anything you like?" Viv asked from the other side.

Riley slid the curtain open and showed her the outfit.

"Meh."

"I agree," Garrett said.

Riley disappeared behind the curtain and tried on another outfit, then another, modeling for Viv and Garrett each time. After a while, she didn't even feel present as they studied her look. She only tried on items she didn't hate.

"Try this." Garrett handed her a denim micro vest that snapped twice across the breasts and laced up in the back.

She torpedoed it back, hitting him in the face. She hoped one of the metal adornments would knock out a tooth.

"Does that mean you don't want to try anything with lace either?" He laughed.

"This is ridiculous. I look like an idiot in these things."

"You want to go onstage wearing your faded jeans and a plain T-shirt, looking like a girl from the South Side of Chicago?"

"Do you have a problem with where I'm from?"

"Of course not, but we're trying to create an image," he said.

"Your taste sucks!"

"No, it doesn't. You're being difficult just to spite me. We're not leaving here until we agree on an outfit."

"It's one stupid concert. You said yourself that it's only two songs. It hardly matters. I'll borrow something from my roommate." She went back into the dressing room, flipping the curtain closed behind her.

As she lifted the T-shirt to pull it over her head, the curtain opened and Garrett slipped in.

Riley yanked the shirt back down and spun around to face him. "Get out!"

"What is your problem?"

"You are!" she snapped. "Do you mind?" The dressing room was tight quarters for the two of them and the heap of discarded clothes at her feet. Her heart raced.

"You didn't seem to mind me too much last night." His gray eyes gleamed.

Her mouth went dry. He had a point. She needed a snappy retort, but no words came.

"Is that what's bothering you?" He leaned close.

"Of course not," she lied.

"Good." He pulled her into his arms and kissed her.

Riley couldn't decide whether to push him away or pull him closer. She'd worried he wouldn't kiss her again after last night, but he infuriated her, too. Still, she couldn't help losing herself in the touch of his lips and comfort of his arms.

He slowly released her. "Still mad?"

"Maybe." She dipped her head and blushed, her knees weak, as a thousand butterflies fluttered in her stomach.

He pushed a lock of hair over her shoulder.

"Why did you kiss me?" she asked.

"It seemed like a good idea." He gave her a half smile that was knowing, wicked, and not the least bit sweet.

"So whenever you don't like what I have to say, you're going to kiss me to make me shut up?" She hoped so, but logic said he was using her.

"I like your thinking."

"I'm serious. You don't even like me. You said so yourself."

"Well, you're growing on me." He shrugged with a lazy smile. "For some reason, the more time I spend with you, the more I can't help myself."

Riley wasn't sure if that was a good thing or not.

43

Riley clutched a large shopping bag as she and Garrett left the shop and headed back toward State Street.

"What's wrong?" He strolled leisurely beside her, carrying a second bag.

"I don't understand what's going on. You and me. What is this?"

"Why does it need a label?"

"It doesn't, but it needs an explanation. One minute you're a jerk, then the next you're nice. And now you're . . ."

"Interested. Kissing you," he said with an amused, cocky grin.

"Yeah. I don't get it."

"You sure like to overanalyze things."

Riley stared down the street. "I don't want to end up regretting anything later."

"Fine. When I saw you with that guy, Emmet—"

"It's Bennett."

"Whatever. I realized that I didn't like the way he looked at you, all hungry and predatory."

"He did not."

Garrett gave her a pointed look that said otherwise. "I didn't plan on doing anything about it, other than making sure you didn't have a free minute to see him. But then I kept noticing your beautiful eyes and that wild ginger hair of yours, and well, I couldn't resist any longer."

Riley flushed with excitement. She couldn't imagine Garrett jealous of anyone. "Ginny told me to guard my heart from you."

"Ah, so I have Ginny to thank for turning you against me?"

"No, you do that well enough on your own."

He smirked. "So, want to do something tonight?"

"I thought we were too busy."

"Not anymore."

She couldn't help but be wary, but there was something especially appealing about the way Garrett took charge when he wanted something, and it seemed that maybe he wanted her. Happy jitters of excitement ran through her.

Before going to the studio, they stopped at Daley Plaza. Garrett bought her a hot dog and soda from a food cart. They sat on a ledge overlooking the Picasso statue. Riley laughed at the look on Garrett's face when mustard dropped onto his white button-down shirt. It seemed that the more time they spent together, the more he relaxed. And this was a side of him that she liked very much.

Later, they rehearsed for the House of Blues gig in the large recording studio designed to accommodate a full orchestra. As she watched Garrett in action, she realized her heart was melting. It was very nice. A new energy buzzed between them as she began to let him in.

They didn't let on to anyone at work the new direction their relationship had taken. Yet every time Garrett joined her on the mock stage and they locked eyes, trills of excitement shot through her. They shared a secret no one else knew.

Riley struggled to concentrate, counting the minutes until she'd be alone with him again. She hadn't crushed on a guy this much since tenth grade when she fell for a drummer in her school band. Those feelings seemed silly and innocent now, compared with the growing intensity she felt for Garrett. How she'd gone from despising him to being unable to think of anything else she didn't know, or care.

Every time he paused to look at her, his smile reached into her heart and hugged her tight.

"I think that's good for tonight. I don't want to overwhelm you. Ready to get out of here and do something fun?" he said as they wrapped up the session.

"Sure. What did you have in mind?" She grinned. She'd actually loved what they'd been doing for the past two hours. Working with Garrett after he'd kissed her and admitted to being jealous had changed everything. She saw a new vulnerability to him that she hadn't noticed before.

"I heard that Grant Park is nice," he said.

"Sounds perfect."

Walking close, their hands brushed together as Riley and Garrett came across a free concert at the pavilion in Grant Park. They chose not to fight the crowds to watch when people recognized Garrett and snapped his picture. Instead they opted for pizza at a concession stand and watched the Buckingham Fountain light show.

Garrett teased her and made her laugh. Riley lost herself in his eyes as they turned a beautiful shade of slate gray in the fading light. He snuck in a tender kiss. Later they found a secluded spot of grass, lay on their backs, and stargazed.

"Oh, I forgot to mention that you have a photo shoot tomorrow." Garrett turned his head toward her.

She sat up. "You forgot?"

"It slipped my mind," he said, which was a lame excuse as far as she was concerned.

Riley leaned over him, linking her fingers with his and pinning his hands next to his head, enjoying the rush of power she held over him. "Could you try a little harder not to have things that involve me slip your mind? I'd like to rate a little higher than an afterthought."

"Trust me, you are no afterthought. In fact, you have

been the first thing I think of when I wake up in the morning and the last thing I think of at night," he said softly, gazing into her eyes.

"You're just saying that." There was no way he could really feel that way. Garrett could have whoever he wanted.

"Nope. It's the truth." Garrett flipped her onto her back, taking up the position she'd had on him. "What do you have to say now?" he asked, his face inches from hers.

"Um," she whispered, at a loss for words, her heart racing and her brain suffering a delicious break in transmission.

"Well, that's got to be a first." He captured her mouth and rewarded her with long, lingering kisses.

Riley must be dreaming, because never in her life would she have imagined she'd spend a warm summer evening in the park, kissing Garrett Jamieson.

But it was no dream.

The next day Riley woke to a text from Garrett wishing her good morning and giving her the details for the photo shoot.

She grinned and did a little happy dance as she lay in bed. Last night they had walked arm in arm to her door. Riley hadn't wanted to part, but they had a busy day ahead. Garrett gave her the sweetest good night kisses that left her longing for him and unable to sleep.

Riley burst into Erika's room and jumped onto her bed,

causing her roommate to shriek, "Are you crazy, woman?"

Riley plopped her head on the pillow next to Erika's. "You'll never guess who I went out with last night."

"And I won't care for at least another hour," Erika mumbled, her eyes closed.

Riley rolled closer and faced her. "Garrett."

Erika's eyes sprung open. "What?"

"Yup." Riley grinned.

"Oh my God. Last I heard, you hated him."

"Hate is a strong word. He and I have been starting to get along the past week or so."

"What happened?" Erika slipped a hand under her cheek.

"Remember how you brought Bennett to the studio, and Garrett went all alpha dog and decided he needed to mark his territory, so he kissed me."

"Yeah, that was two days ago."

"Yesterday we were basically fighting over what I should wear for the concert and he kissed me again. After that he bought me lunch, and then we went out last night."

"That is so wild!"

"I know! Right?"

"So now the two of you are dating?"

"Pretty much. We aren't telling anyone at work because they might all think I'm a slutty whore throwing myself at him."

"Please tell me he didn't say that."

"Of course not. But I don't want people thinking the wrong thing."

"Bennett is going to be so disappointed," Erika said. "There's no way he can compete with Garrett Jamieson."

"Nope. There pretty much isn't. I've gotta get going. I'm meeting Garrett."

"I'm happy you're happy," Erika called as Riley rushed out the bedroom door.

"Thanks!"

Riley showered and dressed, counting the minutes until she'd see Garrett. And like clockwork, he met her outside of the downtown photo studio with a delicious kiss that left her wishing for more.

Garrett met with the photographer while a makeup artist and stylist applied their skills to her.

The clothes they had bought the day before hung on a rack. She pulled on a pair of black, faded jeans, a stone-washed T-shirt, and an awesome cropped leather jacket. The price had been obscene, but Garrett didn't bat an eye. The outfit boasted casual rocker, but with a little edge.

The photo shoot went fast. She remembered several she'd done back on *Chart Toppers* and appreciated that she had experience in so much of this business.

The next days were a whirlwind of rehearsals for the House of Blues gig, working the next songs to record, sharing knowing looks with Garrett, and sneaking into the recording booth for stolen kisses.

They succeeded in keeping their new relationship a secret, which made it even more exciting. Still, Riley worried what everyone at work would think if they found out she'd fallen for Garrett like any other groupie, but that's not how it happened.

It had taken weeks to get to know him and most of that time she didn't especially like him, but Garrett changed and she saw a new side to him now, a side she liked. He let down his guard and allowed her in. That was the Garrett Jamieson she'd fallen for.

They wrapped up a little earlier than usual and went to Garrett's apartment for dinner. They stopped at the tiny market at the base of Marina Towers for a few groceries.

With Brad on tour, they had the place to themselves. Together, they made spaghetti and a small salad, and ate dinner on the balcony with a spectacular view of the city as a backdrop.

Riley sighed with contentment at the new direction her life had taken. As the evening air cooled, she shivered.

"Are you cold? We can go in," Garrett suggested.

They carried their dishes inside, leaving them on the kitchen counter.

"Want to watch a movie?" Garrett asked.

Riley needed to get home and catch up on sleep. She'd been so busy the past couple of weeks, and it had caught up with her, but the idea of cuddling on the couch with Garrett overruled.

"That sounds great," she said.

He brought them fresh drinks and a bowl of microwave popcorn. As they snuggled onto the couch, Garrett scrolled through the list of available online movies. They settled on an adventure flick set on the high seas.

The movie became a backdrop as Garrett trailed kisses down her neck, transporting her to a place of pure bliss. Their hands traveled over each other, and their bodies pressed close, creating a cocoon of passion.

But Garrett didn't push for anything more. Riley wasn't sure if she was relieved or disappointed. She had to concede that he was actually a gentleman.

She yawned. "I'm sorry. I feel so tired all of a sudden."

"You've been working really hard. Close your eyes and relax," he suggested.

"It's like I've been hit by a truck or something. I better not be getting sick."

He put his hand on her cheek and forehead. "You feel a little warm. Why don't you stay? I promise to behave like a Boy Scout. On my honor." He raised his hand in the Boy Scout sign.

She laughed. "I have known some rather naughty Boy Scouts, so I don't think that line holds much water. But now that you mention it, I think I'll close my eyes for a few minutes."

44

Garrett woke to the annoying buzz of the apartment intercom. He opened his eyes. Riley slept soundly in his arms, so sweet and vulnerable with her mass of red hair splayed across his arm like a beautiful blanket. The buzzer sounded again. Riley stirred.

"Shh," he whispered and climbed over her and off the couch to the voice box near the apartment door. He pressed the TALK button. "Yes," he said, his voice groggy from sleep.

"There is a Mr. Jamieson on his way up to see you," the doorman said.

"Which Mr. Jamieson?" he asked, because none of them should be within a thousand miles of Chicago.

"A middle-aged gentleman," he replied.

Shit. He looked at Riley sleeping under a tousled blanket, her hair strewn across the pillow. He pressed the TALK button. "Thank you."

How much time did he have? "Riley." He brushed a lock of hair from her warm cheek.

"Um-hmm," she murmured.

"Riley, you need to wake up. Now," he said with urgency.

She slowly opened her eyes and blinked a couple of times. "What's going on?" she said in a scratchy voice.

"My dad's here."

"Where?" She bolted upright, her eyes darting around the room in panic.

"In the elevator on his way up."

"Oh my God!" She stood up and smoothed down her clothes. "What do I do? Hide?"

"No, it's not like we were doing anything wrong, and he was bound to meet you sooner or later."

"I wish it were later." She collected their drinking glasses and carried them to the kitchen in an effort to tidy up.

A knock sounded at the door. Riley popped back around the corner, fear in her eyes. He grimaced. "That was fast."

"Smooth your hair," she said, running a hand through her own tangles.

Garrett pushed back his hair and ran his hands over his wrinkled T-shirt. Having his dad find him with the girl he was working with first thing in the morning was not the best scenario. "Here goes nothing."

He opened the door. "Hi, Dad. This sure is a surprise."

"I thought I'd spring a quick visit before your mother and I leave for Europe. Looks like you slept in your clothes. Did I wake you?"

"Yeah, you did." Garrett ran his hand through his hair again.

"Sorry about that, but I took the six a.m. flight from Boston."

"Come on in." Garrett stepped aside. His dad entered and stopped short at the sight of barefooted Riley with mussed hair and rumpled clothes.

"Oh, you're not alone," his father said.

"Dad, I'd like you to meet Riley Parks. She's the girl I signed to record." He grimaced, wishing desperately this could be going down differently.

His dad frowned. "I see. Nice to meet you, Riley. I've heard a great deal about you. Your singing talent, that is."

"Hi, nice to meet you," Riley said with a shell-shocked look on her face.

Garrett intervened. "We were up late watching movies, and fell asleep on the couch."

His father nodded but refrained from sharing his opinion. "I can't be here to celebrate the gig at House of Blues tomorrow night, so I flew in for the day to observe your rehearsal."

"That's great. I'd love for you to hear Riley sing," Garrett said. He did want his dad to hear her, but it would have been nice if he called first.

"Well, I should be going. It was nice to meet you, Mr.

Jamieson. I guess I'll see you this afternoon," Riley said nervously.

"I look forward to it, too," he said.

Riley slid into her sandals and collected her phone and purse.

"Garrett, do you have a washroom I can use?" his father asked.

"Right through there." Garrett pointed toward the bathroom.

"Until this afternoon, then," his dad said to Riley and disappeared down the hall.

"Oh my God!" Riley mouthed.

"It's fine. Don't worry about it," Garrett whispered.

"He already hates me, I can tell."

"No, he doesn't. It'll be okay."

"Call me later if you can," she said at the door.

"I will." He kissed her quickly and she slipped out the door.

A minute later his dad reappeared. "You've been busy, I see," he said, looking at the rumpled blanket on the couch.

"It's not like that, Dad."

"Isn't it? I think we'd better have a talk."

"I'm not sleeping with her."

"Garrett, I wasn't born yesterday. I saw the way you two looked at each other. A lot more is going on than recording music."

What could he say? He'd fallen for Riley. And the only reason he hadn't slept with her yet was because he liked her so much, and he wanted it to be special. Feeling this way about someone was new territory for him.

"Son. You're going to do whatever you want. I know that. But as you begin this new venture, do you really want to start out as a cliché? She's an attractive young girl, but if you want to be taken seriously, you need to keep your head in the game and not let your johnson call the shots."

"I'm not!"

"Aren't you? This is ridiculous. Tell me what happens when this little flame you've got going burns out? You've never had a history of longevity with women. In fact, have you ever been with any one girl for more than a week?"

"This is different, Dad. Before, we were always on tour. Or working in different cities."

"All I'm saying is, what happens when this ends? How are you going to manage a long-term working relationship with Riley? You need to create a professional partnership that doesn't include side benefits."

He feared his dad was right. If things didn't work out with Riley, she'd hate him. If after a few weeks or months, one of them changed their mind, it would be difficult, if not impossible, to work together.

"I get it," he said with defeat.

"Good. I only want you to succeed. She'll thank you in the long run."

But how could he let her go, now that he had her?

45

Riley couldn't shake her sore throat, and it had to happen on a day Garrett's dad showed up to hear her sing. He must think she and Garrett had slept together. What a nightmare.

She warmed up in the vocal booth. Garrett had been on the phone ever since she arrived, and when he finally glanced at her, it was with a smile that seemed off. It wasn't forced, but it wasn't natural either. She'd bet money that his dad had given him a hard time.

Garrett finally hung up the phone. Riley was about to ask him how things went with his dad when Mr. Jamieson and Barry came in. She hung by her mic, pretending to be busy, but mostly scraping off the edge of her nail polish with her thumbnail.

"Let's get started," Garrett said to the band from the front of the room. "My dad flew in just to hear you guys, so let's make it good."

The guys in her makeshift band chuckled. Garrett's eyes landed on Riley. She smiled, desperate to connect, but there was that odd, guarded look from him again.

Fine, she could play aloof professional, too. She turned to their drummer, who clicked off the beat, and they began. Performing with the studio musicians was tricky because they weren't used to playing as a group. They were pulled together for this one performance.

Riley knew the recorded tracks that had been laid down, but singing live was always different. If only she had a few more days to work the kinks out.

Garrett stopped them a couple times and offered suggestions. Only once did he approach her.

"Is everything okay?" She covered the mic with her hand and tried to read the thoughts he masked behind his stoic expression.

"It's fine. I'm trying to make sure you're ready. Your voice sounds strained, almost rough."

"I've had a sore throat ever since I woke up. I took something, but it's getting worse."

"I never should have let you stay last night. I should have put you in a cab," he said briskly.

His tone sounded as if he wished she hadn't been there, not because she was getting sick, but because he regretted having his dad find out.

"Are you mad at me?" she asked softly.

"Of course not. We're here to rehearse," he said, but

his posture remained rigid.

"I know that, but you've been acting strange this whole time. Did your dad say something?"

He sighed and looked at her for a moment. Turmoil rolled in his eyes. "You and I need to talk, but this isn't the time."

Without another word he walked away and rejoined his father.

Was he going to break up with her? They'd only been together a few days; how could it already be over? She tried not to let her heartbreak show.

"Try it again from the top, please," Garrett said.

After that, he never looked her in the eye. He consulted with his dad and Barry while she sang, and gave directions on entrances and sound mixing, but never approached her. Her heart ached at how easily he could turn off his interest.

Rehearsal lingered with slow torture as Garrett remained distant and her throat tightened in pain. She wanted the whole thing over so she could get to the bottom of whatever bothered him.

Finally he called a break. As she slid her mic back in the stand, his dad approached.

"You are an enormously talented young lady. I see why Garrett was determined to work with you," Mr. Jamieson said with genuine interest.

Riley let out a breath of anxiety she'd been holding

since rehearsal began. "Thank you. Garrett's been really helpful."

"I have no doubt. When Garrett sets his mind on something, he always finds a way to succeed." He smiled with pride.

Riley found his comment a bit odd. What did he mean by it?

Mr. Jamieson continued. "I wish I could stay longer, but I have a plane to catch. Best of luck tomorrow night. I'm sure it will go well."

"Thank you for coming, and have a nice vacation."

He smiled and turned to his son. "Garrett, would you walk me out?"

"Sure thing, Dad." The two disappeared.

A few minutes later, Riley found Garrett at the curb, waving as his dad rode off in a town car to the airport.

"What did he think?" she asked.

"That you were great. And he gave me a bunch of suggestions that we can work on."

They watched the car disappear around the corner. "Are you okay? You've been acting weird all day."

His jaw clenched. "There's a lot going on. Like I said earlier, we need to talk."

"Yes, we do," she said.

He sighed. Defeat clouded his eyes.

"Garrett, you can talk to me." She put her hand on

his cheek. "Please don't leave me in the dark like this. I'll understand."

He stepped out of her reach, appearing stricken.

Still he said nothing, and her panic reached new heights.

A couple walked past them on the sidewalk.

"Can we get out of here? I'd like to talk in private where it's just you and me and we don't have to worry about who overhears," Riley said.

"I think we should cool things off," he blurted.

She stared. "What?"

He finally looked her straight in the eye. "Things are moving too fast. I don't want our feelings for each other to get in the way of finishing and launching your record."

"Why would it? We both want the same things." At least she had started to once she got to know his softer side, but where was that now?

"We need to have clear lines of communication and letting emotions get in the way will only screw things up."

"Why are you saying this? None of it seemed to bother you yesterday. Is it because of your dad?"

Garrett looked away.

"Oh my God, your dad said something. He doesn't like me."

"He likes you just fine, but he said that this can't work long term. And he's right. The odds of you and me staying together are slim to none, but the odds of you making a real go as a recording artist are huge."

"You'd rather make records with me than be in a relationship?"

"Riley, the whole reason I came to Chicago was to produce records. Not find a girlfriend. I like you a lot, but I can't go sleeping with my clients."

"Now I'm a client? And whoever said I'd sleep with you anyway? Everything was great until your dad showed up, and now you're running away like a scared little boy."

"No. I'm facing the facts. Business needs to come before personal."

"And whose words are those? Your dad's? Geez, Garrett, grow a pair."

"This is exactly why we should concentrate on work. Personal stuff gets in the way. I never should have started this." Garrett turned and walked away.

"I can't believe I fell for you. I am such an idiot," she said as he left her behind. How could she have made such a huge mistake?

46

The next afternoon, Riley downed two more painkillers. Her fever refused to go away. Adding to her problems, Garrett wouldn't answer his phone. Riley wanted to scream, except that her throat burned and every muscle ached. She dreaded having to face Garrett after he broke off their barely started relationship. Tonight she was scheduled to go onstage as an opening act at House of Blues, and she desperately wanted out of it.

Canceling a gig was one of the worst things an artist could do, but then again Garrett deserved it. He treated her like a second-class citizen, springing this performance on her with such short notice, bossing her around, and then dumping her. After she'd cried on Erika's shoulder for an hour last night, Erika said it was no wonder Riley was so sick after all this stress.

Riley sent him a final text. *I'm sick. Can't sing tonight.*

That ought to get his attention. Her phone pinged immediately in reply.

Grab a cab. Come straight here. I'll meet you at the stage door.

No! She just wanted her bed.

Instead, she forced herself into the hot, humid air and hailed a cab.

"House of Blues, please," Riley said, climbing in. She leaned her head back and closed her eyes, only to be startled awake when the taxi pulled up to the Marina Towers. How convenient that her first gig would happen right below where Garrett lived. Talk about a control freak. He probably planned it that way.

As the cabbie announced her fare, Garrett appeared. He peeled off a couple bills and paid the driver.

"You look like hell," he said with a mix of concern and irritation on his face.

"I feel worse."

He put his hand to her forehead. She wanted to swat it away, but the action would have taken too much effort.

"You're warm. Let's get you a Tylenol."

"I've already taken some."

He led her toward the rear entrance. "Well, you're going to need more before the day is over."

Riley stopped outside the stage door. "Garrett, I can't. Seriously. I'm about to fall over. I'm not saying this because I'm trying to punish you. I'm really sick."

He crossed his arms. "I know you don't feel well, and that you don't especially like me right now, but there's not much I can do about that. You're nervous and afraid to appear onstage. You've probably made yourself sick worrying about it. In our business, we don't cancel. Ever."

He stared at her, leaving a long, silent void in the air between them.

"You want me to go on, even if I sound horrible?" she said, her voice sounding scratchy.

"No, I want you to go on and push through it. For two songs, I want you to forget you're anything but perfection. I want you to rock that place and give them a performance they'll never forget."

"I can't." Tears welled in Riley's eyes.

Two guys approached, their cameras clicking.

"Garrett, how are you handling the band breaking up?"

Garrett turned his body away from the photographers, took Riley gently by the arm, and guided her through the doorway.

"Paparazzi are the last thing I need. I swear my whole world is turning to crap." He led her onto the stage. She saw cameras positioned around the stage and on the balcony. The hair on the back of her neck went up.

"Yes, you can perform tonight, because we're filming your music video."

She turned her weary eyes on him and asked with the last of her energy, "And you didn't bother to tell me?"

"And give you more things to freak out about? No. Now go to your dressing room and gargle with some warm salt water. You have sound check in ten minutes." He walked away.

"Where are you going?" she called after him in disbelief.

"To call a doctor."

Riley crossed to the stairs. In the first room at the top of the steps she found her outfit hanging from a clothes rack. A love seat with pillows and a throw blanket occupied the room, along with an armchair and a dressing table with a lighted mirror. A bathroom was off to the side.

Riley closed the door and collapsed on the couch. She flung a pillow across the room in frustration over Garrett's bullying tactics. It's like he had flipped a switch and returned to his former, unlikeable self. He had a lot invested in tonight, especially now that a full-scale film crew had taken over, but did he really want her to go on when she'd sound so sucky?

I hate Garrett, she texted Erika, then tossed her phone on the coffee table. Emotions overcame her, and her throat tightened. She willed herself not to cry; it hurt too much.

A few minutes later she joined the studio musicians onstage. As she ran through a sound check, she tried to hit her marks, but couldn't avoid the sluggishness surrounding her. In the audience, Garrett consulted with the camera guys.

In the middle of the second song, he signaled to cut the music.

"Hold up, guys. Let's take five. Riley, meet me in your dressing room."

Her first instinct was that he wanted to apologize and say how wrong he'd been and that he needed her in his life. But more likely was that she sounded so bad he planned to bawl her out.

She slid the mic back on the stand and trudged up the stairs to her dressing room. A minute later Garrett walked in with a man wearing a sport coat and tie.

"Riley, this is Dr. Vos. He's going to take a look at your throat."

So Garrett wasn't here to declare his undying love.

"Hi, Riley, nice to meet you." The doctor stepped forward and shook her hand.

"I'm an ear, nose, and throat specialist at Northwestern Memorial Hospital. I'm on call when artists such as yourself aren't feeling well, but still need to perform."

"I didn't know doctors did house calls."

"Or House of Blues calls, and from what I hear you're feeling pretty blue," he joked. "Why don't we sit down here on the couch? Is it okay if I look at your throat and do a quick checkup?"

"Sure. Can you cure me by eight o'clock?" She knew there was no escaping the performance.

Garrett watched, concern etched on his brow. Yet he

avoided looking directly at her.

"Probably not, but maybe we can get you through it without any hitches." Dr. Vos took her temperature, pulse, and blood pressure.

Riley struggled to keep her eyes open. She wanted to sink back into the couch and sleep.

"Now let's take a peek at your throat." He shined a light in her mouth and used a tongue depressor. "Your throat is pretty ugly, but it doesn't look like strep. We won't know without a culture."

He pulled some supplies from his bag and cultured her throat.

Riley gagged and her eyes teared as he swabbed the back of her throat.

"Sorry about that." He swabbed his petri dish and then dropped everything into a Ziploc bag.

Garrett held out a tissue. She took it from his hand and wiped her eyes.

"Have you been taking anything?" the doctor asked.

"Tylenol. A couple every four hours."

"All right. We won't know about the rapid strep test for a couple of hours. I'll drop it at the lab right away. If it's inconclusive, we'll leave it for forty-eight hours to see the result."

"Thanks, but that won't help me much tonight," she said, defeated.

"No, it won't. I'd prefer you drank clear liquids and

went straight to bed, but I understand the show must go on. I took the liberty of writing a prescription and having it filled before I came. It's for a much stronger painkiller."

Oh, great. The good doctor planned to drug her. "Won't it make me loopy?"

"This is a common prescription painkiller. You're getting one dose. All this does is mask the pain for about four hours."

"If you want to get through tonight, you need to take the pill," Garrett said.

Riley ignored him.

"The management here will vouch for me, as well as the hospital. Here's my contact information."

She accepted his card. It looked official.

"You don't have to take the painkiller, but it will help you get through the performance. Either way, I will follow up as soon as your test results are back."

Riley took the prescription bottle. A single pill rattled in the bottom.

"Try to rest before your performance if you can. And straight to bed when it's over," the doctor said.

"Thank you."

"One last thing. Break a leg!" He smiled and left. Garrett followed him into the hall.

Erika rushed in.

"What are you doing here?" Riley asked, wishing everyone would go away.

"Protecting you from you know who. I don't trust him not to be an even bigger jerk," she said, sitting next to Riley.

"He's been okay." But Riley missed the Garrett from the past few days who had held her in his arms and made her feel like the luckiest girl on the planet.

"What did the doctor say?" Erika asked.

"He doesn't think it's strep. He gave me a painkiller for tonight, but I don't know if I should take it."

"Stop being such a drama queen. He's a doctor! Take the damn pill." Erika handed her a bottle of water.

"It's just that this is how people become addicts."

"My mother has a stash of these she uses whenever she gets a hangnail. It's a painkiller, not heroin. Bottoms up!"

"I hate you," Riley said.

"Yeah, you've been saying that a lot today."

Garrett returned in time to watch Riley toss the pill in her mouth and swallow.

"Nice job, Erika," Garrett said.

"I'm not talking to you, so save your breath," she answered.

"I could have you tossed out of here," he threatened.

Riley rolled her eyes.

"Try it," Erika dared.

Ignoring Erika, he spoke to Riley. "Were you comfortable with the sound check? Do you want to do anything else out onstage?"

Comfortable? Not even close, but she didn't feel like

going back onstage, let alone getting off the couch. "No, I want to close my eyes." She sighed and leaned back, wishing this whole ordeal would be over.

"There's about two hours before you go on. How about we leave you alone and you try to catch a few z's."

"Are you serious? Maybe you do have a heart in there somewhere." She laid her head on the arm of the love seat.

"Contrary to popular belief, I do. I'll give you one hour. That should leave you time to warm up and get ready."

Garrett pulled the blanket from the back of the couch and spread it over her, which made her sad that he wasn't hers anymore. The softness of the couch cushioned her aching body. She closed her eyes.

"I'm going to leave and let you sleep. I'll see you after the show, but if you need anything, I'm a call away," Erika said.

"Thanks, Erika."

Riley sensed Garrett looming over her. "Good-bye, Garrett."

"I'm leaving."

The light switched off and she was out.

Garrett hated having to play the tough-love card with Riley, but he'd already screwed up and needed to set the right tone from here on out. When she'd climbed out of that cab earlier, he wanted to fold her into his arms and comfort her, but he needed to draw strict lines between them. He couldn't afford to screw up again.

Hopefully a little sleep and the painkiller would get Riley back on track. All the times he'd been sick on the road, his mom had been there to take care of him. She'd bring in the soup, tuck him in, and do a dozen other things to help him feel better. He couldn't cross the line and get too personal with Riley anymore, but there was something he could do.

He moved quietly into her dressing room and snuck her phone off the table.

47

"*Riley,* honey, wake up."

Riley was dreaming again. Wasn't she? Then a gentle shake of her shoulder forced her out of her deep slumber.

"Riley, open your eyes. You have to get ready to sing."

It sounded like her mom, which was so strange, because her mom didn't know she was singing again.

"She's really out," she heard Garrett say.

"She always did like to sleep in."

The voice sounded distinctly like her mother's. Riley's eyes shot open.

"There you are." Her mother's face appeared in front of her.

"Mom! What are you doing here?" She scrambled upright.

Her mother smiled broadly. "Imagine my surprise when I received a call on your phone from none other than

Garrett Jamieson. I thought for sure it was a prank call, because I wasn't aware you knew Garrett Jamieson, let alone were singing again."

Riley turned to Garrett and cried in disbelief, "Why did you call her?"

The smile on his face faltered. "Because you're sick, and I figured having your mom here would make you feel better."

"Oh my God," she groaned.

"And I'm so glad he did, or I might have never known you were singing and recording an album. You shouldn't keep such wonderful news to yourself," her mom chimed.

Riley dropped her head into her hands and swore.

"How are you feeling?" Garrett asked.

She swallowed. Other than the shock of seeing her mother, the cyclone of doom, she actually felt pretty good. "Better. Definitely better."

"Great. I'll get out of here while you get changed. We can do vocal warm-ups as soon as you're ready."

Garrett disappeared, leaving her alone with her mom. Riley braced for the oncoming storm.

"Riley, what is going on here? And why haven't you told me about this?" her mom snapped.

"Mom, I only found out about the concert a few days ago." Parched, Riley reached for her water bottle and drank. It no longer hurt to swallow.

Her mom looked at the clothes hanging on the rack.

"I think things have been going on for a lot longer than a few days." She ran her hands over the stylish leather jacket.

There was no escaping her mom now. "I didn't decide to start singing again by choice. It was the only way I could think of to come up with money to pay for the car that *you* didn't insure and the damage it did."

"You know that wasn't my fault." She slipped the jacket off the hanger and tried it on. "This is really cute. Did your new boyfriend buy it for you?"

Riley snatched the skinny black jeans and acid-washed graphic tee off the rack before her mother could, and slipped into the bathroom to change.

From behind the safety of the closed door, Riley yelled, "He's not my boyfriend, and yes, the car thing was your fault! You never bothered to insure it, even after I asked you to. I do everything for you, Mom, and you shit on me time and time again."

"You said you worked for an insurance company. From what I've heard, that's a total lie, too."

Riley stepped out of the bathroom wearing the new clothes. "Mom, this isn't about you. For once, it's about me."

This day was bad enough, and now she had to worry about whatever horrors her mother was about to commit. She pulled on her stylish new boots.

"Which is why I'm here, to help." Her mother admired herself in the mirror.

Garrett entered cautiously. "Is everything okay? Sounds a little loud in here."

"Everything's great," Riley snapped. "And Mom, I don't need your help. You can go home."

"Of course you do. You can't go out there tonight looking like you do. Not to mention, you never performed well on *Chart Toppers* without my pep talk."

"Oh, like the time when you slapped me right before I went out onstage? That was a great motivator."

Her mother looked stricken. "I never—"

"Yes, you did. Don't deny it just because he's here." She gestured to Garrett, who looked on in shock.

"Why couldn't you ever be a normal mother? Why couldn't you love me?" Tears welled in Riley's eyes and she trembled with emotion. "What made you not even care about your own kids?"

"Of course I care about all of you," she said.

"You lie to us, steal from us, and abandon us!" Riley cried, not caring that Garrett heard the details of her nightmarish past.

He stepped between them. "This has to stop. I can see there's a lot you two need to talk about, but save it until after the show."

"No! You brought her here, and she is going to answer me," Riley demanded. Once and for all, she deserved to know.

Her mother, never one to back down, retorted,

"You have no idea what you're talking about. I've been Goddamned Mother Teresa compared to my mom. Did you ever go without food to eat? Did I ever bring men home that crawled into your bed? No! I protected you. I gave you a roof over your head. I didn't kick you out when you turned eighteen, but you couldn't wait to get away from me."

These were her mom's standards for good parenting? Not throwing her kids out?

Garrett looked at her mom, then at Riley, and then back to her mom again. "I'll give you two a couple of minutes." He disappeared like a frightened child, unequipped to handle two angry women.

"You were never there for me," Riley shouted.

Her mom raised her hands in the air. "Never there? I'm the one who went to LA with you when you were on that show. I hocked everything I had to buy you clothes for all those early auditions. My boss fired me for skipping work so much. Matt and Britta had to live with my brother's ex-wife for a month. I did everything I could to give you a shot at making it, and you threw it all away. I didn't raise you to be weak. I raised you to be a fighter."

"But I was a kid. I was scared, and you told the press everything, all my hopes and dreams, my deepest secrets. You stomped all over any small bit of confidence I had."

"Well, you were a little know-it-all. You always thought you were better than me."

"How could you think that?" she cried.

"The way you'd parade around with Desiree Diamond and laugh with Jason Edgette."

"Desiree was horrible to me. Couldn't you see that? I hated her."

"Well, look who you're acting like now?"

Garrett reappeared in the doorway, his concern turned to panic. "Riley, you really need to get ready. I can't push back the curtain any later."

She sighed. "I know. Mom, you need to leave."

"But I've always been here for your performances."

"I can't do this drama with you right now." She needed to pull herself together, and fast.

"You're the one who started it. I only wanted to help."

"It would help if you left."

"I can't believe you don't want me here. You've never appreciated what I did for you." She picked up her purse and headed for the door.

"Mom?"

"What?"

"Take off the jacket."

Her mom tore off the leather jacket and threw it onto the couch. Garrett scrambled out of the way as she flew past.

After her mom was out of earshot, Garrett apologized. "I had no idea. I never would have asked her here if I knew she was going to stir up family drama."

Riley came at him full force. "No. You didn't think,

did you? Even though I told you how she had me sign loan papers for her and made me liable for her mistakes? You don't know everything about me. Not even close."

"I only meant to help."

"Stop!" She held up her hand. "I really don't want to hear it. I have to get ready to go onstage in front of a packed crowd, even though I'm exhausted, sick as a dog, and just did fifteen rounds with my mom."

To his credit, Garrett left the room without another word.

48

"*How* do you feel?" Garrett asked again as Riley approached the stage. After the screaming match between Riley and her mother, he didn't know if she'd have a voice left to sing with. He had a lot riding on tonight. He'd dropped a load of money to pull this taping together. Now, with the lack of rehearsal time in front of the cameras, and Riley pissed at him for pulling away, it would be a miracle if this thing went well.

"I told you. I'm fine," Riley barked back, refusing to look at him.

They waited backstage, moments before she went on. Riley was a knockout in low-rise jeans with a fitted T-shirt bearing a turquoise graphic. A wide belt with metal adornments hugged her hips, and she wore the cropped leather jacket that she had loved, but insisted cost too much.

"I meant emotionally," he said. "After that scene with

your mom, well, you guys looked like you were about to tear each other apart."

She glared at him instead of responding.

Fine. He deserved that. The edgy streaks of blond in her dark red hair made her look tough, but from what he'd witnessed, Riley was a vulnerable girl who had suffered plenty. All her bravado was just a wall she'd put up.

"At least you look good," he said.

"Gee, thanks," she said sarcastically.

Taped rock music filled the theater, exciting the room full of pumped-up concertgoers. Garrett remembered the early days of Jamieson when they were the opening act. No one wanted to listen to them. The crowd only wanted the main attraction.

But the audience tonight had been informed they would be part of a music video, so hopefully they'd step up and make a good show.

"You remember all the moves I gave you?"

"Of course."

"And be sure to work the whole stage. Damn it, I should have flown Peter here to show you how it's done." He adjusted the collar on her jacket and she slapped his hand away.

"Are you really trying to crush any tiny shred of confidence I still have?" she asked, bouncing nervously on her feet.

Where'd she learn that trick? He always did that with

327

his brothers to relieve stress and up their energy before going on. "Are you nervous?"

"Of course I am, and you're not helping. So would you please shut up?"

He held his tongue. She was right. He was unloading his nerves on her. He would keep quiet.

But then he couldn't help himself. "We didn't have time to rehearse camera shots, so when you get the chance, be sure to take some time to focus on them."

"Garrett!" she barked. "This isn't my first flipping time on a stage."

"What?"

"I've done this before on *Chart Toppers*, a much bigger venue, and on live television with millions of people watching. Some of the best people in the industry were directing me."

"Yeah, but—"

"I never wanted to do this again. I did everything in my power to avoid it, but I'm here. And I'm going to try, with every ounce of energy I have left, not to fail. And if I screw the whole thing up, I screw it up. But I promise you I'll do the best I possibly can. Now if you don't back the hell off, I'm outta here!"

The evil glare she delivered erased any doubt that she'd do exactly that. "All right. I'll shut up and stay out of your way."

"You know how long I've been waiting to hear you

say those words?" she muttered.

And even though it killed him to do it, he stepped away.

The announcer from the radio station sponsoring the headliner, Amnesia, took the stage. After a few quick comments, he said, "And now, without further delay, put your hands together for Riley Parks. The little girl from *Chart Toppers* is all grown up!"

With his hand reaching out to touch her, Garrett stepped up to wish her good luck. He pulled back when he saw the fear in her eyes. For all her bravado, she was scared. He wanted to reassure her, but the time for that had passed.

"Here goes nothing," she said, and ran out onto the stage.

The band hit the opening chords and Riley jumped into the first song without missing a beat.

He watched from the wings like a little kid not allowed to go out and play in the snow. For all the drama Riley caused, there was no question that she was a natural. Her distinctive sound and captivating personality captured the crowd's attention.

He clenched his hands while analyzing every move she made. Riley came to the edge of the stage and belted out the high notes, she pulled back and went quiet and emotional and then amped everything back up for the soaring climax, unleashing the killer power that had silenced everyone in the control room when she sang with Steven Hunter.

He wished Peter was here to see the crowd's reaction to

his song. But it pained him to realize that at the rate he and Peter were going, they wouldn't be getting along for a very long time, let alone seeing each other.

The first song ended and Riley spoke to the crowd. "Hi, everybody. It's great to be here. I know you're really here to see Amnesia."

The crowd erupted and Riley laughed. "I know. Only one more song and I promise to get out of here."

She smiled at the crowd with gratitude and Garrett's heart melted. If only he could get her to smile at him that way again, but he'd probably burned that bridge when he chose business over pleasure. He couldn't blame her, he was an ass, but in the long run, ending their relationship was a smart business decision.

Garrett tensed when the song began. If any of the songs they recorded would hit, this was the one. He'd worked with the crew on the lighting design for days. The camera guys knew what he needed, but if the crowd wasn't into it, or if Riley avoided looking into the cameras, he wouldn't get the needed footage.

But the second song went even better than the first. Riley seemed more relaxed. He heard the strain in her voice, but doubted the audience would know anything was amiss. He wished she'd play more to the cameras, but at least the crowd was fired up.

She didn't work the stage the way he wanted, but she was damn good. Excitement bubbled within as the crowd watched in awe and burst into a roar of cheers and applause when she ended.

Riley smiled, soaking in the audience response. The lights caught her glistening eyes. "You guys are awesome!" she yelled to the crowd. "Thanks for giving me such a great welcome back, Chicago!" She blew them a kiss, waved, and ran to the wings.

Garrett moved to swoop her into a hug, but she side-stepped him. He felt a stab to the heart at her rejection, but knew he deserved it.

49

She'd done it. She hadn't forgotten words or fallen on her face. Garrett waited for her in the wings, but he was the last person she wanted to see right now.

"Nice job." He patted her on the shoulder after she avoided his hug.

"Thanks." She forced a smile.

"But I wish you would have played to camera two more, and you never once looked into the mini cam."

"I was a little distracted after the visit you arranged with my mother. Not to mention the fact I only learned a couple of hours ago that there would be cameras tonight."

"I know that, but you have to pay attention to the small details."

Was he for real? It had taken all the energy she had to step out on that stage.

"Whatever," she said, ready to change out of her clothes,

find Erika, and go home.

"I'm serious. You did fine for your first try, but we need to really put some work in before you take the stage again."

Again? She couldn't think past today and getting out of here. She refused to let Garrett get her down after how hard she'd worked. "You may be right, but the audience was into it, so it couldn't have been too bad."

"Riley, the audience knew they were part of the video. They were told to cheer and be rowdy. You can't expect audience adulation. You have to earn it."

She stared at him with disbelief. "Do you say these things on purpose? Or are you stupid?" She spun on her heel and stalked toward the stairs.

"What?" he said, following close behind.

She stopped abruptly and Garrett almost ran into her. "I have been working my ass off trying to make the best of a bad situation, and all you can do is ruin any small bit of joy I find. You are just like my mother."

Garrett frowned. "You don't understand."

She climbed the stairs. "I understand plenty. You stick your nose into things you shouldn't. You schedule me for appearances, photo shoots, and live recordings without bothering to tell me. Did you ever consider that I might do a lot better if I know about things in advance? A little more rehearsal would have made a huge difference."

"You weren't ready to be told."

She turned on him. "No! You weren't ready to trust that

333

I can handle it. You're out of line. All the flippin' time! And, you had no right to call my mother. She's half the reason I quit singing to begin with. Stay out of my personal life. In fact, stay out of my life altogether."

"Hi, Garrett," a familiar voice called.

Riley turned to see a smiling Tara waving at Garrett from the base of the steps.

"Oh look, your next conquest is here." She stormed up the remaining steps. "I don't know why I ever trusted you. You're nothing more than a manipulative jerk," she muttered, thinking of how he had kissed her into submission. So why was she shocked when he dumped her?

"That's not fair. All I did was kiss you," he said, chasing after her.

"Well, I stupidly thought it meant something. I trusted you, and I've learned the hard way that, like my mother, you can't be trusted."

"You can be pissed all you want, but you're forgetting one little detail. You're under contract. I bailed you out of your bad decision-making. You owe me."

Riley stormed into the dressing room. "You're right, but signing a contract with you was just one more huge mistake, and I plan to fix that right now."

He crossed his arms and leaned against the doorframe, blocking her exit.

She tore off her jacket and hung it on the garment rack. "Screw your contract, your big lawyers, and your constant need to push me around. It's over. Sue me for every penny I owe you. Even if it takes me the rest of my life to pay you back, it'll be worth it."

"You can't," he started, but she cut off whatever he was about to say by disappearing into the bathroom and slamming the door.

"You can't do that," he shouted. "You're sick, tired, and upset. You need to go home and get some sleep. In fact, take tomorrow off."

She changed out of the boots, jeans, and T-shirt and back into her regular clothes. Garrett was such an ass; why hadn't she listened to her gut and kept him at arm's length? She carried the clothes out and fumbled with the hanger. Frustrated, she balled up the clothes and tossed them on the couch.

"I used to idolize you as an artist and performer. Boy, I was stupid. You're no more than a cocky jerk who struts around bullying people until you get your way. News alert, I've dealt with bigger bullies than you. I know your kind. You hide behind all that bravado because you're scared, just like the rest of us."

"Riley, calm down for a sec. You know you can't break the contract."

"Watch me." She sat down and put on her shoes. "And to think I was really falling for you. What a joke. You never cared about me. You wanted me to like you so I'd believe every piece of crap you fed me."

"You're sick. Go home. We can smooth this over in the morning."

"I'm not smoothing anything over. I quit. Do whatever you want with the recordings we finished. I don't care." She pushed past him out of the dressing room. "But I'm not singing another note for you!"

"Riley!" he called out.

"Ever!" she shouted.

50

Garrett was jarred awake by his phone buzzing. Who would call in the middle of the night? Was it possible that Riley wanted to apologize and take back her angry words?

He grabbed for his phone in the dark.

It was his mom.

At three o'clock in the morning.

"Hello?"

"Garrett, it's Mom." Her voice wavered.

He jolted up in bed. "What's wrong?"

"I have some terrible news."

A sense of dread flooded over him.

"It's your father." Her voice broke.

He went stone cold with fear of what she might say next.

"He's gone."

Garrett's world fell out from under him. He gripped the phone tighter.

"What do you mean?" he asked, his voice a whisper, but he already knew the answer.

"He died." And his mother, a pillar of strength, began to cry.

"What happened?" Tears filled his eyes.

"He was fine while we packed for the trip. He was reading in bed, and then said he had an upset stomach. We had ordered Thai food, so I thought nothing of it. He got up to get an antacid and collapsed on the bedroom floor."

His dad couldn't be gone. He needed him. "No, Mom. He can't be." Garrett struggled to breathe as the walls of the room closed in around him.

"I'm so sorry, honey. I wish it weren't true. The doctor says it was a massive heart attack."

Garrett leaned over, his head in his hands. "But I saw him yesterday. He flew all the way out here to see me before you guys left on your vacation tomorrow."

He thought of their conversation and the disappointment his dad had expressed over Garrett getting involved with Riley. Then he remembered his parents' trip. "Oh, Mom, it was supposed to be your anniversary trip."

"I guess it wasn't meant to happen. Twenty-five years is all we got together. One second he seemed fine and the next he was gone."

Garrett pinched the bridge of his nose, trying to hold himself together. What did he need to do? He looked around the darkened room as if the solution would reveal itself. "Mom, are you okay? Where are you?"

"I'm at the hospital, and I guess I'm as well as could be expected. Honestly, I'm probably still in shock."

"Is Peter there?"

"He's on his way now, so that's good. But I don't know how we'll get ahold of Adam. He's somewhere on safari. I'm not sure what to do."

The sadness in her voice broke his heart. He wished he were there and not a thousand miles away. "I'll call Wally. He'll know how to find Adam quickly, and I'll be on the next flight to Boston."

Garrett pictured his kid brother, only seventeen, on his own in a foreign country, and about to get the devastating news that his dad had died.

"Thank you. I'll feel better once I have all you boys back home safe with me."

"Does Grandma know?"

"I thought I'd wait until morning and have Uncle Steve go to her house to break the news. The poor woman."

His heart broke at the idea of Grandma learning her oldest son had died. "I wish I was there now," he said.

"Me too, but you'll be here soon. Garrett, a woman from the hospital is here. I think there are some papers I need to sign. Call me when you know what flight you're on."

"I will. I love you, Mom."

"I love you, too. I'll talk to you again in a little bit."

Garrett hung up the phone, dropped it on the bed, and stared at the walls.

His dad, gone. It couldn't be possible. He'd never see him or talk to him again. And they had so much left to do together.

He dropped his head into his hands and wracking sobs overcame him.

51

Garrett took a hired car service from the Boston airport. The only person from the Jamieson management team who lived in Boston now that the band had broken up was Wally, their manager for the past four years. Wally was at his parents' condo with Peter and their mom.

When Peter opened the door, the pain in his eyes matched Garrett's. It seemed that only a few months ago it was Peter rushing home after their father's first heart attack. Garrett had never forgiven Peter for not being there when it happened. Peter had been off visiting his girlfriend, Libby, in Wisconsin. But Peter possessed a kind soul and hugged Garrett, their embrace thick with grief.

"How's Mom?" Garrett asked.

"She's hanging in there. Wally located Adam's team in Tanzania, and Mom was able to talk to him. He's on his way home, but he has a four-hour ride to the nearest airport and twenty-two hours of flights before he gets here. I don't think Mom will take a real breath until he's home."

Garrett patted Peter's shoulder. "I get that."

He left his hastily packed bag in the entryway and entered the condo his parents had bought a year ago when they relocated the band to Boston.

His mom spoke quietly on the phone, but as soon as she saw him, she handed the phone to Wally and rushed to Garrett. Her eyes were red and she seemed to have aged years overnight.

She hugged him fiercely. "I'm so glad you're here."

"There's nowhere else I'd be," he choked out, his throat tight with emotion.

The day passed with many phone calls to family and close friends. Wally put out a statement to the media, asking for respect for their privacy during this difficult time. Garrett prayed the request worked, because he and his family didn't need to be bothered at a time like this.

They all moved in a fog, struggling to grasp that his dad had died. He and Peter accompanied their mother and helped pick out a casket. His father's body would be flown back to their hometown of San Antonio for the funeral and burial. Even though the Jamiesons had all made Boston their new headquarters, his parents had still kept the family home.

Adam's plane arrived late the next night due to bad weather and rerouted flights. Wally offered to pick Adam up, but Garrett insisted he'd meet him. His brother had spent the past thirty-six hours crossing the globe, surrounded by strangers. The first face he saw would be family.

Peter joined Garrett at the Logan International terminal, right outside of customs. Few people milled about at the late hour. Garrett spotted him first.

Adam walked toward them, taller than Garrett remembered, his clothes and boots still dusty. His loose curls that all the girls loved were longer, and his weary face was deeply tanned.

He reached them and dropped his duffle bag to the floor. Garrett grabbed his kid brother and hugged him. Adam held tight.

"Good to see your ugly mug." Adam spoke softly and with sadness in his voice. No words could express their true feelings.

Adam hugged Peter next.

"You bring half the Serengeti back with you?" Peter asked, trying to lighten the moment as he surveyed Adam's clothes.

"Sorry about that. They don't have closed vehicles with air-conditioning in the village. Most of my clothes look far worse than this. I was going to buy something when I changed planes in Frankfurt, but the connection was tight. I wish I had a chance to clean up before seeing Mom."

Garrett picked up Adam's bag. "She'd never forgive us

if you were one minute later than necessary."

The three walked side by side to the exit. None of them spoke, but Garrett knew they were all sensing the deep void. Never again would they walk with their father.

They were on their own.

52

Riley couldn't get Garrett off her mind. Every second she wondered how he must be feeling with his dad gone. Her dad had never played a strong role in her life, and she hadn't seen him in years. But Garrett had been close to his father, even going as far as referring to him as his best friend. He must be devastated.

"Hey Riley," Logan said, entering the live room.

"Hi, Logan." She was setting up equipment for a group of string instruments. Work seemed so one-dimensional now that she didn't have to juggle rehearsals and recording with Garrett. Her life was quiet.

"Are you going to have enough space in here with those Christmas trees?" He referred to the half-dozen decorated trees occupying the room.

She laughed. "I think so. If I have to move a couple out, Jamie will be crushed. She takes her Christmas theme seriously."

"Listen, I wasn't sure if you'd heard, but the funeral for Garrett's dad is in San Antonio the day after tomorrow."

"No, I hadn't." And she hadn't heard a word from Garrett, either. She'd called him as soon as she learned the news, but had to leave a message. Every time her phone rang, she hoped it was him, but it never was.

She'd quit on him that night. He probably hated her. Oh, what was she thinking? The poor guy just lost his dad. Riley was probably the last person on his mind.

"Barry is going to the funeral. He worked with Jamieson on their last two albums. I guess he knew Garrett's dad pretty well."

She attached a cord to a mic and slipped it into its stand. "Garrett will be glad that he's there."

"What about you? Are you going?"

"No. I only met his dad that one day, and I don't think he approved of me."

"Funerals aren't for the person who died, they're for the people still living," he said.

"I'm sure Garrett has a lot more important people in his world than me," she said, connecting the cord to the wall.

"I don't know. You two looked pretty cozy the last few days."

Riley looked at Logan and then away.

"Don't believe everything you see. A couple of weak moments don't make something real. Garrett isn't interested in me. He only cared about the album."

346

"You have to go," Erika insisted a few hours later. She followed Riley into the kitchen.

"Why? It would be weird," Riley said.

"No, it would be a grand gesture letting him know you care."

"But I don't."

"You are such a liar." Erika cocked her head and gave her an all-knowing stare.

Riley ignored her and opened the fridge, but nothing inside looked good. "You know all the crap Garrett pulled on me. I don't need any more of that in my life. I already have my mom." And yet she couldn't get Garrett out of her mind.

"He's nothing like your mom."

"No? Then why can't he ever be honest with me and open up?" She shoved the door closed.

"Have you asked him?"

"Mostly I yell at him when that stuff comes up. None of it matters anymore anyway because I quit, and now he's in San Antonio to bury his dad and might never come back."

"Have you talked to him since then? A lot was happening that day. You were sick, your mom showed up, and it was your first performance in years."

"No. I called and left him a message, but he didn't return my call." She went to her bedroom. Erika stayed on her tail.

"You were so into him. It's been years since you liked a

guy this much. I'm not gonna let you walk away from possible true love without a good knock-down, drag-out fight."

Riley dropped onto her bed and lay on her back. "I'm tired of fighting."

"It's a figure of speech, I don't expect you to actually fight; then again, making up can be pretty hot."

"But I told him to take the recordings and do whatever he wants with them, that I'm out of it."

Erika crawled on her stomach next to Riley. "Is that what you really want?"

"Yes," she said, but inside, her resolve faltered.

"I don't care what you say, you need to go to San Antonio."

"Even if I was willing to, I don't know where it is, or how I'd get there."

Erika popped up. "No problem. I can handle that. I'll call my aunt. She's a travel agent."

"But I don't have anything to wear to a funeral," Riley groaned, not sure this was a good idea.

"I bet I do. Any other arguments?"

"Only that I have no idea what I'd say to him."

"Trust me. Words won't be necessary."

53

The next morning, Riley sat in a simple pew in the crowded San Fernando Cathedral. The Jamiesons did nothing small. The historic church was from centuries gone by and like nothing she'd ever seen before, with marble carvings, stained-glass windows, and an ancient stone floor.

A mahogany casket, covered with a spray of lilies, commanded the front of the church. Hard to believe that only a few days before, the man had been alive and well, and visiting Garrett in Chicago.

As the service began, Garrett and his family entered. He walked to the front pew with his mother and sat beside her. He looked sharp in a charcoal-colored suit and tie, but the brief glimpse Riley caught of him revealed a subdued Garrett facing probably the most difficult day of his life.

After the priest said a few words and read a scripture, a heavyset man gave a eulogy, describing Jett Jamieson as a devoted father, husband, and savvy businessman. Then the priest said that Jett's sons wanted to sing one of their father's favorite songs, "Teach Your Children Well."

She craned her neck to catch a glimpse as the three famous brothers rose from the front pew and stepped onto the dais, leaving their mother sitting alone. Riley recognized the youngest brother, Adam, from his dark head of curls. Peter stood a slight bit taller, his hair a dusty blond. He wore a somber expression.

When Garrett turned to face the attendees, Riley's breath caught. The fiery challenge in his eyes that she'd grown so accustomed to had been replaced by pain. Her heart ached at the sight of his grief-filled eyes.

The brothers gathered around a single microphone. Adam held a guitar. Their father's casket lay before them.

Riley had seen videos of Jamieson in concert, always so strong and powerful; the brothers owned the stage with spotlights and pyrotechnics. But today was in stark contrast. No band backed them up. No fans screamed their names. The silence of the crowded church echoed as if they sat in a hollow cave.

The three shared a mournful look as Adam began to play. A rich tone filled the church. The glorious sound echoed off the high ceiling as they sang the heartfelt tune. They sang of the love of a parent for his children and that the past is only a good-bye. Their voices rang out strong and pure as everyone in the church paid witness to the sons' tribute to their father.

Riley recognized the low timbre of Garrett's voice, setting him apart from his brothers. How could he sing this soulful song at his own father's funeral? She wiped at her eyes with a tissue.

Their father would have been proud as the brothers' voices blended in perfect harmony, the sound reverberating off the stained-glass windows. Their performance was a beautiful farewell to the man who raised them.

The song ended and one by one, the brothers took their seats. As Garrett passed his father's casket, he paused for a moment, and with his head bowed, laid his hand on it. When he turned to take his seat, Riley noticed the strain etched on his handsome face and wished she could reach out to him, to apologize for making things so difficult, and to take back all the cruel things she'd said.

The ceremony concluded with the sprinkling of holy water, and a hymn. Pallbearers stepped forward and carried the casket down the long aisle. Garrett escorted his mother behind. He glanced Riley's way for a brief moment, as if he knew all along that she'd been there, but then he looked away and passed. Peter and Adam walked on either side of an elderly woman, most likely their grandmother, the shuffle of her feet on the stone floor sounding with the weight of her grief. Slowly the pews emptied.

Outside in the bright summer heat, a gleaming black hearse was parked in the open plaza in front of the church.

Fountains danced in the background as if unaware of the sadness of the day.

The crowd began to disperse, some talking amongst themselves, others waiting to speak to the family. Riley saw her boss talking to a man she didn't recognize. She stood off to the side. She'd come all this way, and the only people here she actually knew were Garrett and Barry.

Eventually Barry, wearing a sharp suit, such a contrast from the relaxed dress at work, moved on through the crowd and spoke to Garrett, his brothers and mother, hugging each one. After walking away, Barry noticed Riley.

"Hi, I didn't realize you would be here."

"It was last minute."

"I'm sure Garrett will appreciate seeing you."

She hoped so. "There are so many people."

"Yes, things like this do bring old friends out of the woodwork. His father was a good man. Those boys are in for a tough adjustment. I feel for them, losing their dad so young. Well, I've got a return flight to Chicago to catch. Do you need a ride to the airport?"

"Not until tomorrow morning. It was the best I could do last minute." It saved her three hundred dollars on her airfare. She'd already spent more money on this last-second trip than anything in her life.

"Well then, be sure to take some time to check out the River Walk. It's only a couple blocks from here."

"Thanks. See you tomorrow," she said.

After Barry left, she mustered up the courage to join the line of people waiting to offer their condolences. She'd never done this before and wasn't sure what to say, but suddenly she stood before Peter Jamieson. His famous face was so familiar to her, yet he was someone so far out of her league.

Nervously she introduced herself. "Hi, I'm so sorry about your dad."

"Thank you," he said, politely shaking her hand.

Did he think she was a fan who snuck past security? "I'm Riley Parks. I know your brother, Garrett, from Sound Sync."

"No kidding?" His smile changed from polite distance to openly friendly. "Nice to meet you. Garrett's told me a lot about you."

"Thank you for writing such amazing songs. I really love them." She didn't have the heart to mention that she never planned to sing them again.

"It's nice to know someone is getting use of my music. This is my brother, Adam."

Adam finished greeting the person in front of her and turned in her direction.

"Adam, this is Riley Parks, the girl Garrett signed to record."

It didn't feel right talking about business when it was their father's funeral, but maybe talking about something else helped.

"Hi, thanks for coming. We really appreciate it," Adam said.

"I'm sorry about your dad."

"Thanks," he said, and then the person in front of her moved on and Garrett spotted her.

He looked tired, but smiled. "Riley, I didn't expect to see you."

"Me neither. It was a spur-of-the-moment decision."

"Thanks. I got your phone message. Sorry I didn't call you back."

"It's fine. I didn't expect you to."

An awkwardness stood between them. Should she hug him? She stood far enough away that it didn't seem natural.

"Are you going back to Chicago with Barry?"

"No, I'm here until early tomorrow morning."

"You should come by the house later. We're having people over for a late lunch after the burial."

She sensed eyes on her, and saw Peter and Adam watching her interaction with Garrett.

"It'll be casual. I'll text you the address. It's not far," he said.

"I wouldn't want to intrude."

"You wouldn't be. It's just family, neighbors, friends. Adam and Peter's girlfriends will be there, too. They're nice. You'd like them."

"Thanks." She appreciated the invite but would have to think about it.

Garrett turned to his mother.

"Mom, this is Riley, the girl I've been working with. Dad met her when he was in Chicago."

A middle-aged woman wearing a simple black dress and heels, with kindness in her eyes, smiled. "Yes, Jett told me how talented you are."

"Thank you. I'm so very sorry for your loss."

"Thank you. Life can change so unexpectedly."

The procession moved on and Riley was on her own.

54

Riley didn't go to Garrett's house. She couldn't picture herself pretending to fit in with his family's friends and relatives. Who was she to Garrett anyway? A friend? A coworker? The girl who was supposed to be recording with him? Or was she the girl he kissed several times and then changed his mind about? And to be honest with herself, she didn't know what she wanted to be to him.

She checked into her budget hotel a few blocks away. The simple room was cool, which was a nice change from the stifling summer heat of San Antonio.

At one point she ventured out and found a tourist area with souvenir shops, a movie theater, and a wax museum. If she went to the museum, would she find a life-size figure of Garrett? She shuddered and then laughed at the creepiness. She checked out the Alamo and ate dinner at a sub shop before retreating to her hotel room.

Riley wondered what Garrett was doing. Probably surrounded by friends and family. He said he'd been avoiding his brothers the past few months. Not much avoiding he could do anymore. What would they do now that their dad had died? Would Garrett ever come back to Chicago? She kind of lucked out with her timing to quit. Now Garrett had much bigger things to worry about than her.

Later that night she lay on her bed watching TV, waiting for tomorrow and her flight home.

It had been nice to see Garrett and meet his brothers and mom, but she probably shouldn't have spent all this money for five minutes with him. Why had she come anyway? Something about Garrett kept drawing her in, as if she had no control over her emotions. Her phone beeped.

A text from Garrett. She sat up.

Are you still awake? he texted.

Yes.

Want to go for a walk?

Her heart took off. *Sure.*

Where are you staying?

She texted him the address.

See you in ten.

Riley hopped off the bed and ran to the mirror, did a couple of quick makeup touch-ups, and ran a brush through her hair.

Stepping outside, she found that the sweltering heat of

the day had subsided into a balmy night. She waited on a bench in front of the hotel, fully expecting him to pull up in a fancy sports car. As the minutes passed, a lone figure appeared from the darkness, just outside of reach of the streetlight. In the dim haze she could tell the stranger wore a cap and cargo shorts. As he came closer, she recognized him to be Garrett wearing a faded San Antonio Spurs T-shirt and sandals.

Riley stood. "I didn't recognize you at first. I thought you'd drive and then we'd go for a walk."

"Our house is less than a mile from here."

"I'm surprised you could get away," she said.

"I had to. We've had nothing but togetherness for the past four days and I think we all need a break from each other. Makes me wonder how we survived on tour for so long. Any place you'd like to go?"

"Wherever you like is fine."

"All right." They set off side by side at a casual pace. "You didn't stop by this afternoon."

"No. I didn't want to intrude."

"You wouldn't have," he said in a soft voice.

Did he really mean it? "How are you doing?"

"Fine, I guess. It's actually a relief to have the funeral over. It feels like weeks since he died, and like the world stopped and nothing else existed outside of our pain. It's weird being out and not surrounded by family and the heavy reminder that Dad died. It's strange seeing people

going about their business as if no huge tragedy just happened."

"The funeral was nice. I think your dad would have
really liked that song you and your brothers sang. It was
beautiful."

"Dad loved Crosby, Stills, and Nash, and especially that
song. He taught it to us when we first started out. He said
it was about how important it was for parents to teach their
children, but just as important for children to teach their
parents."

"Interesting. I never thought of the song that way
before." There was a lot she needed to teach her mom, but
was her mom willing to learn? Probably not.

They entered a busier area, with more traffic and tourists walking about.

"Aren't you worried people will recognize you?"

"Not really. This is home to me. I refuse to let that
get in the way of me getting out to my old hangouts. Plus,
our manager said there's a huge engineering conference
in town. They aren't exactly the Jamieson demographic.
Between that, the heat, and how late it is, I doubt I'll be
recognized. Have you seen the River Walk?"

"No. I was going to, but I didn't really understand
where it was. I did check out the Alamo."

"When I was a kid, our school took us to the Alamo
once a year. But everyone should see the River Walk. Come
on, I'll take you down there."

They took a turn and Garrett guided her to an old stone bridge and a staircase next to it. Down one level, a secret world opened up before her. Where a street should have been, there was a river. Open-air restaurants with bright-colored umbrella tables lined the waterway, and savory scents wafted through the air. Flower baskets burst with color and trees draped with twinkling lights leaned over the river as if helping to hide it from the rest of the world.

"This is amazing."

Garrett smiled. "I thought you'd like it."

People milled about the narrow sidewalks that ran along the river. In some spots dining tables were set inches from the water's edge. Live music played in the distance.

They passed under an old bridge that arched across the river. "There's nothing even close to this in Chicago. San Antonio must have been a great place to grow up."

"It was. My grandparents moved here when they were first married. My grandpa was in the air force and got stationed here. They liked it so much, they stayed. Of course, this area wasn't so built up back then."

They climbed to the top of a small bridge. Lights from the restaurants shimmered over the water.

"I used to come down here with my friends all the time when I was a kid. We'd get in trouble for dropping this concoction we made. It looked like bird poop. We dropped it off the bridges as the guide boats passed below. My dad would get so mad, but then later, I'd overhear him telling my mom and laughing." Garrett smiled at the memory.

Riley could picture a young, mischievous Garrett. "How is your mom? This must be incredibly hard for her."

"She's been so strong for all of us. The only thing my mom ever cared about was family. Then suddenly, the band broke up and all of us scattered. My dad had planned a big trip for him and Mom. They were supposed to leave . . . I guess it would have been a couple days ago. Dad said they were finally going to see the sights instead of being rushed from one concert venue to another. Now it'll never happen."

They walked for a while in comfortable silence, their hands occasionally brushing together, but he didn't take her hand.

"What are your plans?" She wanted him to say he was returning to Chicago, and held her breath waiting for his answer.

"Honestly, I have no idea. I can't imagine abandoning my mom right now. I'd like to be here to help her figure out all this legal stuff she's got to face."

"I understand. Listen, about the things I said at the House of Blues—"

Garrett interrupted. "Don't think twice about it. A lot was going on that night, it was such a mess. It feels like a million years ago to me."

She was about to say that maybe she'd reconsider recording with him if it would bring him back to her, but it sounded like maybe he was giving all that up. She'd turned into a damn yo-yo with her emotions whipping one direction, then another.

"Did you and your mom make up?" he asked.

"Not really. I'm trying to keep her at a distance, otherwise she takes over my life."

"Sounds like a smart idea. It's a lesson that I need to learn, too. I seem to have a problem with overstepping my boundaries."

They saw a bench overlooking the river and sat.

"I've been a real jerk," he said.

"No." She smiled. "Okay, maybe a little."

"I've been doing a lot of soul searching since my dad died, and I don't really like what I've found. I practically forced you to sign on with me." He stared straight ahead as he spoke.

"No, I walked into that knowingly; I needed the money."

"And that's the wrong reason to record. Did you know that I have been jealous of my brothers my whole life?"

"Why?" She couldn't imagine Garrett being jealous of anyone. He was confident, talented, and when he wanted, so charming she couldn't think straight.

"I don't know why, but I always was. When Peter was born, everyone made such a big deal about the new baby. He was this sweet little kid who everyone loved."

"I'm sure they loved you just as much."

"Yes, but I couldn't see it. And then Adam came along

and it was worse. I was supposed to be the more responsible one. I was held to a higher level than my brothers."

"I can relate to that."

"And then they were both more talented than me. Peter could sing, play, and write the best songs. And Adam was this happy, goofy guitar genius. I could play, but never to Adam's level, and I couldn't write, and I wasn't strong enough to be a lead singer. They were always better, so I needed to succeed in other ways. So I made sure I was in charge. All the time. Looking back, it wasn't fair. I interfered when I shouldn't have. I acted like I knew more than they did."

"Why are you telling me all this?"

"Because I wanted to give you a little insight into why I've been such an asshole. I don't want to be that jerk anymore."

"There's a lot more to you than being a bossy jerk."

"We'll see about that. I want you to know that I'm going to tear up the contract."

"But . . ."

"You signed it for the wrong reasons, and the way I pushed you was inexcusable."

Was she experiencing relief or dread? At least she wouldn't have to go to battle with him, but it also ended their time working together.

"It's going to take me a long time to pay back all your money, but I will. I'm not like my mom. I'll do it."

"The money is yours. You earned it."

"I couldn't."

"Yes you can, and you will. It's clear to me that you've had a rough time, and if that money helps get you back on track I'm more than happy to do it. But there's something else you need to know."

"Okay." Was it grief that drove him to say these things?

"You don't need to pay the insurance company back for that accident."

"Now you're sounding like my mom. I'm not going to ignore my responsibilities."

"That's not what I meant. All you need is a decent lawyer to represent you. They'll be able to prove to the court that you were never in possession of the car and couldn't have possibly been driving it at the time of the accident."

"You've given this a lot of thought."

"I have, and I've talked to one of our attorneys. Here's his number. He's offered to represent you pro bono, for free." Garrett handed her a slip of paper from his pocket.

"I really won't have to pay it back?"

"Guaranteed. It's a simple case. I figured that's how it would work when you first told me about it, but I wanted you to need the money, so I didn't mention it. I'm sorry."

He stood and she followed as he walked along the river's edge.

"What about the three songs we finished?" She was proud of what they'd done together. Would those songs ever be heard again?

"Eventually I might like to do something with them, but not right away. I have a lot more to figure out in my life, like how not to mix business and personal. I messed up with you big time. I thought I could mold you into my idea of a star."

"I don't mold very well."

He laughed. "No, you don't. You're one of a kind. Don't let anyone change you. I want to be a better person. I owe it to my dad. Next I'm going to try to fix some of the scars I've inflicted on my brothers. It's the least I could do."

Her heart broke for him. "Your dad was very proud of you. I saw it when he came to Chicago."

Garrett smiled sadly, clearly not believing her.

They got up and continued to walk, coming full circle on the River Walk. After, Garrett brought her back to her hotel.

"Thanks for flying down. You didn't need to, but it was nice that you did. What time is your flight in the morning?"

"Early, six."

"Do you need a ride?"

"It's okay. I already ordered a shuttle."

He nodded. "The walk has been good."

"I'm glad. Are you going to be okay walking home this late?"

"I'll be fine. I wish I could say when I'll see you again, but I honestly don't know."

"I understand. I'm sorry you have to go through all of this."

"Thanks. I should let you get to bed." He gave her a quick kiss on the cheek and then headed off into the darkness, leaving Riley with more questions than answers.

55

The day after his father's funeral was eerily quiet. Garrett found his mom at the kitchen sink washing dishes. The well-wishers were gone, and extended family had returned home.

"Good morning." He leaned against the kitchen counter wearing only an old pair of shorts.

"You slept in. I'm glad." She smiled lovingly.

Still half asleep, he rubbed a hand over his face. "I did."

"How is your friend?"

"Good. I showed her the River Walk. She liked it." Riley was probably back in Chicago by now. At least he'd had a chance to apologize and make things right.

"She seemed like a nice girl. Are you still recording the album with her?"

He went to the refrigerator and pulled out the orange juice.

"We kind of had a big blowup the other day. It was the night that Dad died." He tilted the carton back and drank.

"He told me."

Garrett wiped his mouth with the back of his hand. "He did?"

She nodded. "I overheard him talking to you. It sounded pretty heated."

"It was. Dad wasn't happy with the way I'd handled things with Riley. It was a pretty horrible last conversation. I could hear in his voice how disappointed he was in me." Garrett's heart ached.

"What did you do that upset him so much?" She washed and rinsed another drinking glass.

Garrett grimaced. "I never told Riley about the video-taping until she got there. She was really sick that day, and didn't want to go on."

"Performing sick is never easy."

"I called her mom to come down, because I thought that would make Riley feel better, but it ignited a huge fight. It was out of control." He'd had no idea her mom would be so unsupportive. All he'd ever known from his parents was encouragement.

"Maybe you should have kept her informed."

"But if I told her, she would have freaked out."

"I must ask, do you want to be the kind of businessman who forces people to do what you want?"

"That's pretty much what Dad said." Garrett frowned.

"He was a very smart man."

"Yeah, he was. The last time I talked to him we argued. I can't help but feel if I hadn't upset him so much, he'd still be here."

She wiped her hands dry on a dish towel. "Garrett, you are not responsible for your father's heart attack. He's had heart problems for years, you know that. I'm sorry your last conversation with him was difficult, but you need to let that go. He was so proud of you."

Garrett shook his head in denial. The memory of his father's disapproval broke his heart, and he couldn't do a thing to fix it.

"Listen to me. Your father loved your phone calls. He'd tell me about your conversations and the progress you were making. He talked about how you were reinventing your-self in the face of adversity." She rubbed his back. "You are a lot like your father."

"No, I'm not."

"Oh yes, you are very much like him, and he loved that. I think that's why he pushed you so hard, because he knew you could handle it."

"I miss him so much, Mom," he whispered, his grief threatening to pour out.

His mom wrapped her arms around him. "Me too."

Ten minutes later Peter and Adam returned from dropping Libby and Marti at the airport. The girls had summer jobs to get back to in Boston. Garrett envied his brothers' tight bond with their girlfriends. Riley's face popped into his mind. She would have gotten along well with Libby and Marti.

Now it was only the four of them. They gathered around the patio table, quiet, as they tried to settle into whatever their new normal would be, over cold beverages and a plate of cookies a neighbor had brought by.

"So tell me what your plans are," their mom said, pouring herself a glass of iced tea.

"Nothing, really. I thought I might go for a run later," Peter said.

"I didn't mean for today. I meant for tomorrow, next week, and next month."

Garrett exchanged confused looks with his brothers.

"I'm home now. That's my plan. To be home," Adam said.

"I love you boys more than anything, and losing your father is a terrible blow to all of us, but staying home grieving isn't going to work."

"What do you mean?" Adam asked, looking confused. "You want me to go get a job?"

"No." She squeezed his hand. "While we all need time together to grieve, it's just as important that you boys get back to your lives. You've traveled the world; you are far older than your actual age. It wouldn't be healthy for you to move back to your childhood home. Staying here would make you crazy."

"But Mom, we don't want to leave you alone," Peter said.

She smiled that gentle, loving smile that made her so wonderful. "I'll be fine. I promise you. It would break my heart to see you boys wasting away here. You are so full of life and energy. Plus, I have a lot of work ahead of me. I want to spend more time with your grandmother, and then I need to figure out how to move on with my life, too."

"Dad would want us to be with you," Garrett added.

"No, your father would tell you to get on with living your lives. There have been a lot of changes the past six months, starting with the breakup of the band. You are all still very much in a place of transition. Honor your father by continuing to be the strong, successful young men he raised."

Garrett couldn't imagine abandoning his mom now, and from the expressions of Peter and Adam, they felt the same.

"I've never been more proud of you boys than during this past week. And you're always welcome to be at home here or in Boston, as long as you like. But I know you. In three days, you'll be clawing to get away and do something. Think about it." She stood with her iced tea and went inside.

"She doesn't really mean it, does she?" Peter asked.

"Pretty sure she does," Garrett answered. His mother could be far more stubborn than their dad had been.

"So we're supposed to just leave? I don't want to," Adam said.

"I think Mom is worried that we'll move into the basement and never leave."

"We don't have a basement," Adam said.

"You know what I mean," Garrett said.

"But that's exactly what I want to do," Peter said. "Mom shouldn't be alone."

Adam nodded his agreement.

"Let's give her a day or so. She'll come around," Garrett said.

But the next day, their mother held strong to her convictions that they keep busy. She had them going through old boxes of memorabilia that had been stacked in the garage for years.

"Remember when we went on our first tour in that old van?" Peter said.

"We were packed in so tight. Dad took a picture so he'd remember exactly how to get it all back in after each stop." Garrett laughed at the memory.

"I spent three thousand miles with a duffle bag on my lap," Adam said.

"It feels so long ago. Can you believe how fast things changed?" Garrett said, lifting out a photo album.

"I know. From school auditoriums to Madison Square Garden. It's insane," Adam reminisced.

"Hard to believe it's all over," Garrett said, mourning the band, as well as his dad and Riley.

"It's not over forever. Just for now," Peter said.

Garrett couldn't believe his ears. "I thought you were finished with the band."

"For now I am. The grind was too much. I fried my voice and had to have surgery, but down the road, who knows?" Peter opened a photo album and laughed. "Adam, you look like a baby with those big eyes and round cheeks."

Garrett took a look. "His guitar is practically bigger than he is."

"I can't believe Mom saved all this stuff." Peter paged through the photos.

"Garrett, remember when Mom highlighted your hair so you could spike it?" Adam laughed.

"Yeah, it was my inner punk rocker crying to get out. Look at the one of Peter with a buzz cut."

Peter leaned over to see. "I forgot about that. I fell asleep with gum in my mouth and it got matted in my hair. Dad took out Grandpa's old hair trimmer and buzzed it all off. Thank God Libby isn't here to see this picture. She'd never let me forget it."

"I think I'll frame it and give it to her for Christmas," Adam said.

Garrett wished he had someone special to share his stories with. He hadn't heard from Riley since their walk the other night, but he hadn't called her either.

"Garrett, what's up with that girl who came to the funeral?" Peter asked, as if reading his mind.

"Yeah, she seems way too nice to be hanging around with you," Adam added.

Garrett frowned because Adam was basically right. "Things are pretty much nonexistent ever since the House of Blues gig. The night turned into the perfect storm—if something could go wrong, it did."

"Technical problems?" Adam asked, unfolding a lawn chair to sit on.

"I wish. We'd started seeing each other."

"I knew it," Peter said with a knowing smile.

"Things were going really well, but then Dad showed up and found out." And that guilty feeling squeezed his heart again.

"I bet he had a coronary over it," Adam said.

Peter frowned.

"Sorry. You know what I mean. Dad was never much into letting girls interfere with the band."

That was an understatement. Whenever there was a decision between one of them spending time with a girl or working, their dad was adamant that girls could wait. Garrett had always agreed, until he met Riley.

"Dad told me straight out to end it, so I did. Now I hate myself."

"Dad was great, but if I had let him have his way, I wouldn't be with Libby," Peter said.

"And Dad never would have let me go to LA to see

Marti. I don't want to think how that would have turned out if I hadn't," Adam said.

"That's right," Peter agreed. "Just because Dad's gone, it doesn't mean he was right or that you should do everything he said."

"I don't know. There's a lot more to it. Riley was sick and then she was pissed at me for springing a bunch of stuff on her out of the blue."

"Ah, that sounds more like the Garrett we know and love," Peter said.

"Well, she's pretty much had enough of me. She did the gig, but then chewed me out, said she quit, and stormed out." He'd replayed that scene over and over in his mind the past few days, wishing he could have a do-over.

"Can you blame her?" Adam said. "You can be a real douche bag."

"I guess not. I only meant to do what was best for her career." Yet if someone had pulled that on him, he'd have gone ballistic.

"Where have we heard those words before?" Adam snickered.

"It's over, and I can't blame her." He thought about all the ways he'd manipulated her. He deserved what he got.

"But she flew halfway across the country to attend the funeral," Peter said.

"She did," Garrett agreed, thankful he had one last hour with her that night.

"She wouldn't have come if she hated you," Peter said.

Garrett nodded. She had gone to a lot of trouble to come to the funeral and see him for only a few minutes.

"Did she change her mind about recording?"

"No. I released her from the contract."

Peter looked up from the photo album he held. "Seriously?"

"I couldn't push the issue and force her to finish out the contract after everything that happened."

"I'm speechless. Who are you?" Adam said.

"She's really amazing. I wish you guys could have heard her sing live, but I don't want her hating me the rest of her life. She's the best person I've ever met. I mean, she calls me on my shit. She doesn't back down. She's tough as nails."

"Sounds like Riley got under your skin," Peter said.

"Honestly, I can't stop thinking about her. In the past I never cared if I ticked people off, but with Riley, it's different. It's like she's my moral compass."

"Garrett has a conscience, somebody call the press," Adam said.

"And speaking of conscience," Garrett said, looking from one brother to the other, "I want to apologize to you, too. I was terrible to you a lot over band stuff and girl stuff. I was jealous of your happiness. I'm sorry, and I give you my word, I won't ever do it again."

"Geez, this girl really got to you." Peter laughed.

"You've got it bad," Adam said.

"No. It's not like that," Garrett defended. He just wanted

to set things right with his brothers.

"Oh yeah, you've never cared what a girl thought before. You are toast, man." Adam laughed.

Except that he had no reason to see her again.

56

Riley nestled back into her world of Christmas carols as Jamie Halloway's album neared the finish line. Riley would miss the comfort the holiday decorations had brought her during this tumultuous time.

Perspiration glistened on Jamie's brow as she belted "O Come All Ye Faithful." A part of Riley still yearned to feel that rush of power that singing her heart out always gave her.

It had been three days since she returned from the funeral, with no word from Garrett. She missed him, and that surprised her. She even missed the bossy side of him. Since he'd been gone, work wasn't the same.

Riley noticed Tara at the door holding a pink message slip up to the window. She was unable to enter the room during live recording. Riley came over to see Tara's scribbled message.

Barry wants to see you in his office.

Tara's expression gave nothing away. Had Riley screwed up? She didn't think so. She nodded to Tara that she'd be right there. As soon as Jamie finished the chorus they were working on, Riley slipped out.

As she rounded the corner to Barry's office, she heard a familiar voice. A moment later her suspicions were confirmed when she laid eyes on Jason Edgette.

"Jason!" she exclaimed.

"Riley, look at you!" He opened his arms and gave her a big hug. "You've grown up! How long since I last saw you?"

"I think it was a year ago Christmas. What are you doing here?" she asked, amazed to see him.

"I have some business in Chicago and thought I'd swing by while my wife is shopping to see how you're doing."

"I'm good. Tell her hi." Riley had met Jason's model wife a couple times during the reality show. She was terrific.

"Glad to hear it. I understand a lot has been going on with you."

She shrugged.

"Why don't we all sit down," Barry suggested, and closed the office door.

"I heard you were in Europe on tour," Riley said to change the subject as she sat on the small sofa.

Jason sat on the other side. "I was, but it's good to be

back in the States. We're taking a month off and then the U.S. tour kicks off in Boston."

"That's great, and your new album has been doing really well," she said.

"Thanks, but I'm not here to talk about myself. Catch me up. I was happy to hear you were recording an album with Garrett Jamieson, but now Barry tells me you're not. What's going on?"

She sighed. So much had happened so quickly. "Yes, I was. Basically I agreed to record with him, but things got complicated. His dad died, and we both agreed to void the contract." She couldn't muster the courage to say she quit on him, and that Garrett let her.

"I see." Jason exchanged a look with Barry. "And now you're back working your regular job."

"That's right."

Barry took a seat in the armchair. "You know, Riley. I've been thinking about the album you started but haven't finished. It's a real shame to leave it that way. How would you feel if I said there was a chance you could still finish it?"

"Seriously?"

"Anything's possible," he said.

She never thought finishing her album was an option. She'd been so angry at Garrett that night at House of Blues that she didn't take a moment to let the euphoria of performing again sink in. She had loved every second of being on that stage.

"Are you interested?" Barry asked.

Jason watched intently.

"Um, yeah. I think I would be," she said, and a pulse of excitement rushed in her veins. Maybe things would turn out after all.

She noticed the small curve of a smile on Jason's face.

"Good," Barry said. "Now, in a perfect world, if you were able to finish this album, what would you want?"

"I don't understand."

"Barry and I have been talking about your future. To be totally honest, Riley, I always hoped you'd sing again. That's the reason I asked Barry to give you a job. I wanted you to remember what you were missing."

"Oh."

"And now that you've found your voice again, I want to make sure you get a chance to finish what you started. So, let me ask again. If you were able to finish your album, and do it any way you wanted, what would you want?" Jason asked.

Her mind was a jumble. She couldn't believe Jason had been hoping all this time that she'd sing. And how cool. Suddenly, she knew exactly what she wanted.

"I'd want Garrett back here. He started this whole thing, he should finish it."

Jason smiled.

"Okay. What else?" Barry asked. "You've been working here for a while now. Anything you'd do differently or change?"

"I'd want Garrett to play guitar on the album. And you know what else? I know this is pushing my luck, but I'd love it if his brothers would help with it, too. I think it would mean a lot to Garrett to have their support on the first album he produces. Plus, they were an awesome band, and having them play backup would be a total dream come true."

"That would be quite the star-studded studio band," Jason said.

"You said dream. There you are." She laughed. Then another thing popped into her head. "Oh, and one more thing. Jason, about five years ago you made a prediction about me on the day we met. Do you remember?"

"I do," Jason said with a knowing smile.

Riley grinned. "I want that prediction to come true."

"Are you sure you're ready?" Jason asked.

"I am. It took me a long time to get to this place, but I really believe now is the right time."

"That is so great to hear," Jason said.

"Looks like I have a few phone calls to make." Barry rose from his chair and went to his desk.

"Are you really going to call Garrett?" A mixture of panic washed over her. "I don't know if he'll want to work with me anymore. He seemed pretty adamant about ending it."

"Then I'll create a situation he can't say no to," Barry said, undeterred.

"Okay, but don't tell him that I want his brothers, too. If they agree to this, which I know is unlikely, I'd like to surprise Garrett." She hoped her surprise would be a welcome one, unlike the ones he'd sprung on her.

"I can do that." Barry picked up his phone.

"Riley, if you'd excuse us, Barry and I have some work to do," Jason said. "We'll let you know how it goes."

"Okay." She went to the door. Ten minutes ago, her recording career was over, but now the future held so much promise.

"Don't worry, Barry can be very persuasive," Jason said.

"Thank you." She smiled as hope renewed in her heart.

On her way out, she overheard Barry.

"Garrett, Barry Goldwin here. I have a new up-and-coming artist I'd like you to meet. How soon can you get to Chicago?"

57

Garrett walked down the corridor to Studio B. He was back, still chasing the dream. Only it wasn't the dream he'd hoped it would be. Instead of recording with Riley, he would be working with a new artist that Barry had found.

Barry said the artist was young and hungry to make it in the recording industry. That was the kind of artist Garrett needed. While Riley had the pipes, she didn't have the heart or the drive.

But which studio was she working in today? Was she wearing her holiday sweater and listening to Jamie Halloway crooning Christmas carols? Did Riley even know he was back?

Thoughts of Riley had been his one solace as he moved through the days after his dad's death. The sight of her determined smile and flowing hair as she charmed everyone around her flashed across his mind. Maybe he could request she work with him on this new project. She'd been dying to work at the board. He could finally give her something she really wanted.

He sighed and opened the door to the control room to meet his new artist. But what he found inside was the last thing he expected. Peter and Adam sat at the control board.

"What are you guys doing here?" he asked.

"Barry called and said he had a special project he wanted us to work on. The guy has done so much for us that we figured we should return the favor," Peter said, smirking.

Garrett noticed their guitar cases propped in the corner. "What are you talking about?" None of this made sense.

"Plus, Mom said we were driving her nuts. I think she was thankful to get rid of us for a while," Adam said, spinning his chair like a little kid.

"Barry called you?" he asked.

"That's what I said," Peter answered.

"And what exactly are you going to do?"

Peter grinned. "Play backup."

"On what planet would you ever be willing to play backup on some unknown artist's album?"

"Hopefully she won't be unknown forever," a sassy feminine voice said behind him.

His heart lurched. He spun around.

"Hey, Garrett," Riley said nonchalantly. "You ready to

get to work? We're way behind if we're going to finish this album."

He turned to his brothers. "You agreed to play on her album?"

"Yup. Riley told us she only wanted the best, and frankly, Garrett, you can't handle it by yourself," Adam said.

"I'm a producer now. I don't play backup," Garrett said.

Riley stepped between Peter and Adam. The guys stood and the three faced Garrett as an impenetrable wall. "You will on my album."

"Riley, we've been through this. You don't need to record this album."

"I know, and I appreciate it. But I changed my mind." Riley smiled, a defiant glint in her eyes.

She looked so beautiful, he wanted to steal her away from his brothers.

"Riley, I can't—"

"You can't mix business and personal. Yada, yada, yada. Guys, would you mind if I had a word alone with Garrett?"

"No problem." Adam went for the door and Peter followed.

As Peter passed Garrett, he paused. "This is your one chance. Listen to her. Don't be an idiot and screw this up."

Riley leaned against the edge of the control board with her arms crossed, waiting for him to speak.

"So you've decided to record after all. How'd you

suddenly come to that decision?"

"I had the chance to think about what was important to me and what I wanted to do with my life. A smart person once told me that chances like this only come around once. I figured maybe I should give it my best shot."

"And why are my brothers here?"

"I don't want any old studio musicians. I want the best." She arched an eyebrow and leveled a determined stare at him.

"And who put you in charge?"

"The owner of the studio asked me what my dream scenario would be and I told him."

"And you wanted me?"

"Very much." The corner of her mouth turned up in a delicious smile.

"But I told you I can't mix business and personal."

She took a step toward him. "And I don't care what you said."

"But my dad was right when he said—"

"Your dad was a very good businessman, but I'm not going to let him dictate who I can fall in love with."

He cocked his head. "Those are pretty strong words."

"Well, I'm a pretty strong girl. I've decided to go after the things I want."

"You know, I'm used to being in control."

"How's it feel to have someone turn the tables on you?" She took another step closer.

"How did you know I'd go for this?"

"I didn't know." She kept coming. "Sometimes you have to play big to win big."

"But what if we don't work out and you come to hate me?"

"I'm sure we'll knock heads. Trust me, yours is thick as a brick. If we don't work out, I can survive that. But not even trying? That I could never live with."

"Sounds like you've given this a lot of thought."

She stood before him, beautiful and perfect. His heart pounded.

"I have. And imagine if we do make it? How fun would that be?" She slipped her arms around his waist. His breath hitched.

"That would be fun." He wrapped his arms around her, looking at her pert nose and devilish mouth.

"You know we'll fight," she said.

"That's true."

"But we have to stay on track. We have a tour to get ready for."

He startled. "What tour is that?"

"The one Jason Edgette offered me when I was thirteen. He said I could be his opening act. It starts in a month."

"You've been very busy. You'll have to quit your job here and get straight to work."

"I already quit."

He pushed a lock of hair behind her ear. "Is there

anything you didn't think of?"

"Probably, but that's why you're here, to make sure we do this right."

"I'm glad I'm good for something."

"Oh, you're good for a few things." She ran her finger across his jawline. "One of which is playing on the album."

"But I told you, I'm here to produce."

"I'm not making the album without you playing on it. That's my deal, take it or leave it."

"And you come along with the package?"

"Yes, I do. So are you going to kiss me or argue with me?"

He lowered his mouth to quiet any more demands she might make.

Acknowledgments

A huge shout-out to all the readers who begged for Garrett's story. He is the character you all loved to hate in previous books. I hope you feel I gave him his due.

Many people helped out with the creation of *Under the Spotlight*, from research to critique partners to beta readers. Thank you and big squishy hugs to Mary Kay Adams-Edgette, Sue Balthazar, Deb Barkelar, Kris Hebel, Amanda Hensen, Arianna Pajtash, Linda Schmalz, Scott Singletary, Kristi Tyler, and Margo Zimmerman, and not to be forgotten, the constant love and support from my family.

Thank you to my lovely agent, Jane Dystel, and everyone at Dystel & Goderich Literary Management. You are an awesome team of professionals.

To the Madison Media Institute, Ron Dettwiler, Jonathon Schaub, and Audrey Martinovich for allowing me to observe classes in the recording studio and learn about your industry, as well as answering so many of my questions.

And also to the extraordinary James Dylan, who shared his knowledge of the ins and outs of recording studios, musicians, and touring.

Thanks to Emily Becker for sharing stories of life as a police officer and helping make this book more authentic.

Huge thanks to Joanna Hinsey and Judy Bryan, who saved me in the eleventh hour when I got stuck. You're a writer's best friend.

And finally, a warm hug of gratitude to Rosemary Brosnan for discovering *Rock and a Hard Place*. Your kindness will never be forgotten. And a special thank-you to Karen Chaplin and my team at HarperTeen for your hard work and dedication.

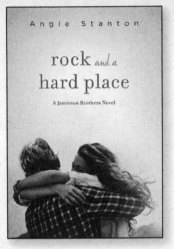
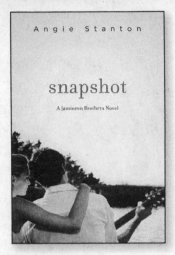